# Critical Acclaim For AARON ELKINS AND GIDEON OLIVER

# ICY CLUTCHES

"Not even a glacial avalanche can cover up murder when Gideon Oliver, the physical anthropologist, is given some rags and a few old bones to examine 30 years later... a challenging puzzle."

—*The Washington Post*

➢

"Gideon Oliver, that most engaging forensic anthropologist, solves a lulu here... Aaron Elkins is witty and oh so clever with that final twist."

—*New York Daily News*

➢

*more...*

"Murder, a singular detective, a winning supporting cast, humor—what more could we want from a mystery?"

—*Chicago Sun-Times*

➢

"Aaron Elkins' archaeologist detective, Gideon Oliver, has dug out a niche all his own. A latter-day Dr. Thorndyke, he's a forensic whiz known as "the skeleton detective." Show him a few bones and he'll not only describe who died, and from what, but how he or she lived."

—*Detroit News*

➢

"A real detective story, with all the clues placed fairly before the reader—but we'll bet Elkins will keep you guessing."

—*Denver Post*

➢

"It is when Gideon uses a few charred scraps of a human body to describe a man, his height, weight, age and smoking habits, that a new Sherlock Holmes rises before us."

—*Houston Post*

➢

"The hero's enthusiastic lectures on human bones make him fascinating company."

*—New York Times Book Review*

➢

"A pleasure...sit back and enjoy while wallowing in all that deliciously obscure and newly-learned information."

*—USA Today*

➢

"A literate, amiable story...enhanced by a credible plot, a likable hero, and a thoroughly detailed picture of Alaska through a vacationer's eyes."

*—Kirkus*

➢

"Elkins writes with a nice touch of humor ...Oliver is a likeable, down-to-earth, cerebral sleuth."

*—Chicago Tribune*

➢

"Our hero has but to look at a piece of human bone and, like Sherlock Holmes, can tell everything about the person to whom it belonged. Since he knows more about hominid phylogeny than Sherlock did, he can look at a tibial fragment 113 millimeters long and say, 'this one was nearly forty. And Japanese. And built like a wrestler, say 145 pounds.' Great stuff."

*—New York Times Book Review*

*The Professor Gideon Oliver Novels*

ICY CLUTCHES

CURSES!

OLD BONES (1988 Edgar Award-winner for Best Mystery)

MURDER IN THE QUEEN'S ARMES

THE DARK PLACE

FELLOWSHIP OF FEAR

*Also by Aaron Elkins*

A WICKED SLICE (with Charlotte Elkins)

A DECEPTIVE CLARITY

A GLANCING LIGHT

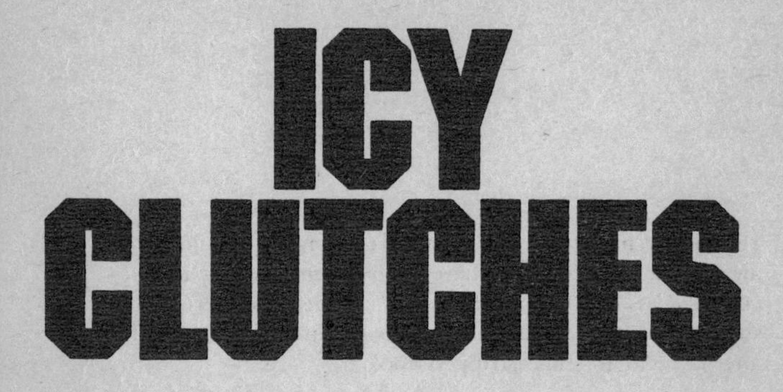


# ICY CLUTCHES

AARON ELKINS

THE MYSTERIOUS PRESS
New York • Tokyo • Sweden • Milan
Published by Warner Books
 A Time Warner Company

If you purchase this book without a cover you should be aware that this book may have been stolen property and reported as "unsold and destroyed" to the publisher. In such case neither the author nor the publisher has received any payment for this "stripped book."

This is a work of fiction. The characters, incidents, and dialogues are products of the author's imagination and are not to be construed as real. Any resemblance to actual events or persons, living or dead, is entirely coincidental.

MYSTERIOUS PRESS EDITION



Cover illustration by Stanislaw Fernandes

The Mysterious Press name and logo are trademarks of Warner Books, Inc.

Mysterious Press books are published by
Warner Books, Inc.
666 Fifth Avenue
New York, New York 10103
A Time Warner Company

Printed in the United States of America

Originally published in hardcover by The Mysterious Press.
First Mysterious Press Paperback Printing: December, 1991

10 9 8 7 6 5 4 3 2 1

## ACKNOWLEDGMENTS

Gideon Oliver has always relied on the kindness of his real-life counterparts. For *Icy Clutches*, particular thanks are due to several practicing forensic anthropologists. First, it was Dr. Michael Charney, Director of Colorado State University's Forensic Science Laboratory, who gave me the focal idea for the plot over a friendly cup of coffee one morning.

Later, others cordially and generously filled in gaps in my knowledge with their own formidable expertise, viz: Peggy Caldwell of Rutgers University and the New York City Medical Examiners Office; Dr. Rodger Heglar, consultant in forensic anthropology, San Diego, and Professor Emeritus, San Francisco State University; Dr. Ted Rathbun, Chairman of the Anthropology Department, University of South Carolina; and Dr. Ed Waldrip, Director of the Southern Institute for Forensic Science, New Orleans.

David W. Spirtes, Chief Ranger, Glacier Bay National Park and Preserve, was equally generous with his time and considerable knowledge.

Glacier Bay Lodge, where much of the story's action occurs, is a real place, and is as described. My thanks go to owner Bob Giersdorf for his permission to use this remote and romantic hotel as a setting for some fictional foul play.

# PROLOGUE

*Skagway Herald*, July 27, 1960

### AVALANCHE NEAR GLACIER BAY SCIENTIFIC RESEARCH TEAM FEARED LOST

*Four scientists are believed dead in an avalanche near the foot of Johns Hopkins Inlet in the northeastern arm of Glacier Bay, Alaska. The avalanche, apparently triggered by yesterday's earthquake tremors, is believed to have ended the lives of all four members of a botanical survey team from the University of Washington headed by Professor Melvin A. Tremaine, chairman of the Department of Botany. The team was making its way across a spur of low-lying Tirku Glacier when the earthquake struck. They had been studying periglacial vegetation in the Glacier Bay region.*

*In addition to Professor Tremaine, 40, the other*

*missing members are graduate students James Pratt, 24, Jocelyn Yount, 25, and Miss Yount's fiancé, Steven Fisk, also 25.*

*A fifth member of the project, Assistant Professor Walter Judd, is uninjured. Judd, 30, accompanied the others on the flight to Johns Hopkins Inlet from Gustavus, but became ill shortly after landing and remained at the shoreline, a mile from the path of the avalanche.*

*Three other members, including the assistant director, Dr. Anna Henckel, 31, a research associate at the university, had remained behind at the project's headquarters in Gustavus.*

*Aerial search missions for the missing scientists are continuing, but little hope of finding them exists, according to Glacier Bay National Monument Superintendent Albert Stutfield.*

*Skagway Herald*, July 28, 1960

## SCIENTIST FOUND ALIVE
## BURIED IN ICE FOR 21 HOURS

*In what was termed a "miracle stroke of luck," Melvin A. Tremaine, leader of the botanical survey team believed lost in Tuesday's avalanche at Glacier Bay, was discovered alive late this morning. Tremaine, who had survived for over 21 hours trapped in a glacial crevasse, was found when a search plane pilot spotted his red parka from the air.*

*The scientist, who was unconscious when rescuers reached him at 11:00 A.M., was wedged into a shallow 90-foot-long cleft in the ice. He was flown to Bartlett Memorial Hospital in Juneau, where his condition is listed as critical. According to a hospital spokesman,*

*Tremaine's injuries include lacerations, frostbite, internal injuries, and fractures of the skull, leg, and both arms.*

*The search for other survivors is continuing.*

*Skagway Herald*, July 30, 1960

**GLACIER BAY SEARCH ENDS**

*Glacier Bay Monument Superintendent A. D. Stutfield announced late yesterday that the search for survivors of last Tuesday's avalanche has been called off after three days.*

*"We've done our best," Stutfield said in commenting on the termination of the search. "There is absolutely no chance of anyone still being alive."*

*The sole survivor, expedition director Melvin A. Tremaine, remains at Juneau's Bartlett Memorial Hospital. His condition is listed as serious but stable. According to hospital spokesman Raymond Stouby, Tremaine is now intermittently conscious. He is expected to regain full use of his faculties.*

*Anchorage Daily News*, September 8, 1964

**HUMAN REMAINS IDENTIFIED**

*GLACIER BAY—A man's platinum ring engraved with the inscription "To Steve, Love Forever, Jocelyn" has led to the solution of a grisly mystery. National Monument officials have now confirmed reports that the fragmentary human remains recently discovered at the terminus of Tirku Glacier are those of members of a botanical research party killed in a 1960 avalanche.*

*The ring, found in association with a small number of bone fragments and some tattered items of clothing and equipment, was identified by Robert Fisk of Boise, Idaho, as belonging to his brother, Steven Fisk, a member of the ill-fated Tirku survey team. The ring had been a gift from his fiancée, Jocelyn Yount, also killed in the avalanche.*

*According to A. D. Stutfield, monument supervisor, the remains washed out of the glacier after being locked in the ice since 1960. "They may have been lying out in the open for months," he said. "It's not an area that gets much in the way of foot traffic."*

*A skeletal-identification expert has subsequently identified the bones as those of Fisk and James Pratt, both graduate students at the University of Washington. No trace of Miss Yount is believed to have been recovered.*

*Reached at his home in Seattle by telephone, the expedition director, Professor Melvin A. Tremaine of the University of Washington, said that he was "too overwhelmed with emotion by this new development to offer meaningful comment." Tremaine himself was trapped in a glacial crevasse for 21 hours in the avalanche's aftermath.*

*The assistant director, Dr. Anna M. Henckel, was unavailable for comment.*

# 1

Glacier Bay Lodge, September 10, 1989

"I think it only fitting," Professor Tremaine said, rising with a feline grace not often seen in a man of sixty-nine, "I think it only fitting that we conclude our first dinner together with a toast."

He inclined his handsome, scarred face downward while the waiter glided noiselessly around the table with a towel-wrapped magnum of Piper Heidsieck, the third of the evening. When each of the six fluted glasses had received its portion of champagne, Professor Tremaine lifted his head. With a tanned and graceful hand he casually brushed back the lock of thick, strikingly white hair that fell so often and so artlessly over his brow. His lean shoulders under the cashmere jacket were squared, his back straight. He raised his glass.

"To the memory of three young people," he said, "three brave young people who gave their lives—so full of promise—in the pursuit of the advancement of human knowledge. To Jocelyn Yount, to Steven Fisk, to James Pratt. We who remain behind . . . remain and grow old . . . we salute you."

He made as if to speak further, then stopped with a small shake of his head and raised his glass.

Five glasses besides his own were raised. Five throats besides his own gurgled with champagne. Here and there an eye glistened. It was a poignant moment, a moment satisfactorily replete with memories and emotions. It would, Professor Tremaine thought serenely, make a moving opening to his book, far better than the one he'd been planning.

> *In mid-September of 1989, in a warm and pleasant dining room, I looked out*—make that *gazed out.* Make that *gazed pensively out—across a chill, gray Bartlett Cove toward the ice-choked inlet where it had all happened so many years ago. I raised my glass. "To the memory of three young people," I said, "three brave young people who—"*

His train of thought interrupted, Professor Tremaine scowled. "What?"

No one responded, but he knew what he'd heard.

"What a crock of shit," somebody had said.

And unless he was very much mistaken, it had been uttered in the distinctly Teutonic tones of the eminent Dr. Anna M. Henckel.

The subsequent angry thump with which Professor Tremaine set his glass on the table was not quite loud enough to carry to the far end of the Glacier Bay Lodge dining room. There, at the only other occupied table—actually four tables pushed together—sat twelve men and two women in the gray and green uniforms of the National Park Service. And one tall, quiet man in cotton slacks and a much-laundered, pale blue sweatshirt. Most of those in uniform were engaged in a vigorous after-dinner argument on the merits of the conventional prusik sliding-friction knot versus those of the Kleimheist. The lone civilian, by contrast, was gazing (abstractedly rather than pensively) out the window at the placid, darkening waters of Bartlett Cove and the sunset-reddened glaciers of the Fairweathers beyond. Occasionally he lifted his coffee cup to his lips, or sighed, or crossed his restless legs, or uncrossed them.

Gideon Oliver was beginning to wonder if coming along with Julie to her training session had been such a good idea. It had made sense when they'd planned it. His fall classes at the University of Washington–Port Angeles would not start for another week, and his notes were fully prepared. He had finally finished the proto-hominid evolution monograph on which he'd been working for most of the summer and sent it in to the *American Journal of Physical Anthropology*. The one case he was handling for the FBI (two skeletons buried under the parking lot of a membership discount department store in Tacoma) was on hold; he'd finished his analysis and wouldn't be called as an expert witness until the case came to trial in November, if then.

So why not use the unaccustomed free time to accompany Julie on a trip to the pristine far north, to Glacier Bay, Alaska, which neither of them had seen before? Wouldn't it be better than being separated for a week? Her days would be taken up, of course: She would be attending the five-day Glacier Search and Rescue training course. But he could spend his days in long, cool, solitary walks, and look at icebergs floating in the bay, and maybe take one of the excursion boats up Tarr Inlet to see the glaciers calving. Or read a novel. Or just relax and do nothing for a change. And the evenings and nights would be all theirs. This would be a great vacation, a tonic for both of them.

Only it wasn't going to work out. There were only two trails in the thickly wooded vicinity of the lodge, totaling three and a quarter miles; he had already been around them twice. They had forgotten to bring any novels and none were available at the lodge, the newsstand having closed when the tourist season ended a week earlier. And there wasn't an iceberg to be seen; the nearest ones floated out of sight, thirty miles beyond the Beardslees, in the bay's northern reaches. And the excursion boats to the glaciers had, of course, closed down along with the newsstand.

The one good thing was that the nights *were* all theirs, and that would make up for a lot. Just being wherever Julie was made up for a lot. Still, it was going to be a long week. Here it was, not quite the end of the first day, and already he was bored stiff. He turned an ear to the discussion around him in hopes that the subject had changed to something more amenable.

". . . feel that way about it, what's wrong with a mechanical prusiker?" someone was spiritedly demanding. "The Heibler clamp, for example?"

This was met with incredulous laughter. "The *Heibler?* You gotta be kidding! The minute you put any lateral load-bearing stress—"

Gideon tuned out again. He looked out over the quiet water. He looked for a while at the other party across the room. The silver-haired man at the head of the table, wasn't he familiar? No, he decided; he simply looked like the generic Hollywood version of the Great Novelist, as seen on movie screens a hundred times: long, wavy white hair, craggy features, cashmere jacket, even an ascot tucked into an open-throated shirt. Gideon's interest wandered, and he looked out the window again. He uncrossed his legs. He toyed with the dessert menu card. He sighed.

Julie turned toward him. "Gideon? Anything wrong?"

"No, just a little restless. Too much coffee, I suppose."

"I don't think that's what it is. I don't think you enjoy being my spouse."

"I love being your spouse. It's my all-time favorite occupation."

"That's not what I mean."

He nodded. "I know."

What she meant was that he didn't like tagging along to someone else's meeting with no role of his own to play. And she was right.

"I think it was the 'and spouse' that did it," she said.

"I think you're right."

A list of attendees had been waiting for them in their room when they'd arrived. "Julene Oliver," the sixth entry had read, "Supervising Park Ranger (GS–13), Olympic National Park, Washington. And spouse."

When he'd seen that, he'd had terrifying visions of the "spouses' programs" awaiting him. "My God," he'd said, "I can see it now. 'Morning bus tour to Kumquat Village, where you will be greeted by lifelike Indians and served a traditional Indian lunch of mud-broiled salmon cakes, to be followed by a program of authentic Indian war dances. In the afternoon, a leisurely visit to nearby Totem Shopping Mall.'"

"I wouldn't worry about it," she'd said. "The closest mall's in Juneau."

"I'm glad to hear it. I must be lucky. Come to think of it, I guess there won't be any bus tours either."

There wouldn't be any bus tours because there weren't any roads; none besides the dirt strip between the lodge and the little airport at Gustavus ten miles away. The only way in or out of Glacier Bay was by boat from the coast, or by airplane—one scheduled flight a day in, one out; a tree-skimming, thirty-minute hop between Juneau and Gustavus.

That had all been this morning. By the end of the week, he now feared, he'd be more than ready for a visit to Kumquat Village. Maybe by tomorrow.

The harried-looking man on Julie's other side detached himself from the general conversation and leaned across to them.

"You're talking about spousal activities?" he asked Gideon. "You're not finding enough to do?" The possibility seemed to cause him real concern. "It's a shame you're the only spouse here. If we had a few more I'd have arranged something interesting. Maybe," he said, his eyes brightening, "I could—"

"That's okay," Gideon said quickly. "That's all right. No problem at all, Arthur."

In the absence of the superintendent of Glacier Bay National Park and Preserve (on vacation in Hawaii) Assistant Superintendent Arthur Tibbett was the ranking park official and the host at the welcoming dinner for the class. A soft, compact man with a vaguely beleaguered air, he seemed a fish out of water at this table of fit, outdoorsy men and women; a paper-pusher among the nature children. Already he bore the mark of his kind, the bureaucrat's habitual little pucker of anxiety between his sandy eyebrows. His interest in—and probably his knowledge of—prusiks and Kleimheists had run out early. For the last twenty minutes he had been going through the motions: here a minuscule nod, there a preoccupied murmur of agreement, here a vacant smile while his fingers tapped restlessly on the table.

Spousal programs seemed to be more in his line. "Last year," he told Gideon with his first show of enthusiasm, "we flew them to Haines to see *Lust for Dust,* which is really a great show. And did you know they have the world's tallest totem pole there? But I just can't justify the cost for one person. My budgetary allocation for—"

"Really, I'm fine, Arthur." Spousal activities. Was the term itself repellent, lascivious even, or was it just his mood? "I'm having a great time. Don't give me a thought. Really." He tipped his head toward the table at the other end of the room. "The white-haired man over there . . . he looks awfully familiar. You wouldn't happen to know who—"

"Oh," Tibbett said lukewarmly, "you mean Professor Tremaine."

Gideon snapped his fingers. "Tremaine! That's M. Audley Tremaine, isn't it?"

"It *is?*" Julie said, impressed.

The three of them looked across the room at the suave and celebrated host of "Voyages," television's preeminent science program and king of the Sunday-afternoon ratings, if you didn't count football season.

"He looks exactly the way he does on television," Julie said. "Will you just look at that tan?"

"He didn't get it around here," the pallid Tibbett said, managing to make it sound like an accusation.

"What's he doing here?" Gideon asked. "The lodge is closed for the season, isn't it?"

"Technically, yes, but it's kept open for Park Service training at this time of year, and he just horned in, to put it candidly. The man doesn't have a scruple about bypassing regulations. A friendly telephone call to his good friend the deputy secretary of the interior, and here he is with his entourage, working on his great opus."

That would explain Tibbett's animosity. The assistant superintendent was not a man to look with favor on the bypassing of regulations.

"Opus? Is he writing a book?" Julie asked.

"Yes. You've probably heard about his being involved in an avalanche here at Glacier Bay years ago?"

Julie nodded. "He was the only survivor."

It had happened almost three decades before, but it was everyday knowledge. Tremaine, who had been heading a botanical research team, had been trapped in a crevasse on Tirku Glacier for a day and a night. Later, he had used this ordeal as the cornerstone of his career. It was a rare episode of "Voyages" that didn't have some reference to it, however oblique. The pitted facial scars from a barrage of two-hundred-mile-an-hour ice spicules and the limp caused by the loss of three toes to frostbite had added to his allure, visible reminders of a life filled with danger and exotic adventure. His eaglelike profile and elegant, nasal baritone hadn't hurt either. He had begun appearing on talk shows in the seventies, had introduced "Voyages" with immediate success in the mid-eighties, and had been America's best-known science popularizer ever since. Somewhere along the way he had left his academic pursuits—some said his academic integrity—behind him, although guests on his show were still instructed by the producer to address him as "professor."

"Well," Tibbett explained, "now it seems he's writing a tell-all book about it. *Tragedy on Ice.*"

"Sounds like something starring Peggy Fleming," Julie said under her breath. Tibbett guffawed immoderately, then turned it into a discreet cough.

"Who are the others?" Gideon asked. "Why would he need an entourage?" Anything was better than Heibler clamps and lateral load-bearing stress.

Tibbett peered at them again. "The gray-haired woman is Dr. Anna Henckel. She was Tremaine's assistant on the original survey. And the, ah, portly gentleman next to her is Dr. Walter Judd; he was on it too. The others—well, I don't have their names straight, but I understand they're relatives of the three people who were killed. Tremaine is using them all as resources, I gather."

"M. Audley Tremaine," Gideon mused after a moment. "I'd sure like to meet him."

Julie stared at him. "Are you serious? The only time I remember you watching 'Voyages' was when it covered human evolution. You ranted and fidgeted through the whole thing. You were yelling at the television set. You called him a pompous charlatan, as I recall."

Tibbett blinked and eyed Gideon with transparent respect.

"That's because the man got everything so completely screwed up," Gideon said. "In one hour he single-handedly managed to set popular understanding of evolution back ten years. Remember how he 'traveled back in time' and talked to those 'Neanderthalers'? Those actors with fur pasted on them, grunting and squatting and hopping—*hopping*, for God's sake—all over the place, like big, hairy fleas?"

"I remember," Julie said. "You made your point very clearly at the time. Or at least very loudly. So then why do you want to meet him?"

"Because of the work he did back in the fifties, before my time. Before he was M. Audley Tremaine, for that matter."

"Come again?"

"He used to go by his first name; Milton, or Morton . . ."

"Melvin," put in Tibbett. "Melvin A. Tremaine. I suppose it isn't dashing enough for him nowadays."

"Right, Melvin A. Tremaine. He was a pioneer in the study of postglacial plant succession; very important stuff for physical anthropology. Some of the definitive work on late Pleistocene human skeletal dating was based on his research on vertical pollen distribution analysis."

Julie nodded. Tibbett's eyes glazed slightly.

"He and I are colleagues in a way," Gideon said. "He was at U-Dub twenty or thirty years before I was."

"U-Dub?" Tibbett echoed.

"He's speaking native dialect," explained Julie. "It means University of Washington."

"I see," said Tibbett, who obviously didn't.

"U-Dub," Julie said. "It's short for U.W."

"Oh." Tibbett searched visibly for something to talk about. He didn't want to go back to Heiblers either. "You know, next year is the thirtieth anniversary of the Tirku project, and the department is going to put up a memorial near the site of the avalanche." His lips twitched their disapproval. "No possible connection to the publication of his book, of course," he said tartly. "Well, tomorrow I have to accompany him and his party out to the site—as if I didn't have anything more important to do—where they'll choose the location for the plaque."

He snorted. "Probably an idea dreamed up by his press agent. I know no one consulted *me* about it. The whole thing's ridiculous. It's not as if anyone ever goes in there, in any case, so who's going to see it? He's simply exploiting the majesty of the United States government to promote his book, that's what he's doing."

Tibbett grumbled on in this vein for a while, not without Gideon's sympathy. Still, Tremaine's contribution to post-glacial plant succession was a real one, and Gideon's respect for the man as a scientist was high.

He drained his coffee. "Do you think he'd mind if I went over and said hello?"

But as Gideon put the cup down, Tremaine and his party began getting up. Tremaine nodded curtly to the others and headed for the exit, his limp quite marked. He was smaller than he appeared to be on television, perhaps five-nine. His path brought him within a few feet, and Gideon stood as he approached.

"Dr. Tremaine? My name is Gideon Oliver. I'm a great admirer of your work—"

He stopped, startled. The dessert menu card he'd absently continued to hold had been snatched from him by Tremaine. "Certainly," the silver-haired television star said. "Delighted."

Tremaine plucked a pen from the inside of his jacket, scrawled something across the card, thrust it back into Gideon's hand, and went on his way.

Gideon stared at his back for a moment, then looked down at the card.

"Happy voyages," it said. "Best wishes, M. Audley Tremaine."

As he did most mornings, Gideon awakened just before the alarm clock was due to go off. And as he did most mornings, he found himself nestled against Julie's back. He sighed, nuzzled her neck, and reached out to click off the alarm before it buzzed.

Julie stirred and muttered into the pillow, "It can't be six o'clock already. It can't be."

"I'm afraid it is."

She groaned softly and turned herself into him, snuggling her chin into the hollow of his shoulder. For a while they lay quietly, pressed against each other, dozing and content. For Gideon, this was perhaps the best part of the day. Was he at heart such a pessimist that he should awaken each morning filled with gratitude, with relief, almost with amazement, at having her lying by his side?

"I love you," he said. He bent his head to kiss her hair.

She murmured something, worked herself closer still, and fell asleep again, her breath warm and sweet against his chest.

At 6:10 he disengaged himself, got shivering into his robe, and turned up the room's thermostat. He put up some coffee in the automatic coffee maker on its own little shelf over the sink and stood waiting for the water to boil, staring numbly at his wild-haired, unshaven reflection in the mirror. Morning coffee was his responsibility; that was one of several mutually agreeable arrangements they had worked out by trial and error. Cooking chores were evenly split, but Julie did the dinner dishes, in exchange for which Gideon hauled himself out of bed to make coffee every morning.

It was a system that seemed eminently equitable in the evenings, but somehow less fair in the mornings, especially in a cold, burnt-rose Alaskan dawn when there had been no dinner dishes to do the evening before. Maybe a little renegotiation was in order. He scratched a sandpapery cheek and smiled at his reflection. What the hell, why not just admit that he enjoyed making coffee for her, carrying it to her, watching her stretch and come awake smiling?

"Mmm," she called, "smells wonderful." She yawned, shoved some pillows up against the headboard, and pushed herself partway up with her eyes still screwed shut. Julie was like a zombie in the morning, barely articulate and only marginally coherent until she'd had a cup of coffee or been awake for an hour. Whichever came first.

He brought the pot and the cups to her on a tray, put them on the nightstand, and sat on the side of the bed. She had nodded off again, chin on her chest. He kissed her cheek, at the corner of her mouth. She mumbled something. He kissed the side of her throat. With her eyes still closed she murmured some more and lifted her arms to go around his neck.

"Mmm," she said again, while he continued nuzzling, "'zis serious?"

"I'm afraid not," he said. "You have to be dressed and out of here in twenty minutes." He loosened her hold and poured coffee into the Styrofoam cups for both of them, then stuck hers in her hand, closing her fingers around it. "What's on your agenda anyway?"

Julie took another swallow to gather strength for speaking. "Latest techniques in victim location. All-day field trip. You?" Complex sentences, or even complete ones, were not to be expected first thing in the morning.

"Me? I'm not doing anything. I'll relax, that's all."

Her eyes finally opened to regard him doubtfully. "You're going to spend an entire day doing nothing?"

"Absolutely. With pleasure. I've gotten too goal-oriented, that's my problem. From now on I just take life as it comes."

# 2

Professor Tremaine was not altogether pleased with the way things were progressing. Oh, they had gone reasonably well during the introductory dinner the night before (Anna's characteristically vulgar comment aside), but now, at breakfast, he sensed an undercurrent of tension, of reserve. In the cases of Anna Henckel and Walter Judd he could guess at the reasons, ridiculous though they might be, but what did the others have to be touchy about? By the end of the week there would be cause enough, but why now? They had never met each other before. They were enjoying a quite luxurious stay at Glacier Bay at his expense, were they not? Well, perhaps not at *his* expense, but it amounted to the same thing, didn't it? If they didn't want to come, why were they there? Had anyone forced them?

Or was he imagining things? Might they be not touchy but star struck, now that they grasped that they would actually be working directly with him for the next few days? Sometimes he forgot the impact that meeting a celebrity had on ordinary people. Absurd, really—he was quite the same as anyone else—but there it was, and he supposed it was up to him to do something about it. The better their initial relations, the better things would go later.

He pushed the remains of his buttered English muffin away, signaled for another cup of coffee, and got out his box of Dunhills. He lit up, sucked in a deep lungful of smoke, tucked a loose end of his paisley ascot into his shirt collar, and cleared his throat. "We have twenty minutes before we leave for Tirku Glacier," he said, "and it occurs to me that there may still be some unanswered questions about just why we are here. If so, please feel free to ask them."

He peered at them with warm sincerity and lifted his eyebrows to indicate that such questions were welcome. More than welcome.

Gerald Pratt's lean, weathered hand went slowly up. Everything Gerald Pratt did went slowly. In that way he reminded Tremaine of Pratt's brother James, killed in the avalanche in 1960. Physically, too, the resemblance was there if you looked for it: the bony nose—broken and poorly mended in Gerald's case—the long face, the lantern jaw. Was this what James would have come to if he'd lived? James, too, had sometimes been maddeningly measured in speech and manner, but there had been a spark, an intensity, flickering beneath that quiet surface. This the dark, gaunt, torpid Gerald lacked utterly. But Gerald was in his fifties, of course. James, his younger brother by a year or two, had never reached thirty. Ah, well, Tremaine thought with the tinge of melancholy that often came with his first cigarette of the day, there was something to be said for dying young.

He smiled tolerantly. "There's no need to raise our hands here, Mr. Pratt."

Pratt lowered his hand. "I'm no scientist," he said in the laconic, deliberate way that had already begun to grate on Tremaine's nerves. "Comes to that, I'm not much of a reader either. So . . ." His cheeks hollowed as he drew on his pipe. "So . . ." One cloud, two clouds, three clouds of nauseous, yellowish-brown smoke emerged in slow procession.

Tremaine made a conscious effort to keep from tapping his foot with impatience. The tolerant smile began to congeal. "Yes . . . ?"

"So I'd appreciate it," Pratt finally droned, "if you'd tell us just why we're here and what's expected of us. Sort of in a nutshell."

"You didn't get a letter from Javelin Press?"

"I saw it," Pratt said. "Didn't make a whole lot of sense." He ran a hand through lank, black, thinning hair.

"Well, then, let me see if I can make it clearer." In Pratt's case, Tremaine suspected, the problem was not awe, or touchiness either. The man was permanently out to lunch, that was all. "As you know, I am nearing the completion of a book on the Tirku botanical survey party of 1960. Until now I have never discussed those last fateful hours on the ice with complete candor. Now I think it's time to tell the story, the full human story, which no living person but myself knows. It is scheduled for publication in May of next year—1990 being the thirtieth anniversary of the expedition."

He lifted his coffee and sipped. "The idea came to me that before I prepared my final draft it would be a good idea to review the material with people who might have some unique personal or scientific insights into it. Thus, some weeks ago, I asked my publisher about the possibility of gathering a small group together for that purpose.

Javelin Press readily agreed, and here we are. As I mentioned last night, I will be reading the manuscript aloud over the next several days, and all of you will be free to make whatever comments or suggestions you care to, as I go along."

"Mm," Pratt said, sucking at his pipe and looking no less thoughtfully obtuse than he had before. He was wearing oil-stained orange coveralls. Yesterday, it had been oil-stained brown coveralls.

"I have great confidence in the value of the contributions to come," Professor Tremaine said. "Dr. Henckel here was the assistant director of the project, of course, and I'm sure she will have much to offer. The same applies to Dr. Judd, here on my right, who is the only other surviving member. You, Mr. Pratt, and Ms. Yount next to you, and Dr. Fisk there, as close relatives of the three young people who lost their lives, are in a position to provide many insights into their personalities and characters, of which I could hardly be aware."

He paused for a beat, as they liked to say in television. "I need hardly add that all of your contributions will be gratefully acknowledged in the book."

Out of the corner of his eye he saw Anna Henckel stiffen at that. He was right, then. Still nursing that ancient and absurd grudge, was she? Well, he'd forgotten it long ago. Not that her savagely vindictive letters to the *Journal of Systematic Botany* wouldn't rankle even now, if he let them. And what about that virulent and unjustified attack on him at the 1969 American Society of Plant Taxonomists congress in Phoenix? If anyone had the right to a grudge, he did. Fortunately, that wasn't the kind of person he was. As far as he was concerned, bygones were bygones. Water under the bridge.

He smiled again at Pratt. "Does that clarify things, Mr. Pratt?"

"I suppose so," Pratt said with a shrug. He poked with a finger at his thin, dark mustache. "Tell the truth, though, I don't really see what I can add."

There Tremaine agreed with him. He didn't see what *any* of them could add—for what he'd told Pratt hadn't been quite true. This gathering hadn't been his idea at all. It had come from Javelin Press; from their attorney. Javelin had been on the losing end of an invasion-of-privacy settlement not long before, and they were still skittish. The best way to avoid problems, the attorney had said, was to "co-opt potential adversaries by involving them in the developmental process." If they chose not to participate, they would be asked to sign a statement so indicating. But they had chosen to participate.

At first Tremaine had thought it was a terrible idea, but as time passed he began to see some value in it. There were going to be some unsettling revelations in his book, and no doubt some—probably all—of these people were going to be upset. Better to deal with that before the book came out, rather than after. It might make for some unpleasant moments this week, but he could deal with that. He was no stranger to confrontation.

"Be glad to do what I can to help, though," Pratt said around the stem of his pipe. Laconic he might be, but the man had a way of mumbling on. And on.

"Thank you." Tremaine's crisp nod was meant to terminate the exchange.

"And whose idea was it to meet here, of all places?" Anna Henckel asked tartly. "Also yours, Melvin? To add a touch of sentiment?"

Anna was baiting him, of course. Aside from her sarcastic tone, she knew very well that he'd dropped the unfortunate "Melvin" when he'd begun to host "Voyages." Well, she had been a mean-spirited woman twenty-some years ago. Had he really expected her to change? She certainly hadn't changed much physically. At sixty, she was as boxy, stone faced, and stern as ever; blankly impassive, magisterial, humorless, detached. Even that chopped-off, battleship-gray hair (a few decades ago it had been battleship dun) seemed like a self-righteous reprimand to his own carefully groomed white mane.

And yet hadn't there been a time, so long ago that it was hardly credible now, when he had seen her in a different light? When her now-guttural speech had been husky and soft, her thick body narrow-waisted and lush? When he had actually believed—briefly, to be sure—that the young and exotic Anna Henckel, with her camellia-petal skin, might be the woman he . . . With an imperceptible shake of his head he dismissed the repellent thought. Well, at least he had made it through that demented phase without blurting out some mortifying amatory declaration to her.

"Yes, also my idea," he said benignly. As always, the sound of his own rich, confident baritone pleased and soothed him. "It seemed to me it would be fitting."

That much was true. He had suggested Glacier Bay as the logical meeting place without giving it much thought. And now he was quite pleased that he had. The idea was already producing dividends. That toast last night was going to make a fine opening scene for the book (sans Anna's muttered contribution, naturally). And now, happily, they would be leaving in a few minutes to choose a place for the memorial plaque. And that little excursion would surely furnish the material for a splendidly poignant final chapter for his book. It would provide a needed sense of completion, of a circle come closed. Or would it do better as an epilogue? More sense of closure that way . . .

*Dwarfed by the ghostly white immensity of Tirku Glacier, we stood silent and bareheaded in the wan sunlight.* Or would *mist* be more evocative? Yes, make that *mist.* Who was going to remember? *We were there to pay tribute to Jocelyn Yount, Steven Fisk, and James Pratt, whose remains were forever locked in the great ice flow, but my thoughts were—*

"*I* have a question."

Tremaine surfaced. "Dr. Fisk?"

At forty, Dr. (of dentistry) Elliott Fisk was the youngest of the group, a balding, unappetizing man whose remaining fringe of hair had been allowed, perhaps even encouraged, to grow into a stringy curtain that hung limply from the level of his ears. A close-cropped but equally offensive gray-splotched beard straggled over his face and neck, growing in all directions. With rectangular gold-rimmed glasses framing glittery eyes, a pinched nose, and a tight little mouth working behind the sparse beard, he was like a cartoon anarchist from the editorial pages of Tremaine's childhood. All that was needed was a spherical bomb with a sputtering fuse in each hand.

Astonishing that he should be a dentist. Tremaine could conceive of no circumstance, no emergency, under which he would allow the man to insert his fingers into his mouth. Elliott was the nephew of Steven Fisk, whom he resembled not at all, and Tremaine had taken a near-instant dislike to him on meeting him the day before.

Little wonder. Like his uncle, Fisk had a way of provoking confrontation. But whereas Steven's combativeness had been the natural result of a thin skin, an absurdly high opinion of himself, and an unfortunate predilection for brawling, Elliott seemed like a man who had consciously chosen a carping churlishness as the *manière d'être* best suited to his philosophy of life and who worked doggedly at maintaining it. Despite his bohemian appearance he was a smug, captious faultfinder who had taken up an inordinate amount of time at dinner the night before with his aimless quibbling over what he persisted in calling "administrivia."

"Why couldn't . . ." he had asked in his sulky, complainer's voice a dozen times, and Tremaine had worn himself out fending him off with shrugs and smiles. Why couldn't they be given per-diem expense accounts instead of having to keep track of and record every individual expenditure? (Because that's the way Javelin's accounting department wanted it.) Why couldn't each of them be scheduled to attend only those sessions to which he or she might have something to add, instead of having everybody sit through every minute? (Because arranging individualized schedules was too damn much work.)

The detestable Fisk had even gone out of his way to sneer at the book's title, *Tragedy on Ice.* Tremaine was still seething about that. What business was it of his? Besides, it most certainly did *not* sound like something starring Dorothy Hamill.

Dr. Fisk's question this morning was in character. "I'd like to know why you couldn't just give us copies of the manuscript to review individually instead of making us spend all this time sitting around while you read the stuff to us." He used his forefinger to probe at something—a bug, probably—in the scrubby hair at the corner of his jaw.

Tremaine's chin lifted. Because that's the way I want it, that's why, you repulsive creep. I'm not about to have six copies of my unpublished manuscript floating around. He made himself relax. "That's a good question, Doctor," he said with an appreciative and thoughtful nod, "but the fact is"—he patted the thick burgundy-leather binder in front of him—"that this is the only copy of the manuscript in existence."

"Is something stopping you from making more? How much would it cost? If you look at it from a cost-benefit perspective, the time saved would more than compensate for the few out-of-pocket dollars expended."

Cost-benefit analysis? Dollars expended? Was the man a dentist or a bureaucrat? Both, now that Tremaine thought about it. If he remembered correctly, Fisk owned a seedy chain of dentures-while-you-wait establishments in Chicago.

Tremaine turned the full force of his craggy smile on him. "I'm sure you're right. It's just that it seems to me that the, er, relational dynamics produced by our, our interfacing would produce a productive level of, of . . ." He took a breath and finished strongly. ". . . of metacommunication over and above that possible in a series of essentially one-on-one transactions."

This dubious and high-flown mélange had come from a "Voyages" program on "communication science," which his producer had talked him into doing a year or so ago. The entire subject had seemed like pretentious claptrap to him at the time, and still did. But it had gotten good ratings, and here it was, proving quite useful after all: Fisk, after opening his hairy mouth somewhat in the manner of a startled carp and making a few chewing motions, fell back silent.

"Well, then," Tremaine said smoothly, "if there are no further—"

"May I ask a question? If there's time?"

"Certainly, Shirley—I mean, *Miz* Yount," he said with exaggerated emphasis and a resolutely gracious smile. He had called her "miss" on meeting her the evening before, and she had been quick to reprimand him in that twangy, chalk-on-blackboard voice of hers. Shirley Yount was the dead Jocelyn Yount's fraternal twin sister, a ropy, toothy woman of fifty-three with plucked eyebrows and upswept coppery hair straight out of the fifties. Here, too, the family resemblance was apparent, but once again the years had taken their depressing toll. Her sister had been a striking six-footer, dreamy, athletic, and sveltely seductive. Shirley, equally tall, was gawky and mannish. In the square neckline of her blouse her collarbones jutted out aggressively, and the deeply tanned skin on her flat chest was as coarse as pebbled cowhide.

What a difference: Jocelyn the svelte, leggy colt; Shirley the tough and sinewy old mare.

During dinner the evening before, she had wormed her way into sitting beside him and had yammered away endlessly, telling him at least three times how thrilled she was to meet him in person. (Was there another way to meet someone?) But of course Tremaine was used to this kind of cretinous gushing, and long resigned to it, particularly from middle-aged spinsters like Shirley Yount.

He was, however, irked by a side-of-the-mouth archness of manner, as if even her most vapid remarks—of which there were many—were really sly, private digs of wit and substance. Tremaine, who prided himself on his perceptiveness about such things, had been unable to decide whether there really was malice behind that tediously saucy facade. Or whether it was a facade at all. Either way, by now it had gotten well under his skin. (Considering that this was only Monday morning, there was quite a lot about this ill-assorted group that had already gotten under his skin.)

But what could she have to be hostile about? Here she was, an unattractive, unmarried department-store buyer in Cincinnati or Cleveland or some such place. Thanks to Tremaine's doing, she was enjoying the trip of a lifetime: an all-expenses-paid stay at the premier vacation destination of western Alaska. She would be talking about it—and about what M. Audley Tremaine was *really* like (in person)—for years at her mah-jongg meetings, or wherever such people gathered socially nowadays.

She leaned forward to frown through gargantuan, hexagonal glasses. "One thing I've always wondered is—oh, is it all right to ask something about the survey? Is that permitted?" There it was again; that annoying ability to make a seemingly innocuous question sound like a tongue-in-cheek insult. Our Miss Brooks getting ready to slip one to the high-school principal.

"Of course," Tremaine said.

"Well, I can't help wondering why it was that Dr. Henckel and Dr. Judd weren't out there with everyone else that day at the glacier. I've always wondered about that. Or shouldn't I ask? If I shouldn't, I'll just shut up. I don't mean I wish they *had* been there, I just mean . . ." She trailed off, as she often did, into a macawlike squawk. "Ha-HAH!"

Ah, was that what was bothering her? The fact that her sister had been cut off at twenty-five while an uncaring Providence had allowed these two overstuffed, middle-aged people who had played it safe to plod comfortably on with their lives? Fine, that was all right with him. It was their problem; let them handle it.

As he expected, it was Walter who crumbled first. As all who knew him came sooner or later to learn, Walter's tugboat of a body; his jolly, chuckly, zesty air of enjoying life to the full; and his ruddy complexion (latently apoplectic, if you asked Tremaine) hid a constitution forged in tapioca.

"Well, now, I wouldn't exactly say I stayed *behind*," Walter said, chuckling on cue.

Tremaine shifted restlessly. Between Walter's chuckle and Shirley's squawk, it was not going to be an easy week. Almost equally irritating, Walter had become a belly flaunter in the years since Tremaine had last seen him. The way some men thrust out their chests, he joyfully displayed the blimplike protuberance at his front. He wore his suspenders wide and his pants low, the better to accommodate it. If he wasn't patting it, he was rubbing it. If he wasn't rubbing it, he was tapping it with a rolled-up magazine, or a pen, or even a ring of keys.

"No," Walter continued, setting his hands on that great belly and closing his eyes, "the fact of the matter is that I flew out there with the others in the morning, fully intent on executing the commands of our glorious leader." He opened his eyes. A jocular wiggle of tufted brows was directed toward Tremaine, but Tremaine, keen observer that he was, noted the accompanying tic just above Walter's padded jawline. He smiled back coolly.

"However," said Walter, "the Fates intervened." He chuckled meaninglessly. "Or perhaps the Furies. A medical crisis developed shortly after we deplaned, and I was unable to continue." He paused for a rumble of throaty, empty laughter. "Down for the count, so to speak. So I had to remain behind at the shore, where the plane would pick us up later."

"Yes, that's the part I'm not too clear on," Shirley persisted with a smile that revealed rather too much wet, pink gumline. "The medical crisis." She eyed him coyly, her long, purplish nose honed. "Or isn't it any of my business? I mean, I'm just curious, so tell me to shut up if . . . well . . . ha-HAH!"

"No, no, my dear lady—my dear Shirley, if I may—that's all right. As a matter of fact it was . . ." He leaned forward and paused theatrically, then finished in a stage whisper: ". . . a mosquito bite!"

The words appeared to penetrate Gerald Pratt's lethargy. "A *mosquito bite,* did he say?" The murmured question floated out of a haze of turgid brown smoke. "Is that right?"

"An *infected* mosquito bite," Walter said, "despite which I was heroically bent on continuing my mission." A pause for another forced chuckle. "But our glorious leader, in his greater wisdom, forbade it. I ask you: What could I do but submit as gracefully as I could?" He concluded this annoying performance with an exasperating tattoo played out on his abdomen.

How inexplicable were human emotions! Tremaine almost shook his head with wonderment. For almost three decades, it appeared, Walter had maintained this foolish resentment against him because—well, why? Because Tremaine had almost certainly kept him from being killed in the avalanche, wasn't that what it amounted to? Was that what the man would have preferred? Not that it wouldn't have been what he deserved, inasmuch as it was his fault they had to be out there in the first place.

In any case, Tremaine's insistence that he remain behind had surely been correct. The infected bite had been ugly, with long streaks of brilliant red radiating from the wrist almost to the armpit. Walter had been on penicillin for ten days afterward. With a condition like that, one remained quiet; one did not stimulate blood circulation by scrambling up and down glacial flows. Even if he had survived the avalanche, he would probably have come away with gangrene. Was that what he wanted?

And yet Tremaine sympathized to some extent. There was something undeniably absurd about being kept from a rendezvous with destiny by a mosquito bite. But then that was the sort of person Walter was; a man of limited scope and inconsequential vision, fated by a feeble character to be stymied by minor obstacles. He had hardly protested very vigorously that morning when Tremaine "forbade" him from continuing. What could Tremaine have done if this whale of a man had insisted on going with them? Clamped him in irons? But of course he hadn't insisted at all. He'd merely whined and submitted, as the manuscript made quite clear—one of several things poor Walter was not going to be very happy about.

Tremaine wondered how happy he was with his life as a whole. Probably not very. A few years after the survey, when Walter failed—deservedly—to gain tenure, he had moved to Alaska, first to take an undemanding teaching position at a community college in Barrow, a school whose chief (only?) distinction was that of being the northernmost institution of "higher" learning on the North American continent. From there he had found his way into state government and a lackluster career in the Department of the Environment. Now it was rumored that the governor, apparently no judge of competence, was about to appoint him head of the department, a highly visible, cabinet-level post. Well, good luck to the Alaskan environment, was all Tremaine had to say.

Anna barely waited for Walter to finish before she got in her two cents' worth. "As for me," she announced in that contentious way of hers, "I *did* remain behind in Gustavus on the day of the avalanche. We were correcting some errors in the mapping and distribution analyses."

She flicked a glance at the shiny-faced Walter but didn't bother to explain that it was his bungling and incompetence she was talking about. Well, no surprise there, Tremaine thought; it was *him,* Tremaine, she was saving her ammunition for.

Turning, she stared at Shirley with stolid condescension. "Is this satisfactory to you?"

Just like Anna, Tremaine thought. Never pass up an opportunity to make waves.

Shirley smiled glassily. "Well, if it's all right with you, it's certainly all right with me, dear."

Now there. That was an example. Had that been a gossamer-cloaked jab of some kind? Had some electric current imperceptible to the masculine nervous system passed between them? Had Anna—unthinkable idea—been bested in some mysterious female clash of personalities? Anna herself seemed to think so. With a sulky shrug she fished in her bag for her pack of cigarillos.

Tremaine almost chuckled himself. This wasn't something that happened to the formidable Dr. Henckel very often.

And on this pleasant note their breakfast meeting came to an end. Arthur Tibbett, the assistant superintendent who was to accompany them to the glacier, made his appearance.

"Tibbett, Tibbett," Tremaine mused aloud. "Do I know you?"

"I don't think so," the administrator said.

"We haven't met?"

"Not to my knowledge."

Rather a stuffy sort, Tibbett; every inch the minor functionary. Well, well, no matter. Tremaine was not about to let the puffy manner of a petty bureaucrat affect his sunny mood. On to Tirku Glacier.

# 3

Tirku Glacier is hardly one of Glacier Bay's great attractions. The cruise ships that ply the waters so majestically do not stop near its foot to view it. It is not one of the famous tidewater glaciers fronted by a vertical, spired facade of blue-white ice from which skyscraper-sized chunks split off and crash slow-motion into the bay with booming, spectacular explosions of water. Its receding, grimy snout is now half a mile inland on a gritty plain of its own making, and it is not a gloriously photogenic wall of ice at all, but a squat, humped protrusion one hundred and fifty feet thick, black with dirt and boulders, and shaped something like an enormous bear's paw laid flat on the ground.

On a low, rocky moraine at the northeastern edge of this ugly, imposing paw, seven people stood shivering in a freezing miasma that oozed from the glacial face like carbon dioxide from a lump of dry ice. They had walked, speaking little, from the catamaran beached on the barren gray shoreline. Tremaine had expected some emotion from them, but there seemed to be only a bored restlessness. Now they began to wander off individually, poking spiritlessly at rocks and chunks of gray ice that had fallen from the glacier face. Anna, who affected a six-foot ebony staff, like some ancient Watusi queen, was using it to prod the glacier itself.

"Well," Tremaine said, perhaps a little too heartily, "I suppose we'd better go ahead and pick a spot for the plaque. That's what we're here for." No one replied. Silence, awkward and uncomfortable, hung over the little group. The raw fog—not quite the "mist" Tremaine had had in mind—was sharp in their nostrils, smelling like cold iron.

Gerald Pratt, lighting his pipe, presently looked out from behind hands cupped to protect the flame from the dank wind. A blue woolen guard cap jammed down over his ears made his skeletal face look like a death mask. "So this is where it happened," he said conversationally.

"Not quite," Tremaine said, for once glad to hear even from Pratt. "We were on the glacier itself when the avalanche struck. We were crossing this tongue of it, oh, a few hundred yards back. Over there somewhere. It's difficult to say. The snout's moved back quite a bit since then."

Pratt followed his gesture and nodded slowly. "There, you say."

"Of course I don't know about these things," Shirley Yount said in that maddeningly arch way, as if implying that of course she knew everything there was to know about them. "But if that's where it happened, why don't they put the plaque there?"

"I'm afraid that wouldn't work," Arthur Tibbett told her. "Glaciers move, you see. In ten years nobody would know where it was."

"And where would you suggest?" Tremaine asked.

The assistant superintendent started. "Me? Well, it's up to you, of course. I wouldn't want to say." He had been that way all morning.

"Nevertheless," Tremaine said, "we would value your opinion enormously."

"My opinion? What about here on this ridge, right on that big boulder with the notch? That's going to be here for a while."

"Fine, then just *do* it," Elliott Fisk said disagreeably, "before we all freeze to death. What's the difference? Who comes here, one person every ten years? Who's going to see a plaque, a bunch of polar bears?"

"Just like a dentist," Pratt mumbled inscrutably to no one.

Fisk's pale eyes fixed him. "And what is that supposed to mean, if anything?"

"Just say the word 'plaque' and he comes unglued," Pratt said amiably.

Tremaine looked at him, surprised. Did a dormant sense of humor actually lurk somewhere in that gaunt and dour frame?

"I am not unglued," Fisk replied pettishly, "I just want to get on with the damn thing."

Tremaine wanted to get on with it too. "Well, I'd say that wherever Mr. Tibbett—"

He was interrupted by a cry from Walter, who had been wandering aimlessly, shoulders hunched and hands in his pockets, kicking without point at chunks of gray, decaying ice. "Good *God!*" he shouted. "What in the world . . ."

The others turned to him to find him staring at the ground at his feet. On the wet gravel, lying among the softening pieces of ice that had fallen away from the glacier, lay a glistening ivory shaft of bone, six or eight inches long, broken roughly off at one end.

The thought leaped among them like a spark, almost visible in the whitish air. Once before, a few years after the tragedy, the glacier had disgorged some grisly shreds of the dead expedition members. Had it happened again? They stared, fascinated and appalled. Were they looking at a piece of James Pratt? Of Jocelyn Yount? Steven—

Shirley made a gagging noise. "Look, another piece," she said, pointing. "Oh, God." She shuddered and moved closer to Tremaine, presumably for support, but looming some three inches over him. "Are they . . . are they human? Can you tell?"

Tremaine shook his head. "I'm not sure. I believe they might well be. How horrible, how utterly horrible." His heart was leaping with joy. It was too good to be true; he couldn't have dreamed up better publicity himself. Perhaps the publication schedule could be moved up to make the best use of it. He would have to call Javelin as soon as—

"Probably bear," Pratt said offhandedly. "Plenty of 'em around here."

Tremaine glared at him. He didn't care for the bear hypothesis at all. "Mr. Tibbett? Do you know?"

"Me?" said Tibbett, who seemed to respond habitually in this disingenuous and annoying fashion. "Well, they could very well be bear, all right. And then again, maybe not. I'm not a naturalist myself," he finished lamely (and unnecessarily), "I'm more in the administrative line."

"Well, I'm a dentist and I've seen human bones before," Fisk announced, "and I say those bones are human." For the first time Tremaine almost liked him.

The matter was settled beyond doubt by Anna Henckel, who had been rooting in the glacial detritus while the others stared at the bones.

"Look," she said flatly and held out a waterlogged, brown, ankle-height shoe, rotted and misshapen, the lugged sole curling away from the leather upper. "A Raichle boot," she said.

When nobody, including Tremaine, seemed to grasp the significance of this, she added darkly: "It is the shoe we were outfitted with."

"Still," said Walter, who seemed thoroughly shaken, "what does that prove? Other people wear Raichles. Anyone could have thrown away a shoe, or—"

Grimly, Anna shook her head. "There is no mistake." She dipped it so that they could look into the opening in the top. Inside, in a welter of rotten, dirty-gray wool, was a jumble of narrow bones.

Shirley shuddered convulsively. "How can you *touch* that?"

This was followed by a long, tortured silence, broken at last by the familiar, elegant baritone of M. Audley Tremaine.

"Will this cursed glacier," he cried in a voice laden with passion, "never let their bones rest in peace?"

He glanced around, swiftly and surreptitiously. Had he overdone it? No, they all seemed genuinely moved. (Not the immovable Anna, of course.) What a line it would make in the book, what a marvelous scene. He didn't know about the "cursed," though. A little too melodramatic? He'd have to think that through.

"I imagine we should bring these remains back with us," Anna said, still holding the shoe. She looked at Tibbett. "Is there a suitable container on the boat?"

"Seems to me," offered Pratt, "that we ought to leave 'em where we found 'em. Been here for thirty years. Don't see much point in moving 'em."

"Not much *point?*" Shirley was shocked. "Are you nuts, or what? This could be what's left of your brother, for God's sake! Do you want to leave it for the animals to chew on?"

"Bears been chewing on 'em all this time," was Pratt's unsentimental reply. "Don't see much point in moving 'em now."

"Jesus," Shirley said, having recovered enough by now to speak out of the side of her mouth again, "can you believe this guy? Look, this could be my sister too, you know, and if it is, I don't want her lying out here anymore." To Tremaine's amazement, her horsey face suddenly bunched up and reddened; tears spurted from her eyes. "Damn," she said, and turned away.

Pratt shrugged and shifted his weight from one foot to another, looking abashed. "Either way," he said around his pipe. "Dudn't much matter to me."

"Mr. Tibbett, what is the proper course?" Tremaine asked, not overly optimistic about getting a definitive reply.

"Oh," Tibbett said, still looking at the shoe with extreme distaste, "well." He cleared his throat. "I'm not absolutely sure, to tell you the truth. I'll go back to the boat and radio my chief ranger. He's more familiar with this . . . this sort of thing, you know. He'll know the right way to go about it."

"And in the meantime," Anna said decisively, "we look some more and see what we can find."

"Mort, how would I claim a set of Lego blocks?"

FBI Special Agent Morton Kessler resignedly clicked off the microphone of the dictating machine into which he was recording a memo to file and looked wordlessly at his colleague. It was the sort of question you expected John Lau to ask, and Kessler had learned not to be surprised. Other agents' expense statements listed hotel bills, taxi rides, and meals, but John Lau wasn't quite like other agents. He had come to the FBI late, in his thirties, and unusual expense statements were the least of the many ways he didn't quite fit the mold.

Kessler had gotten to know Lau well in the four years since the big Hawaiian ex-cop and former NATO security officer had joined the bureau. What with the partitionless bullpen arrangement on the sixth floor of Seattle's federal building, you learned a lot about the other agents in your squad. The desks were placed in groups of three, arranged in a triangle, with the agents facing in toward the center. It wasn't very often that all three agents were in off the street at the same time, but even so, you got to know your desk mates pretty well.

"Like anything else," Kessler said. "Put it under *miscellaneous* and hope for the best."

"Right, thanks."

Kessler tried without success to go back to his memo. Again he flicked off the machine. "John, I know I'm going to be sorry I asked, but what the hell is a set of Lego blocks doing on your claim form? I mean, it's not something you see every day."

"Well," John said, continuing to write, "this informant was getting mixed up drawing the layout of a house in Renton, so I thought if I got him a set of Legos he could—"

"—build you a model. Right. Of course. It's obvious." He got up out of his chair. "I need to get a file in rotary. If anybody calls I'll be back in ten."

The single telephone shared by the three desks rang. Kessler hung back while John picked it up.

"Five-Squad. Lau."

"Mr. Lau, this is Annie. Will you hold, please?"

"For me," John mouthed to Kessler, who waved and headed for the filing unit.

"The SAC wants to speak with you, Mr. Lau," Annie went on.

Abbreviations and acronyms were not John's long suits; no more than claims and paperwork. "SAC?"

From halfway across the room Kessler turned. "Special agent in charge, for Christ's sake!" he hissed. "The boss." He shook his head once, briefly raised his eyes to the fluorescent lights, and continued on his way.

John waited, ear to the telephone. The special agent in charge of the Seattle field office was Charlie Appletree, a veteran from the old school who still wore a dark suit and white shirt to the office every day, and still sported a crew cut, although there wasn't much to cut anymore. He had been a confidant of every director since Hoover, with the exception of William Ruckleshaus, whom he had openly regarded as a naive, pipe-smoking do-gooder. "I don't know where you came from," he was reputed to have told the gentle Ruckleshaus in a celebrated exchange, "or who the hell you are, but you sure as hell aren't the director of the FBI."

Generally speaking, however, he was more restrained; soft-spoken, intelligent, subtly political.

"Hello there, John. How are you today?"

"Fine, sir."

"Look, I've just had a call from Dan Britten, the SAC in Anchorage . . ." He paused, familiar with John's small failings. "Uh, you know what SAC means . . . ?"

"Sure." John laughed with amusement at the question. "Special agent in charge."

"That's right, that's right." Appletree sounded pleased. "Good. Well, it seems Dan got a call from the resident agent in Juneau, who got a call from the National Park Service people at Glacier Bay. They've turned up some bones there, apparently human, and they need some help."

"Foul play involved?"

"No, nothing like that. It's a matter for the NPS, not the

bureau. They're pretty sure they're the remains of a scientific party that was lost years ago in an avalanche. No question of murder."

"Uh-huh." John toyed with his pen. "I guess I don't see how we're involved."

"We aren't, really. But they need a forensic anthropologist to sort out the bones and tell them what they have, maybe get them positively identified. The Glacier Bay people asked the Juneau agency to help them out, but the woman they usually use is somewhere in South America at the moment. So Juneau called Anchorage, and Charlie remembered that anthropologist you've brought in a few times—"

"Gideon Oliver."

"Right, Oliver . . ." The name seemed to start him thinking. John heard the creak of his high-backed leather chair. Appletree was no doubt leaning back, tapping his lower lip with one of the pencils he used instead of pens. "He does tend to stir things up, though, doesn't he?"

"In what way, sir?" John asked. Not that it wasn't true.

"Well, I have nothing against him, you understand. He's done some good things for us. It's just that whenever we put him on some simple, cut-and-dried case, it . . . well, it always seems to turn out to be anything but cut and dried. Or haven't you noticed?"

John smiled. "I noticed. It's just that he's good at what he does, that's all. He finds things other people miss." He paused. "At least that's what I think it is."

"Well, what the hell, this one will be Anchorage's baby, not ours. Can you get hold of him? Do you think he'd be available to go up to Glacier Bay and help them out for a few days?"

"To Glacier Bay?" John leaned back in his chair and laughed. He and Marti had gone out to dinner with Julie and Gideon the night before they'd left for Alaska. "Yeah, I think he'd be available."

"Good. Can he get out there right away? Where is he now?"

"Boss, you wouldn't believe me if I told you. I'll get right on it."

"I just don't know, Owen." Tibbett shook his head darkly. "It isn't . . . well, seemly."

Chief Park Ranger Owen Parker threw up his hands and disagreed succinctly with his supervisor. "Seemly? What's *seemly* got to do with anything? It has to be done, Arthur."

"*Why* does it have to be done? We brought the remains in, didn't we? We know who they belong to, don't we? *Why* do we have to go through all this forensic analysis crapola?"

"*Because* . . ." Parker couldn't keep a matching note of irritation out of his voice. Arthur had already approved the process of calling in a forensic expert to identify the bones; he was just being difficult, just covering his ass in case there were some kind of administrative repercussions; although why would there be repercussions? But of course you never knew. No doubt the ever-prudent Arthur would write a memo to file, expressing his reservations, just in case.

Parker's exasperation was, as usual, short-lived. What the hell, it wasn't really the guy's fault. He'd spent too many years behind a desk in D.C., that was his problem. You just had to be patient with him.

"Because," Parker said more quietly, "how else do we deal with the remains? They'll have to go to the nearest relatives, right? Do we just divide the bones into three piles and split them between them? For that matter, how can we be absolutely positive those bones are from the expedition until—"

Tibbett waved him down. "Oh, come off it, Owen, really. Of course they are."

Parker shook his head. "A lot of people have disappeared out there, Arthur."

"Right on the edge of Tirku Glacier? Practically on the spot where the avalanche happened? Don't be ridiculous."

Parker shrugged. "I don't know. We're just lucky we have Dr. Oliver here"—he tipped his head in Gideon's direction—"to help us out."

Gideon nodded back with a smile, but in fact he shared some of Tibbett's discomfort. Working on a set of bones—two sets? Three sets?—with the putative next of kin practically looking over his shoulder was going to be a peculiar experience.

Tibbett began to rock rapidly, or rather to vibrate, in his swivel chair. "Well, I don't want the press making some gruesome, sensational story out of this. We don't need that kind of publicity for Glacier Bay."

"I absolutely agree," Parker said. "No need for it at all."

Owen Parker made a marked contrast to his pudgy, skittish supervisor. Decisive, easygoing, quietly self-assured, the chief park ranger was a handsome, copper-skinned black man of forty with the trim physique of a swimmer, a physique earned in 1968 when he'd made it to the Olympic trials. His gray polyester uniform shirt, with its crisp, permanent-pressed creases, lay as neatly against his flat belly as a shirt on a department-store mannequin.

"No need for it at all," he repeated soothingly.

The three men sat in the cluttered, one-room frame building that served as the ranger station, about a quarter of a mile from the lodge, part of the National Park Service complex in a wooded nook on Bartlett Cove. The gray, white-trimmed building was rustic, almost primitive, the location remote and serene. Otherwise it was like just about every other federal office Gideon had ever been in. The walls were layered with notes, charts, annotated calendar pages, and dog-eared cartoons ("You want it WHEN???"). The furnishings were standard GSA-issue: three aged gray-steel desks with Formica tops, three gray-steel file cabinets, gray-steel bookcase, gray-steel table, and gray-steel chairs enlivened with spinach-green seats and backs of waterproof, tearproof, maybe bulletproof plastic. The furniture was ranged along the walls, leaving a small open space in the middle, where the three had rolled chairs to face each other.

Gideon had been hunted down by Park Ranger Frannie Martinez an hour earlier, at loose ends and leafing without interest through a copy of *Alaska Geographic* in the lodge lobby. His new non–goal-directed approach to life had not been a marked success, and he had almost hugged the woman when she told him what it was about: The Tremaine party had found some bones at Tirku Glacier a couple of hours before; the bones had been brought back by boat; the FBI in Juneau had been asked for a skeletal expert and they had recommended him. Would it be possible for him to enter into a limited consulting arrangement with the National Park Service (a) to determine if the bones were human, and (b) if they were, to identify them to the extent possible? The standard hourly consulting fee of $32.50 would, of course, apply.

Yes, he had told her gratefully, yes, it would be possible, it would be highly possible. Forget the fee.

She had driven him in a Park Service pickup truck to the compound and left him at the station. Since then he had been listening to Parker and Tibbett go back and forth over the same ground: Tibbett indecisive, cautious, obstructive; Parker calmly reassuring and consistent.

"And you, Gideon?" Tibbett said.

Gideon's attention had been wandering. "And me what?"

Tibbett continued his nervous rocking. "How do you feel about publicity?"

Tibbett's attitude toward him had become more subdued, more wary, since he'd realized that Gideon was the Skeleton Detective (a sobriquet hung on him by an overimaginative reporter who'd participated in a case at another national park, Olympic, a few years earlier). Gideon was sympathetic; he wasn't too keen on being the Skeleton Detective himself.

"I'm sorry, Arthur. What do you mean, publicity?"

"I'm asking if you see any problem with low-profile involvement here?"

"Low-profile—" He caught himself before he laughed. This was what came of being the Skeleton Detective. "Arthur, I'm happy to help out on this if I can. As far as I'm concerned, I don't see the need for any publicity at all."

Tibbett, mollified, finally brought his chair to a halt. "I'm relieved to hear that. Fine, then. I just wanted to hear you say it."

"Well, then," Gideon said, "maybe we ought to have a look at the bones."

Parker shot him a grateful look and was out of his chair before Tibbett had a chance to do any more vacillating. "Here they are, right here."

They were in a Del Monte tomato-sauce carton on top of the bookcase. Parker took the box down, used his forearm to clear a space in the center of the table, and put the box there. Tibbett unobtrusively pushed off with his feet to roll his chair a few inches farther away.

Gideon got up to look into the open carton. There wasn't much. A warped, split shoe, still damp, with the bony remains of a foot inside; the upper third of a right femur; and most of a mandible with a single tooth still in place. There were some animal bones too: part of a sacrum and two ribs—mountain goat, probably.

He handed the animal bones to Parker. "Not human."

One at a time the ranger flipped them basketball-style at a wastepaper basket. The sacrum took a second try. Tibbett watched the acoustical-tiled ceiling with practiced forbearance.

"Well, there isn't much," Gideon said, "but I think we ought to be able to come to a few general conclusions about just who we have here. Tell me, do you lose many people out there?"

"We don't lose *any,*" Tibbett said defensively. "Well, a few every year, of course, what with crevasses, and slides, and people who refuse to take commonsense precautions, but as far as I know, the only people who ever died right there, right on Tirku Glacier, were the ones in 1960."

"So these pretty much have to be from the expedition?"

"Well, yes, certainly, I'd say so. Narrows it down, doesn't it?"

"To three people," Gideon agreed. He pulled some old newspapers from the top of a file cabinet, spread them on the table next to the box, and took the boot out. "Got something that will cut through this?"

Parker produced a utility knife. Gideon used it to cut the still-knotted leather thong, then slit the boot itself down the middle from toe to heel, and peeled the two halves downward. The mildewy smell that had hung in the air thickened noticeably.

Tibbett made a face and rolled himself a little farther back. Parker flinched but held his ground.

"The smell's not from the bones," Gideon reassured them. "It's just rotting wool." He tugged gently at the soggy, moldering tufts of material and pulled them easily apart, revealing a complete set of tarsals—ankle bones—

somewhat crushed but still pretty much in place, and most of the metatarsals and phalanges—the foot and toe bones—considerably jumbled. Here and there were shreds of brown skin and shriveled ligament.

"Ah, would you prefer that we leave while you examine them?" Tibbett asked hopefully. "We wouldn't want to get in your way."

"It's up to you. This'll probably take no more than half an hour, but I don't really think you'll find it too fascinating."

Tibbett leaped at the opportunity. "Well, then, we'd better get going. We have things to do."

"What things?" Parker asked.

"Things," Tibbett said.

"Actually," Gideon said, "if you wouldn't mind, maybe one of you could do me a favor and get some information from Tremaine, or maybe from Judd or Henckel."

Parker brightened. "Sure, what do you need?"

"I want to know what the three people who were killed looked like. Height, weight, build, that kind of thing. Distinguishing physical characteristics. And if they know about any old injuries that might show up on the bones."

Parker nodded. "Sure, you bet." He hesitated, frowning. "Am I wrong, or didn't I read somewhere that you didn't want to be told those things when you were working on a case?"

"No, you're right. Anthropologists are like anybody else. Other things being equal, they see what they expect to see. I'm more objective if I don't know who I'm supposed to be looking at. But by the time you come back I'll be done, and we can see how well my findings match what you find out."

"Right, got it." Parker took his flat-brimmed hat from a peg on the wall. "Anything you need here, Gideon? Paper . . . ?"

"No, thanks. This is just going to be a quick-and-dirty run-through. I called my department from the lodge and asked them to Fed-Ex my tools. They ought to be here tomorrow or the next day, and that's when I'll get down to the nit-picking."

"Well, there's coffee if you want some." He placed the hat on his head and carefully adjusted it. "I wouldn't mess with those donuts if I were you. Been here about three weeks."

# 4

Gideon started with the mandible. He picked it up in both hands, turning it slowly, his elbows on the table. Considering that it had spent thirty years or so grinding along in a glacier, it was in pretty good shape. It was male; he knew that at once from the ruggedness, the large size, and the double prominences of the chin. (In the old days, before the sexest terminology had undergone rehabilitation, males had had square jaws. Now they had chins with double prominences.)

And it was Caucasian, although here he was on less certain ground. Race was trickier than sex—to start with, you had more choices—and mandibles didn't offer a lot of clues. Like most physical anthropologists he didn't always find it easy to say precisely how he knew from looking at it that a certain mandible was Mongoloid, or black, or white. But—like most physical anthropologists—when he knew, he knew. And he had little doubt that the sophisticated calculations of discriminant-function analysis would bear him out when he got his tools to make some measurements (and his calculator to do some arithmetic).

Aging was more straightforward. The mandible had belonged to an adult; that was obvious from the one tooth in place; a third molar, a wisdom tooth with a good five to ten years' wear on it. Exactly how old an adult? Well, if you took the average age of third-molar eruption—eighteen—and added that five or ten years to it, you came up with an age of twenty-three to twenty-eight, and that was Gideon's guess.

But here he was on shaky ground again. Eighteen might be the average age that wisdom teeth came up, but betting on averages would make you wrong more often than right, especially with something as wildly variable as third-molar eruption. As he liked to point out to his students, an awful lot of people had drowned in San Francisco Bay, which was just three feet deep—on the average.

And as for that "five or ten years of wear," it sounded fine, but it was even less reliable. Tooth wear depended on what you chewed. If you ate a lot of gritty, abrasive stuff, your teeth were going to wear down quickly. If you lived on puddings and jellies, on the other hand, you'd have a few problems, but worn teeth wouldn't be one of them.

All of which suggested that twenty to thirty-five would be a more prudent estimate than twenty-three to twenty-eight. But what the hell, Gideon thought, why not go with his first impression, which was (as he often told himself) no mere shot in the dark, but the soundly based if intuitive assessment of a highly trained scientist? Well, make it twenty-five, plus or minus three. That would narrow things down and still be reasonably defensible.

Was there anything else the mandible could tell him? No dental work on the molar, of course; that would have made it too easy. And no signs of pathology. Eleven of the twelve tooth sockets were empty, but their margins, where they hadn't been broken or abraded, were crisp, without any sign of bone resorption, which meant that there had been no healing. Which meant in turn that they had loosened and fallen out after death. Which is what usually happened in skulls that took any kind of tossing around. The only reason the third molar was still in place was that it was slightly impacted, wedged crookedly into the angle of the ramus.

There were a few signs of trauma: a curving crack in the cusp of the molar and some crushing at the back of the left mandibular condyle, the rounded projection that fits into a recess just in front of the ear. And there were a few fracture lines radiating from the broken edge where the right side of the jaw had been sheared off just behind the empty socket of the first bicuspid. All bore signs of having happened right around the time of death—what pathologists called perimortem trauma. Nothing surprising there. When you were done in by an avalanche, there were bound to be a few dings.

So: What he had was a male Caucasian of about twenty-five, probably of at least average size and in apparent good health, with nothing to suggest that he hadn't been killed in an avalanche and a few things to suggest that he had. He'd go over it more carefully when his equipment arrived, but he didn't think there was anything else to learn from it; at least nothing that would help in making an identification.

He put it down and picked up the femoral fragment. It was the upper six or seven inches of the bone, and it had taken more of a beating than the mandible. It had obviously been well chewed over, and apparently by more than one kind of animal: bear for certain, and something smaller, a marten or weasel. From the looks of it the crows or ravens had had a go at it too. Still, there was always something to be learned . . .

He fingered the head, the caput femoris, the golf-ball-sized hemisphere that fitted into the acetabulum to make the ball-and-socket joint of the hip. Most of it had been gnawed away, but he could see enough to tell that it was mature; the very end of the bone, the epiphysis, was securely attached to the shaft, which happened at seventeen or eighteen for this particular union. And the sex was male. He didn't need measuring calipers to see that the diameter of the head was somewhere near fifty millimeters, well above the normal female range.

And that was all there was to say about the femur. No way, unfortunately, to tell if it had come from the same person as the mandible. Later he'd try calculating a total height estimate from it, but for now he had to settle for adult male, period.

That left the contents of the boot, and there wasn't much to learn there. The twenty-six bones of the human foot—seven irregularly shaped tarsals comprising the ankle and heel, five long metatarsals forming the arch, and fourteen stubby little phalanges making up the toes—were singularly lacking in information of use to the forensic anthropologist. Either that, or feet had understandably failed to capture the forensic anthropological imagination enough to stimulate any detailed studies.

Whichever it was, all Gideon could say about them after he'd cleaned them, arranged them, and briefly examined them was that the foot, like the mandible and femur, had belonged to a fairly large adult male. The large talar surface told him that, and the bulky metatarsals. (Not that it took an anthropologist to figure it out. How many people were there walking around in size twelves who *weren't* male, adult, and reasonably large?) He'd know more after his tools and tables came, but even then he wasn't expecting much of anything to come from it.

He stretched, wandered around the room until he

found a chipped mug on the bottom shelf of the bookcase, and poured himself some coffee from the automatic maker on the corner of one of the desks. He gave serious consideration to the two withered cake donuts in the open Hostess box, but decided in the end to heed Parker's warning. No place to wash his hands first anyway.

He stepped out onto the wooden porch. The crisp breeze, straight off the glaciers, sent a shiver crawling down his back (or was that the bitter black coffee?), but it felt good to be out in the fresh air after bending over those stale, sad fragments. He felt a little stale himself, or perhaps just disappointed. He hadn't come up with much of anything. He didn't even know how many people were represented on that table.

He changed his mind about having a donut, went back in, got a paper towel to hold it in, and came back out, munching slowly.

The scanty results weren't his fault, of course; there simply were no distinctive features, nothing to separate one individual human being from another; no healed fractures, no signs of surgery, no distinctive anomalies or peculiar genetic formations. The only interesting features, really, were those perimortem injuries to the mandible. Funny, when you thought about it, how much they . . .

He frowned, finished off the donut with his third bite, and went back inside. He picked up the mandible again, thoughtfully stroking the broken margin with his thumb. Then he fingered the cracked molar, the crushed condyle. Was there something to think about here after all, or was he just—

The door opened. "Hey, are you still at it?" Parker asked. "You need some more time?" He waited at the door. Behind him Tibbett peered warily over his shoulder.

Gideon glanced up at the wall clock. They'd been gone almost an hour. It had seemed like fifteen minutes, but he was used to that when he got absorbed in skeletal material. Reluctantly he put the mandible down: He could give it some more thought tomorrow, when he had a decent lens.

"No, come on in," he said. "I'm just about finished."

Parker approached. Tibbett kept pace with him, remaining a gingerly half-step behind.

Gideon told them as much as he was relatively sure of. The mandible was from a male Caucasian of twenty-five, give or take three years, probably above average size. The femur and the foot were also both adult male, both above average size. No indicators of race, but no reason to think they weren't also Caucasian. That was it. His materializing questions about the mandible he kept to himself for the time being.

"Well—does that mean they're all from one person?" Tibbett asked.

Gideon spread his hands. "It could be one person, could be three. There isn't any duplication of parts, so there's no obvious proof that it's more than one, but that doesn't mean it isn't. And the appearance of the bones isn't different enough—or similar enough—to say for sure whether they all belong to the same person. And except for the bones in the boot, none of them are adjacent to each other in the living body, so we can't even put them together to see how well they fit or don't fit."

Tibbett's eyebrows went up. "*That's* the way you tell?"

Gideon smiled. Explaining skeletal analysis was like telling someone how you made a matchstick disappear or plucked a coin out of nowhere. A lot of otherwise intelligent people were disappointed when they found out there wasn't any magic involved.

"Well," he said, looking soberly at the assistant superintendent, "I'm thinking of applying the Baker and Newman regression equations for determining bone association from relative weights in ostensibly commingled remains. If I can get an accurate scale."

"Ah," Tibbett said, his sense of propriety restored. "We'll certainly see that you get an accurate scale."

"Well, it's not three people," Parker said. "I can tell you that right now."

Gideon looked inquiringly at him.

"There were three people on that survey team," Parker said, "but only two of them were men. The other was a woman, Jocelyn Yount. And since these bones are all from men, they can't be her, right? That leaves James Pratt and Steve Fisk."

"Why, that's right," Tibbett said appreciatively.

"But we still don't know for a fact that these are from the survey," Gideon said.

Parker shook his head. "Nah, those are the only missing people we've ever had in that section of the bay. Since they started keeping records, anyway. Arthur's right about that."

"Well, of course I am," Tibbett agreed.

And he probably was. Certainly there was nothing about the bones that suggested that they hadn't been there for twenty-nine years. True, they still had a trace of the distinctive candle-wax odor that meant the fat in the marrow was somewhere beyond the rancid stage but short of the dried-up stage. Ordinarily this would mean the time of death had been anywhere from six months to four or five years earlier. But this too was wildly variable, depending on conditions, and cold could slow it down tremendously, as it retarded all degenerative changes in dead tissue. And with bones that had been in a glacier for two or three decades, you were going to get one hell of a slowdown.

"Owen," Gideon said, "did you have a chance to talk to anyone about what these people looked like?"

"Sure did. Dr. Henckel and Professor Tremaine both."

"And? Did either of the men fit what we seem to have here? Caucasian, twenty-five or so, tall, probably well built?"

Parker laughed, dropped into a wheeled swivel chair, and pushed off a few inches, heels in the air. "They both did. Both big healthy guys, twenty-four, twenty-five years old."

Gideon hesitated. "Did they say either of them had anything wrong with his face?"

"His face?"

"A wired jaw, maybe; something like that?"

"No, why?"

"Yes, why?" Arthur asked. "What are you getting at?"

"No matter. Well, the bones could belong to either of them, or both. I'm afraid I can't do any better than that."

"Well, that's that, then." Tibbett rubbed his hands briskly together. "All we can do is what we can do. Thanks so much for your help, Gideon. I'll initiate procedures to see that the remains—"

"Wait a minute, Arthur," Gideon said, "I think you're jumping the gun. I haven't given those bones a decent going-over yet. Besides, you're going to want to go back to the Tirku area to see if there's anything else out there."

"I'm going to want to do no such thing." Tibbett's voice ratcheted up a notch. "We've already searched. *I* found that horrible jawbone. It was the most macabre experience I've ever had in my life." His eyes rolled up. "Alas, poor Yorick."

"I think Dr. Oliver's right," Parker said.

"Why? What is there to be gained? What—"

But the ranger knew how to get his supervisor's attention. "We'll have to submit a recovery report on this. How will it look to Washington if we can't put down that we instituted a systematic search for remains?"

"I just told you—"

"With equipped, professional park-ranger personnel."

Tibbett sagged. "All right, all right. Let's get it done. What do you suggest?"

"Jesus Christ," Parker said abruptly, looking at the empty Hostess box. "You ate one of those donuts?"

"I get hungry when I work," Gideon said. "It wasn't that bad."

"Yeah, but still—"

"Owen, this is serious," Tibbett snapped. "Now what do you suggest?"

Parker grunted good-naturedly. "Bill Bianco's taking the glacier rescue class up Tarr Inlet for tomorrow's field training. Why don't Russ, Frannie, and I hop a ride on the boat? They can drop us off at Tirku and pick us up on the way back. It'll give us a good three hours or so to look around."

"Fine," Tibbett said, sighing. "You have my approval."

"You'll probably want to come too, Dr. Oliver," Parker said.

"I sure do."

Tibbett made fluttery motions with his hands. "Just a minute. I don't know about that. We have to be careful here. Our insurance provisions wouldn't cover anybody who isn't on official government business."

"Well, what the hell would you call this?" Parker asked, then added, "sir."

"Well, I don't . . . Gideon, would you say it's *absolutely* necessary for you to be present?"

Gideon leaned forward. "Absolutely," he said earnestly. "If they do find some more bones, it'd be extremely important for me to observe the contextual and relational conditions firsthand."

It would also beat hell out of spending the day moping through the rest of the *Alaska Geographics*.

* * *

The resident manager of Glacier Bay Lodge had been doubtful about the wisdom of opening the Icebreaker Lounge from 5:00 to 6:00 P.M. each day with only two small groups staying at the hotel. Servicing a bar for a total of twenty hotel guests, Mr. Granle thought, was likely to be a losing proposition. As it turned out, he was wrong. The members of M. Audley Tremaine's group were on all-inclusive expense accounts and drank accordingly. The Park Service people were not on all-inclusive expense accounts, but they drank like it anyway. For the second evening in a row, there wasn't an empty table, and most people were on their second rounds, a few on their third.

M. Audley Tremaine himself was holding court at the bar, oozing urbane charm. In attendance were a tipsy, wisecracking Shirley Yount, who had obviously started her cocktail hour in her room, and half-a-dozen star-struck park rangers in jeans and sweaters. Anna Henckel, Walter Judd, and Gerald Pratt made an unlikely trio at a table by the big window looking west over the cove. Anna, reading from a sheet of paper, was grimly and methodically ticking off points. Judd, not overly responsive, chuckled and joshed. Pratt, between them, was leaning back out of the way in his chair, Seven and Seven in one hand, pipe in the other, equably gazing over their heads at the clouds obscuring the Fairweathers, and himself off somewhere in clouds of his own making. Elliott Fisk was nowhere to be seen.

Most of the other tables were taken up by park rangers in groups of two or three, and Julie and Gideon had been lucky to find a table of their own near the stone fireplace.

"You want my honest opinion?" Julie was saying.

"Of course I want your honest opinion."

"I think you're . . . well . . ."

"Inventing things?"

"No, not inventing. Reaching . . . exaggerating. It's natural. You're at loose ends, and you're bored, and I just wonder if your imagination isn't getting the better of you."

Gideon leaned back in the comfortable captain's chair, stretched out his legs, and crossed them at the ankles. He'd been wondering the same thing himself. "Maybe so, but I'm not exaggerating that break in the mandible."

"I don't mean that you're exaggerating the physical facts, I mean that you're exaggerating—inventing—well, the—"

"The cause of them?"

"No, not the cause. The—"

"Antecedents. Determinants."

She sighed and picked up her white wine. "How am I supposed to argue with you if you keep telling me what I mean?"

He smiled at her. "Are we arguing?"

"No, we're just—I guess we're just—"

"Speculating. Deliberating. Conferring."

Julie raised her eyes to the rough-beamed ceiling. "I'm going to kill him. All right, tell me what you found."

"I already told you. I spent fifteen minutes telling you."

"I was in the shower washing my hair. And you were yelling from the other room. I missed a word here and there. Tell me again."

"All right, I found—"

"It might help if you kept it to words that a simple, unsophisticated park ranger is capable of understanding this time."

"Such as yourself?"

"Such as myself."

"A park ranger who minored in anthropology."

"Nevertheless."

"Uh-huh." Gideon took a few kernels of popcorn from the bowl on the table. "All right, I found that the mandible was broken off on the right side, a sharp, vertical break, and the broken margin was beveled, not jagged. And the fracture lines were what we call 'stepped.' That means, well . . . stepped. Like stairs. Okay?"

"Okay."

"I also found that the left M3 mesiolingual cusp had a menisciform fracture."

She eyed him over the rim of her wineglass.

"The left third molar had a sort of crescent-shaped crack," he explained.

"That I can handle."

"And, finally, there were signs of pressure damage on the posterior surface of the left mandibular condyle, which is—"

"The little round thingy on the back of the jawbone, that fits in that socket on the skull. Right?"

He sipped his Scotch and soda. "Not bad for a simple park ranger."

"Watch it, don't press your luck. And in your mind all this adds up to what? In a nutshell, please."

Gideon helped himself to a handful of popcorn while he put what it all added up to in a nutshell. "If that mandible had been found in a shallow grave near Green Lake, and I'd been asked for my opinion—my *expert* opinion, I modestly call to your attention—I would have said that this particular profile of indicators is consistent with an extremely forceful ante-mortem impact in the region of the protuberantia mentalis."

She nodded soberly. "Sounds like you, all right."

Gideon let it pass. "An extremely strong blow to the point of the chin. The living chin."

"All right, I'm with you so far. Where you lose me is when you say it wasn't caused by the avalanche."

"I'm not saying it wasn't, Julie. I'm just saying that every time I've ever run into that particular combination of injuries up to now, it was the result of one human being hitting another human being. Either with his fist, if he happened to have a fist like a gorilla's, or more likely with some heavy object, like a rock, or maybe a bat or a hammer. It just makes me wonder, that's all. Which is what they're paying me to do. Or would be, if they were paying me. Want another drink?"

"Nope." She munched popcorn for a while. "Would a blow like that have killed him?"

"Impossible to say. The specific injuries to his jaw, no. But he was hit *hard*. There might easily have been associated injuries to his brain or his spine."

"So you're saying this may have been a murder."

He spread his hands. "I'm saying that just before he died, this guy—either James Pratt or Steven Fisk—was hit in the face with tremendous force."

"But how can you be so sure it was before? How do you know his jaw wasn't damaged long after he was killed, even years later, by pressures in the glacier itself?" She shook her head. "We sure have the damndest discussions."

"I know for several reasons. First, the collagen fibers in the bone tissue were intact at the time—which I know because the distortion of the trabeculae—"

She held up her hand. "I'm convinced. All right, then, why—dare I ask—was it 'just' before? Why not a week before, two weeks before? A separate accident, a separate fight?"

"Again, several reasons. No signs of healing. No signs of treatment—and that jaw would have needed wiring. Also, for what it's worth, Tremaine and Henckel don't remember either of the men having anything wrong with his jaw."

"What did Arthur say when you told him all this?"

"Are you serious? Just having the bones turn up is about all the poor guy can handle right now. I'm not telling him we might be dealing with a murder until I have more than this to go on."

She ate some more popcorn, kernel by kernel. "Look," she said reasonably, "you've never examined anyone who died in an avalanche before, have you?"

"No."

"So you don't really know firsthand what avalanche injuries look like."

"Well, no, not firsthand."

"You said that getting hit on the chin with a rock could do this. There would have been rocks flying around in the avalanche, or at least big pieces of ice, right? Why couldn't one of those have done it?"

"Right smack on the point of the chin?"

"Why not?"

"No other signs of injury; no impact points but this one, flush on the jaw?"

"Why not?"

He finished his Scotch and considered. Why not, indeed. True, it would be odd for a piece of flying ice to duplicate this kind of injury so exactly, but he had run into things a lot more improbable than that.

He put his glass on the table with a thump. "Maybe you're right."

Julie looked at him, head cocked. "But?"

"No 'buts.' I've been jumping to conclusions. You're right, that's all."

She was still recovering from this when Tremaine appeared at the table, one hand in his jacket pocket, suave and amiable.

"Dr. Oliver? I hope I'm not intruding?"

"Of course not. This is my wife, Julie."

"Mrs. Oliver, my pleasure."

Gideon gestured at the third chair at the table. "Please."

"No, thank you, I'll just take a minute of your time. I'd

like to apologize for not knowing who you were yesterday, Dr. Oliver."

"No reason why you should. I just wanted to tell you how much I admire your work."

"Well, 'Voyages' isn't a one-man show, you know." He smiled with practiced modesty. "I get all the glory, but a great many people are involved behind the scenes, each making his own unique contribution to the whole."

"Ah," said Gideon. There didn't seem to be any point in explaining that it was not "Voyages" he admired.

Tremaine leaned both hands on the table. "I wonder if I might ask a favor. Do you know why I'm here at Glacier Bay?"

"I understand you're working on a book about the Tirku survey expedition."

"Yes, it's quite close to finished, really, and I'm being assisted by several people who are either members of the original team or relatives of the members who were killed. Well, naturally, today's discovery of those, ah, remains has stimulated a great deal of interest among them. They were wondering if you'd be good enough to spend a little time with us and tell us what you've found."

"I'm afraid there isn't a lot to tell. There's no way I can make a positive—"

"Would tomorrow at ten be convenient? We meet in the upstairs lounge."

"No, tomorrow morning I'm going out to Tirku myself to have a look around."

"I see. What about the afternoon, then? Will you be back by four?"

"Well, I'm not really—"

"Sure you will," Julie said. "You're getting a lift with my class, aren't you? Bill said he'd have us back by four."

"Splendid," Tremaine said. "We'll see you at four then,

Dr. Oliver. I'll look forward to it." He inclined his shaggy but well-groomed head at Julie. "Mrs. Oliver."

"Uh, did I do something wrong?" Julie said when he had left. "Do I detect a little reluctance on your part?"

Gideon shrugged. "No, that's okay. I'm not reluctant, exactly. It just makes me uncomfortable. I mean, what am I supposed to do, bring in the bones for a show-and-tell?"

"I've never known you to object to talking about bones before."

"But these are their relatives—brothers, sisters, whatever. That makes it different."

"Yes, I see what you mean. Sorry about that. Are you going to tell them about the fractured mandible?"

"Not a chance. No reason to."

There was a pause. "You're not going to tell Tremaine either, are you?"

"I'm not telling anyone. Just you. Not until I put in some more work."

"Because, you know, I just realized," Julie said, thoughtfully running her finger around the rim of her empty glass, "if you just happen to be right about how that mandible got broken—"

"Which we've agreed I'm not."

"—and there *was* a murder all those years ago—"

"Which we've agreed there wasn't."

"—then the finger of suspicion would have to point to M. Audley Tremaine himself, wouldn't it, since he was the only one who got out alive?"

"Well, not necessarily, but I admit the thought did cross my mind."

She leaned across the table toward him. "All right now, tell the truth. Do you or don't you think that jaw damage came from the avalanche?"

"I don't know," Gideon answered honestly. "Intellectually, I think you're right about it. But intuitively I can't help—"

"Oh-oh, intuitively. That's always a bad sign."

He laughed. "Okay, you're right." He reached up and stretched luxuriously. "I'm letting my imagination get the better of me. Maybe I'm just looking for some way to get him off the airwaves before he fouls up the American mind for good."

"Come on," Julie said, standing up. "You've been sitting around deducing all day, but I've been working and I need some crab-stuffed halibut."

# 5

Sailing into the upper reaches of Glacier Bay is a spectacular experience for anyone, but for those whose interests turn toward natural history it is matchless, an adventure to be found nowhere else in the world. As the ship moves out of Bartlett Cove and swings northwest past the Beardslees and into the great bay proper, one sails backward in time. With every mile, the land grows newer, more raw, as one closes on the shrinking glacier that carved out the bay in the first place. In three hours one traverses two hundred years of postglacial history.

The evidence is there even for the untrained eye. At Bartlett Cove itself the ice has been gone for two centuries. The roots of mature Sitka spruce and western hemlock have taken firm hold under the mossy forest duff, and the green, soft, richly wooded land amenably shelters the lodge and the Park Service complex. But sixty-five miles away, where the present upper end of the bay terminates at the foot of the Grand Pacific Glacier, there are no plants at all—only bare rocks and gravel, still wet from the ice that had covered them for millennia. Sailing between the two points mimics the glacier's withdrawal; every mile covered is three years of glacial retreat. In less than half an hour the stately hemlock along the shores begin to disappear, and then the spruce give way grudgingly to tangled stands of alder and cottonwood, which in turn make way for willow, ryegrass, fireweed, and dryas, and finally for the coarse, primitive black crust of algae that marks the first scrabbling hold of the plant kingdom on newly exposed rock.

For over an hour Julie and Gideon had sat relaxed in airplane-style seats in the boat, mostly hand in hand, watching the scenes slip by. The living attractions of Glacier Bay had made their appearance as if programmed. They had seen a trio of humpback whales lolling in the water; black bears swinging lustily along the shore; mountain goats on the high rocks; nesting kites and puffins tucked in stony crevices among the Marble Islands; seals and sea lions and bald eagles; clownish, red-beaked oyster catchers awkwardly stalking mussels.

They had watched the blue water gradually turn milky green from the infusion of "glacial flour," the powdery silt from glacially pulverized rock. The first icebergs—eroded, small, bizarrely shaped—appeared near Rendu Inlet at about the time they were breakfasting on minced ham and scrambled eggs from the ship's galley. And by the time they'd finished their second cups of coffee, they had caught up with the glacial flows themselves. At Lamplugh Glacier the boat slowed and stopped. With everyone else they went upstairs to stand on the top deck and gawk at the two-hundred-foot-high face of brilliant white, shot through with cracks of glowing turquoise blue. And to listen.

Unlike mountain glaciers, tidewater glaciers are never quiet. The grinding noises are predictable enough, but the other sounds from the straining ice come as a surprise to those who haven't heard them before. Sharp *cr-a-aks* indistinguishable from echoing rifle shots. Long, slow *boooommms* like cannon fire in mountain passes. Gurgles, clicks, rattles, even wheezes and moans. Gideon and Julie stood for half an hour, hunched against a dry, scraping wind. With the others they murmured with pleasure when huge chunks of ice came away and slid ponderously into the water, making great splashes that left the icebergs rolling about in their wake.

When the captain started the ship up again they went downstairs, poured cups of hot chocolate to warm themselves, and found their seats.

"Julie," Gideon said, balancing his cup as he slid in beside her, "there are some things I don't understand about glaciers."

"Like what?"

"Like how they work."

"How they work?" Although she had seen her first tidewater glaciers here in Glacier Bay only the day before, she knew plenty about the glaciers in general. Olympic National Park, where she worked, had a dozen of them, and she herself had given lectures on glacial ecology. "Well, they start when snow accumulates faster than it melts over the years, and the old snow underneath is compressed by new snow, so that ice crystals—"

"No, I understand how they form. I don't understand how they work, how they move."

She twisted to face him more fully. "*You* don't understand how glaciers move? The world's leading authority on Ice Age man?"

"Just because I know something about human evolution in the Pleistocene doesn't mean I'm particularly well acquainted with glaciers. The Ice Age has been over for some time, you know." He gulped from the steaming cardboard cup. Beyond the window was what looked like an Ice Age very much in progress. "Anyway, I'm not the world's leading authority on Ice Age man."

"*One* of the world's leading authorities, then."

"That's different," he said gravely.

"Either way, I still can't believe that you don't understand—"

"I understand the theories of Ice Age progression. I understand the theories of glacial advancement and withdrawal on a global level. I'm fine with the theories. Sometimes I just have a little trouble with mechanics, that's all."

She batted her eyes, or came as close to it as Julie ever did. "Do tell."

"Hey, is that a crack about the cabinet I tried to put up in the den? Because if it is, there's no way that can be considered my fault. In theory those toggle bolts should have . . ." He grinned at her. "Okay, I see what you mean. I admit it: Operational details aren't my strong point."

"Really."

"Now wait a minute. The only reason the back door won't hang straight is—I mean, sliding doors are not as simple as you think. How the hell was I supposed to know . . . What's that look supposed to mean?"

"Gideon, have I told you that I loved you today?"

He shook his head. "Not a word."

"Well, I love you."

They leaned together and kissed gently, barely touching. "I love you too," he said quietly. Her soft, glossy black hair fell against his cheek. He closed his eyes. What astonishing power she had to move him. He tipped her head toward him. They kissed again.

"Hey, we don' 'low none of that stuff 'roun' here," a ranger rumbled from across the aisle. "Eyes front."

They separated, smiling.

"Now," Julie said, "exactly what do you want to know about glaciers?"

"Basically, I want to know how those bones got where they did. Look, as I understand it, Tremaine and his people were on Tirku Glacier itself, about two miles above the snout, when the avalanche came down on them. Since then, the snout has retreated about half a mile inland. Which means that it's now one and a half miles below where they got hit in 1960."

She sipped from the cup, basking in the steam. "That's the way I understand it too."

"But the avalanche came from Mount Cooper, to the southwest, which means it hit Tirku sideways, so it wouldn't have carried them down the length of the glacier toward the snout."

"True. What's the problem?"

"The problem is, how did those bones wind up at the snout? How did they get carried forward that mile and a half down the glacier? If Tirku had been advancing all this time I could see it, but it's retreating."

She studied him. "You really don't understand how glaciers work, do you?"

"That's what I've been trying to tell you."

"That's amazing. How can you be a full professor, a recognized—"

He sighed. "Do you ever hear me going on about minor deficiencies in your education?"

"Are you serious?" She tucked in her chin and frowned, the better to affect a deep, masculine voice. "No need to be ashamed, my dear. You are not dumb; merely ignorant."

"Julie . . ."

"Okay, okay. Well, what you have to realize is that there's

a difference between glacial retreat and advance on the one hand, and glacial flow on the other. Even when a glacier is retreating, the ice is still flowing forward, it's just melting at the snout faster than it's flowing. It's like a . . . oh, like a big conveyor belt that's working fine but being dragged slowly backwards. Whatever's in the ice keeps moving forward all the same."

"I see."

"Bill!" she called over his shoulder.

Bill Bianco, the course instructor, stopped at their seats. A blond, easygoing thirty-five-year-old who looked twenty, he was a much-published expert on glaciers, particularly on crevasses. ("How did you get to be an expert on crevasses?" Gideon had asked him the evening before. "Fell into enough of 'em, I guess," he had replied.)

"Bill," Julie said, "what's Tirku's rate of flow?"

"Tirku? On the average about a foot a day, maybe a little less."

"Say three hundred feet a year," Julie said. "In twenty-nine years that'd be, uh, between eight and nine thousand feet." She smiled at Gideon. "A mile and a half. Voila."

Gideon laughed. "I'm impressed."

The boat slowed again.

Bill looked out the window. "This is your drop-off point," he said to Gideon. "Tirku Spit. We'll be back for you in about three hours." He looked at his watch. "At about one. Have fun."

The bottom of the boat grated against rock. An aluminum ladder was hooked on a couple of cleats and lowered over the bow of the *Spirit of Adventure*. Gideon, Chief Park Ranger Owen Parker, and two subordinate rangers clambered down onto a narrow gravel shore and stood back as the digging tools were tossed down to thunk against the pebbles. The boat backed off, gunned its engines, and turned slowly around. There was a glimpsed wave from Julie, and the big, white, three-level catamaran glided northwest toward Tarr Inlet, already looking small and faraway in the immense bay.

Gideon shivered. Tirku Spit was not an amiable place. To their right the flat gray beach stretched around a curve and into Johns Hopkins Inlet. To their left was a long black ridge clotted with a scum of gray-green vegetation. Beyond it, the freezing upper reaches of Lamplugh Glacier could be seen, and then, far off, Mount Crillon and the ice-buried, ill-named Fairweathers. Ahead, the lumpy gravel, seamed with crisscrossing, inch-deep rivulets of water, sloped uphill for half a mile to Tirku Glacier, a grimy, humped excrescence oozing from an ice field somewhere beyond Mount Abbe.

The shore itself was bare except for a border of beached, decaying icebergs at the waterline; melted down into grotesque gray-white shapes two or three feet across, they looked like a scattered row of bleaching mammoth bones, as if the remains of some prehistoric kill had washed up. Under a bleak, slaty sky of cirrostratus the day was gloomy but clear. Gideon could see at least thirty miles in every direction; three or four thousand square miles all told. And in all that vast space there was no sign, aside from the inconsequential, diminishing speck of the boat, that any other human beings existed on the planet Earth, or had ever existed. Or animals. Or plants, other than the hummocked, foot-high mat on the ridge. Nothing but ice, black rock, and water the color of pewter. It was like being back at the beginning of the world.

He shivered again, glad to have the rangers' company.

They headed for the big notched boulder Tibbett had told them about, each carrying some equipment. Gideon shouldered a couple of spades, Owen Parker a pickax, Russ Davis another pick and some food, and Frannie

Martinez a knapsack of hand tools—trowels, small hammer, forceps, chisels, brushes. These had been brought at Gideon's request. Probing for bones was delicate business. If he could help it, those picks and shovels weren't going to get within five feet of any skeletal remains.

Walking to Tirku's foot was easy going. The slope was gentle, the wet, pebbly land scoured smooth by the glacier during its long advance. Avoiding the small streams of water and the isolated boulders left behind when it retreated created little difficulty, and they covered the half mile in fifteen minutes.

When they got to the moraine where the bones had been found the day before, Gideon put down the spades and stared up at the dirty, seeping snout. Gritty and black with soil, it was more massive than it had appeared to be from the shore; well over a hundred feet high and five hundred feet across, a bulging, irregular protuberance furrowed with cracks and pockmarked with holes. There were steady sounds of trickling water from all across its face. The area in front of it was littered with lumps of dingy, melting ice that had fallen from it, some the size of snowballs, some as big as automobiles.

"Ugly sonofabitch, ain't it?" Russ said cheerfully. He was working his first season at Glacier Bay, a hulking, wonderfully clumsy kid from Arkansas with the scrubbed, pink, innocent face of an angel.

"Not my favorite glacier of all time," Owen agreed. "Well, let's get to it. We'll divide the area up into quadrants and split them up between us. That sound all right, Gideon?"

"Sounds fine."

It took only twenty minutes for Russ to find (by stepping on them) the twisted aluminum frames of a pair of wraparound sunglasses that might or might not have belonged to the survey team. And ten minutes after that,

Owen let out a whoop and held up a picklike tool with about eight inches of splintered wooden handle, from which dangled a looped leather strap.

"Ice ax!" Frannie said excitedly. "Were Tremaine's people carrying them?"

"We'll sure as hell ask them," Owen said. He brought it over to show it to them. "It was right at the base of the snout. Must have fallen out of it in the last few days."

"An ax?" Gideon said after a moment. "What would a botanist want an ax for?"

Aside from hitting a fellow botanist in the jaw with, of course. The steel head was a long, vicious-looking affair with a tapering, blunt point at one end and an adzelike blade at the other. Gideon ran his hand slowly over the cold metal, as if he could somehow feel its history. Careful now; his imagination began to get the better of him again.

"Nothing strange about it," Owen said. "You can chop with it when you're climbing, but mostly people use it for walking on ice, sort of like a cane or a ski pole. You hold it by the head—the strap goes around your wrist—and there's a whatchamacallit, a ferule, in the other end of the handle that you poke into the ground. Gives a lot of security on a slippery ice field."

A little later the sharp-eyed Frannie spotted a ragged strip of red-and-black plaid material trailing from a typewriter-sized chunk of smoke-colored ice. The rangers wanted to smash the ice open with a pick, but Gideon insisted on working with a cold chisel and a small hammer, tapping away for forty minutes to carefully chip the material free. To no avail, however. When the ice was reduced to a pile of shavings there were only a few more inches of woolen plaid to be found. No bones.

"Maybe Tremaine or one of the others can identify it," Frannie suggested, but without conviction. Twenty-nine years was a long time to remember somebody's shirt, let alone distinguish it from a million other shirts made of the same common material.

In the next hour, nobody found anything. By noon, when they stopped for a lunch of ham sandwiches and coffee, Gideon was discouraged. He was also cold. Julie, knowing she would be out on the glaciers, had brought her warmest coat to Alaska, a hooded, quilted parka that encased her like a sausage in a bun. But Gideon, expecting to spend his time around protected Bartlett Cove or in a warm tour boat, and believing the tales of fifty-degree weather in September, had only a thinly lined, waist-length windbreaker. It probably was fifty degrees back at Bartlett Cove, but here, on this desolate glacial shelf, it was fifteen degrees colder at least, and the frigid vapor that hung over the glacier made it seem colder yet. His nose was running, his fingers numb and red, his wrist cuffs sopping from poking in the ice, his trousers soaked at the knees from kneeling in the gravel.

All the same there was a time-spanning magic here if you looked for it. These rotting gobbets of ice littering the gravel had traveled eleven or twelve miles from the Brady Ice Field, Owen had told him. At three hundred feet a year, that meant it had taken two hundred years for the ice flow to make its slow way down. Now, today, you could pick up a fusty gray chunk with the knowledge that it had fallen as rain or snow at about the time George Washington was first taking office on the other side of the continent.

Russ saw him staring thoughtfully at a dingy, melting chunk of ice in his hand. "What's up?" he asked curiously, around a mouthful of sandwich.

"When this fell," Gideon mused, "Mozart was still alive."

"No shit," Russ said.

"Keats hadn't even been born, or Shelley. Paganini was

just a kid. The Reign of Terror was just beginning in France."

"Yeah, I guess," Russ said, and went back to his sandwich.

Nothing more was found after lunch, and they were more than ready to call it a day by the time they spotted the white, welcome shape of the *Spirit of Adventure* rounding Russell Island and heading their way, twenty minutes early.

It was only after they gathered up the picks and spades—left leaning carelessly against a rock when they arrived and untouched since—that Gideon saw it.

"Hold it," he said sharply.

They stopped. "What, what's the matter?" Russ said with the tone of someone who expected to get blamed for it, whatever it was.

Gideon pointed toward the ground at the base of the boulder. "That's a human skull. Part of it, anyway."

It took the others a few seconds to locate it.

*"That?"* Russ said, his eyes popping. "I saw that before, when we put the tools down. I thought it was, you know, some kind of upside-down crab shell. That thing's a piece of somebody's *head?"*

His surprise was understandable. It was half imbedded in the soil, a stone-gray, slightly concave disk about five inches in diameter, thickly caked with dirt over much of its surface, rough-edged, and furrowed with deep, branching grooves. And it was thoroughly beaten up, looking every bit as if it had spent thirty years or so grinding along in a glacier. It lay no more than a dozen feet from where Russ had found the glasses.

Gideon knelt to have a closer look, rewetting his knees but not noticing this time. "It's a parieto-tempero-occipital fragment," he said.

"No," Owen murmured. "You're kidding me."

"The right side of the cranium," Gideon explained, and used his hand to trace the area on himself. "From a little in front of the auditory meatus—the ear hole—to the occipital protuberance at the back of the head, and about halfway up the cranial vault."

"Those grooves," Frannie said. She was leaning intently over, hands on her knees, her dark face taut with interest. "What are they?"

"Those are channels for blood vessels."

"Blood vessels?" She seemed confused.

"The veins and arteries that supply the brain." He looked up at her. "This is the inside of the skull we're looking at."

"Oh." She grimaced but kept her place.

They all looked at him, waiting, he supposed, for some Skeleton Detective wizardry.

"There's not much to be told from the inside," he said. "I'll need to turn it over."

They waited. Gideon put a finger against one edge and pushed gingerly. The fragment didn't move.

"Stuck," he said. "I don't want to push too hard. The bone seems sturdy enough, but it might be wet through and I don't want to take any chances. We better dig it up with the soil it's on. I can get it out later."

With a trowel he quickly scooped out a foot-wide trench around the fragment, then used one of the spades to undercut the central pedestal of gravelly dirt and lift it out, parieto-tempero-occipital fragment and all.

"Damn," Owen said, "I forgot to bring a box."

"We can carry it down to the boat right on the spade," Gideon said.

Russ reached for it. "I'll do it!"

Gideon looked at him. *"Carefully."*

"You bet!" Holding his breath, Russ took the spade from

Gideon and held it stiffly in front of him, moving erectly downhill with exquisite care.

Seen from the *Spirit of Adventure* they must have seemed an odd procession: four people in a row, marching slowly down the barren slope, led by a uniformed giant gravely bearing something before him like a treasure on a salver. Later Julie would say that the scene had started her humming the triumphal march from *Aïda*.

# 6

The question is," Bill Bianco said, holding up a liter-and-a-half plastic bottle of Jim Beam at the front of the passenger cabin, "will Chief Park Ranger Owen Parker over there agree to forget about it if I break the rules and pour us all a little something to warm us up? Or will he turn us in?"

"Why, what bottle is that, Bill?" Owen asked mildly, to a chorus of cheers.

Gideon had reboarded the *Spirit of Adventure* to find Julie and her classmates almost as cold-looking and bedraggled after their session on Margerie Glacier as he was after Tirku. He had gotten a mutually warming hug from her, downed a cup of hot chocolate, and just begun to unthaw when Bill broke out the bourbon. And very welcome it looked.

The instructor moved slowly along the aisle, pouring a couple of fingers of the amber liquid into the plastic cups that were held out to him. With Julie, Gideon went to the rear and topped off their cups from the hot-water urn.

Julie gestured at the galley. "I bet I can find us some lemon in here."

Gideon went with her. Russ had put the skull fragment and its bed of earth on the galley's counter, carefully setting it on the sliced-off lid of a Del Monte ketchup carton. (Gideon was going to have to write a letter of appreciation to Del Monte if this kept up.) In the warmth of the boat's interior, the bone seemed drier, less fragile. He was anxious to have a look at the outer side, the side pressed into the earth, where any potentially useful information was likely to be, but it didn't pay to take chances with it. What was the rush? His tool kit had probably arrived at the lodge during the day, and this evening he could take whatever time was needed to free the skull from its context. It always paid to do it right.

But leaving Gideon Oliver with an unexamined skull fragment was like handing a four-year-old a candy bar and telling him to leave it alone until after dinner; it wasn't realistic to hope for too much. He poked it with his finger. It felt solid enough. With a fingernail he scraped at a little clotted black dirt. It came away without taking any of the bone with it. He scraped some more.

"Found one," Julie announced. "Some cinnamon too." She got a kitchen knife from a rack, set the lemon on the counter next to him, and sliced out a couple of wedges.

Gideon glanced up from the piece of skull. "I'm not sure the health department would approve of this setup."

"I'm not sure I do," she said with a sidewise glance at the silvery gray bone. She squeezed the wedges into their cups, then dropped them into the hot liquid while Gideon rubbed away some more dried mud. "Want some sugar?" she asked.

He shook his head. "Look at this."

"At what? That little clump of dirt in the middle?"

"That little clump of dirt is plugging a hole, Julie. See? You can just make out the margin over here."

"Oh boy, a hole," she said. "Here we go again." She set down her cup. "What's so strange—this is not an argument, okay?—but what's so strange about a hole in a skull that's been through an avalanche, followed by twenty-nine years of tumbling along inside a glacier?" She gestured at the fragment. "The skull itself's been smashed to pieces. Why shouldn't it have a few holes in it?"

"Well, you have a point." He sipped at the toddy. "Mm, perfect." The sharp, lemony fumes seemed to drift up, warm and pungent, behind his eyes, then fan out to heat his throat and shoulders. "All the same, I'd sure like to get this thing out of the dirt and see the other side."

He got three fingertips around the occipital margin where the bone was thickest and tugged lightly. Nothing happened. He held his breath and tugged marginally harder. The bone popped cleanly and satisfyingly out of the dirt.

"Ah," he said.

Owen Parker put his head through the doorless entry. "Oh-ho, I figured that's what you'd be doing back here. Finding out anything?" He came in, bourbon in hand.

"I don't know yet. You're just in time to see. Grab a paper towel and put it on the counter, will you?"

With Owen and Julie watching closely at either side, Gideon turned the fragment carefully over, brushed away most of the clinging dirt, and set it on the towel, outer side up. The hole was still filled and mostly hidden, plugged by its clod of dried mud. He pushed cautiously at the dirt. It didn't budge.

If this hole was what his gut—or rather his soundly based but intuitive assessment—told him it was, it wouldn't pay to take chances with it. Preserving the margins would be important.

"You think there might be something thin and sharp in one of those drawers?" he asked. "A skewer, maybe?"

Julie rummaged until she found a seafood fork with a narrow, probelike end, and Gideon began to push gently at the clod.

"Looks delicate," Owen said.

"Mm. It's damp, which doesn't help." He continued to pick at the stubborn dirt. "You wouldn't happen to have some acetone at Bartlett Cove, would you?"

"I think there might be some in the naturalists' work-room. Smells like it, anyway."

"Good. When we get back we can put this in a bath of it to drive the moisture out. And if there's some alvar or acrylic resin around I can make a preservative sealant for it tomorrow. The other bones too."

"I don't know about acrylic resin," Owen said.

"Duco cement?"

"Yeah, I think there's plenty of that."

"Good enough."

Owen watched for a while. "Any idea who it belongs to?"

"Adult male," Gideon said without raising his head. "Mid- to late twenties, fairly large . . . the same as every-thing else so far."

"Does it go with the jaw they found yesterday, do you think?" Julie asked.

"Impossible to say. If we had the whole jaw we could try fitting the condyle into the mandibular fossa here in the skull and see if they go together. But unfortunately we have the right side of the skull and the left side of the jaw. The only—"

He stopped. A pea-sized gray pebble had dislodged itself from the clod. A few seconds later, with some additional prodding, the rest of the dirt fell away to reveal a roughly triangular hole about an inch wide. With painstaking care Gideon ran a finger slowly around the edge of the hole, stopping twice to explore particular features. Then he turned the fragment over and did the same thing on the other side. Five minutes passed.

"What's with the hole?" Owen finally asked him.

Julie laughed. "Don't bother, Owen. At times like this he's oblivious to everything. Completely impervious to human contact. You'll get used to it."

Owen was silent a moment, then persisted. "But what's so interesting about a hole?" This time the question was addressed to Julie.

"Um, if it's all the same, I think I'll let Gideon explain it to you."

Gideon went to an adjustable table lamp at the far end of the counter. He held the fragment six inches from the bulb, and his face six inches from the fragment, tilting it so that the light slanted across the surface to highlight the texture. After another two minutes he straightened slowly up and came over to them with the fragment.

"I was not impervious. I was simply focusing my powers of concentration." He tapped the bone. "Got something funny here, folks."

"Oh my," Julie murmured and downed the rest of her toddy.

"What do you mean, funny?" Owen asked. "What's going on? I mean, I know I'm just the chief park ranger here, but couldn't somebody tell me what's happening?"

Gideon told him. "Whoever this was, he was murdered."

"Murdered!" Owen stared at him. "But these people were killed in the avalanche. They—" He looked from Gideon to Julie and back again. "Weren't they?"

"I don't think so. Buried by it, maybe. Killed, no. Not this guy."

Owen looked down at the fragment in Gideon's hand,

lips pursed. "That's a bullet hole? Is that what you're saying?"

Gideon shook his head. "Too big. And if it was a bullet hole it'd be round and beveled, with the inside table of the bone sheared away. That's if it had been an entrance wound. If it was an exit wound . . . well, never mind. The fact is, this didn't come from a high-velocity projectile going either way. See here around the edges, how the bone has been crushed inward, not just blown away? See how the sides of the hole are conical, not straight? See this crack radiating—"

"Well, what then?" Owen said impatiently. "Look, why does it have to be murder? Why couldn't it be from a falling rock or something? The guy was in an avalanche!"

"You're wasting your time, Owen," Julie told him pleasantly. "Believe me."

"Somebody hit him in the head with something heavy," Gideon said. "If this *is* the same guy whose mandible they found yesterday, he was cracked in the jaw first—hard. He fell, and then he was hit in the head—even harder."

"Wait a minute, Gideon," Julie said. "Just hold on there. Credibility is being strained here. How can you talk about sequence? How can you possibly say that he was hit in the jaw *first?*"

"Jaw?" Owen was muttering. *"Jaw?"*

"I can't tell from looking at the bone," Gideon said. "It's a matter of deduction, of reasonable inference."

"Oh-oh," Julie said to Owen. "Watch out now. Hang on to your wallet."

"Nothing tricky," Gideon said. He put his forefinger through the hole. It went in all the way to the knuckle without touching the edges. "I just can't see much point in cracking him in the jaw *after* someone put a hole like this in his head, can you?"

She made a face. "Ugh, I see what you mean. Yes, I

think you're right. As he usually is," she said to Owen. "It's very annoying."

"The hole is just anterior to the mastoid angle of the parietal . . . about here," Gideon said, touching a point about an inch behind his own right ear.

"Wait a minute, isn't that pretty low for getting hit over the head?" Owen asked. "And pretty far back?"

"Not if you were hit from behind or—more likely—had collapsed onto your face after somebody'd just broken your jaw."

"*What* jaw, dammit? That jawbone we found yesterday—somebody broke it?"

"I'm afraid so. I wasn't positive, but it's looking more likely now."

Owen expelled his breath and watched while Gideon replaced the fragment on the table. "Christ," he said, staring at it, "that's awful. What would make a hole like that?"

"Something heavy," Gideon said. "And pointed."

"Well, yeah, I guess *so.*" He looked suddenly at Gideon. "Christ, you don't think . . ."

"I sure do, Owen. Where'd you put it?"

Owen pulled the broken ice ax from a shelf under the counter and offered it to Gideon.

"No, you hold it," Gideon said. "Point-up. Prop it on the counter so it doesn't move."

Owen grasped it firmly in both hands, where the splintered handle joined the head, and pressed the adze-shaped end against the counter top. The picklike part was held upright and unmoving.

Gideon turned the skull fragment so that the convex exterior side was down and lowered it steadily onto the point. The dull metal spike slid smoothly through the hole, millimeter by millimeter. When the bone was finally seated against it, the fit was snug and perfect, like a peg in a pegboard.

Gideon let go of the fragment, which clung to the spike without even a wobble. Five inches of curving, pitted steel jutted evilly through the hole—and into the braincase, had there still been a braincase. The sight was riveting.

"How horrible," Julie said softly and looked away, out the small window over the counter.

As they often were at moments like this, Gideon's feelings were mixed. On the one hand, he was pleased with himself. With nothing but highly ambiguous evidence to go on yesterday, he'd tentatively reached some manifestly unlikely conclusions about that mandible. His instincts, his experience, had told him something was very wrong. And now, apparently, it turned out that he'd been correct. And he'd quickly recognized this hole in the parietal for what it was too. Simple enough to do on a skeleton found in someone's basement; not so obvious in bones that had been through what these had gone through. Yes, he had reason to be satisfied with his work.

On the other hand, his years of forensic activity had done little to harden him to the unfailing repulsiveness of murder, especially violent, bloody murder. When he was eleven his Uncle Jack had taken him to a wax museum, and Gideon, being a normal enough kid, had dragged his uncle into the chamber of horrors. The first tableau had been enough, a shockingly realistic recreation of a famous ax murder and bathtub dismemberment. Gideon had stumbled out, white-faced and shaken, never to return.

With time, he hadn't changed much, despite his decades-long fascination with bones (the older and drier the better). The sight of the spike piercing this fragile remnant of a young man's head made him want to look away too. His imagination was every bit as active as Julie's, and his knowledge of the human body greater. He knew how abundantly supplied with blood vessels the scalp was. He knew the consistency and color of living brain tissue. He knew . . .

With both hands he lifted the fragment from the point and set it back on the paper towel.

Owen put the ice ax down on its side and made a final try. "Look, couldn't the avalanche have knocked it out of his hands and driven it into . . . No, huh?"

"Come on, Owen."

The ranger sighed loudly, puffing out his brown cheeks. "Arthur's gonna have a fit."

"What do we do now?" Gideon said. "Who has jurisdiction in a case like this, the FBI?"

"Hell, no," Owen said, bridling. "The NPS. Me."

"You're going to investigate a *murder?*" Gideon winced even as he said it. But he would have been surprised if Owen had ever had to deal with a homicide before, let alone a twenty-nine-year-old homicide.

"As chief ranger, I'm responsible for all law-enforcement matters at Glacier Bay," Owen said frostily.

"Fine," Gideon said. "It's all yours. Where do we go from here? What do we do next?"

Owen leaned stiffly back against the counter, then abruptly relaxed and grinned. "The next thing I do is get on the horn to the FBI in Juneau," he said, "and ask them what the hell we do next."

# 7

*For untold eons it had hung there, this huge mass of densely compressed ice nestling in a remote flank of the towering mountain range that would one day be known as the Fairweathers. Even when the Great Warming had set in fifteen thousand years before, it had managed to survive. But the immense ice field of which it had been a part had sagged, cracked, shrunk. Where slow, grinding seas of ice had flowed and carved out deep valleys, rivulets of water now trickled. Land that had lain frozen and barren since the beginning of time emerged at last. The mastodons came—and went—and then the wolves, and badgers, and bears. And still the nameless hanging glacier endured, remote and proud.*

The rich, distinctive voice of M. Audley Tremaine resonated, then seemed to float up toward the beams of the rustic A-frame ceiling twenty feet above. In the arched fieldstone fireplace of Glacier Bay Lodge's upstairs lounge a fragrant log fire snicked and crackled, a welcome counterpoint to the gray, raw afternoon visible through the floor-to-ceiling dormer windows. Six armchairs were drawn up to the hearth, their occupants in various postures of repose.

Rather too much in the way of repose, Tremaine thought with mounting annoyance as he turned over the manuscript page. Lunch had been heavy and long—they hadn't finished until two—and the wine had flowed freely. Did these stuffed and slumbrous people have any idea what he was ordinarily paid to read aloud? Did they know how many millions of Americans tuned in every week to hang on every word? Perhaps he should talk to the manager about lightening the midday meal.

Or perhaps he shouldn't. What did it matter if they were drowsy? If Walter was three-quarters asleep? In a way it was very much better. Certainly the afternoon was proceeding a great deal more smoothly than the morning, when he had been interrupted by one silly quibble after another, on everything from the financing of the La Pérouse expedition of 1789 (Anna Henckel) to the dubious correctitude of terminal prepositions (the know-it-all Elliott Fisk). Since lunch, however, they had been logy and unresponsive, which was all to the good. These sessions were their opportunity to take issue with his book, and if they passed it up, that was the end of it. They had no recourse to further objection; so it said quite clearly in the agreement each of them had signed with Javelin Press.

Now that he thought about it, maybe he ought to ask the manager about supplying wine with breakfast, too. He sipped from a glass of Perrier and continued.

> *More time passed. The glacier-scoured furrow at the foot of the mountains was no longer choked with a barren, mile-thick mass of ice. In its place was a*

*tranquil, surpassingly beautiful estuary of blue-green water studded with icebergs that had calved from the ends of the surrounding glacial tongues. Glacier Bay, the Europeans called it. Adventurers came to explore, and geologists to study, and, eventually, tourists to marvel from the decks of steam-powered excursion boats.*

*And still the hanging glacier clung precipitously to its mountain aerie. Tlingit Ridge, the white man called this peak now. The long, twisting glacial tongues below had names too. Lamplugh, Tirku, Reid. But the hanging glacier itself, one of the last of its kind, isolated and dying, had no name and would never have a name. By the year 1960 of the Christian calendar its hold was finally loosening. Poised precariously over Tirku Glacier, it had shrunk to just four hundred million cubic meters.*

*Only ninety million tons.*

He sat back with a sigh of contentment. "That," he said, "is the end of chapter two." And a damned fine ending it was, complete with masterful narrative hook. Not that any of these undiscriminating boobs would know a narrative hook if it bit them on the ear. "If there are no questions I'll go directly—"

He gritted his teeth at a barbaric yawp of a snore followed by several snuffles, all of this coming from Walter, who wriggled, rumbled, fussed, and then melted deeper into his chair, his head tipping backwards to the accompaniment of other, indescribable noises from his throat. For Walter, even sleep was a form of theater. Like a big dog he woke himself up with a snort, muttered and fussed some more, and settled into silence if not quite wakefulness. Reflections from the flames danced on his nose.

Tremaine glowered briefly at him—at the others, too, for good measure—and read on:

CHAPTER THREE.
*July 26, 1960, 12:04* P.M.

*In the United States Geological Survey Monitoring Station near Palmer, the needle of the seismograph stopped its gentle bobbing, hesitated, and then jerked sharply, scratching a series of spiky black lines onto the paper-covered drum.*

*Ranger Parnell Morgan watched the needle intently, but soon relaxed. As things went in this part of the world it wasn't much of a tremor; 4.1 on the Richter scale. Not the big one they'd been worrying about, just another little jiggle in a part of the world that averaged four a day. There would be no frantic telephone calls on this one, no buckled roadways or twisted bridges, no collapsed buildings or broken water mains.*

*The epicenter seemed to be somewhere in the Fairweathers, in the uninhabited area north of Glacier Bay. A good place for it, he thought, and went back to the half-eaten tuna-fish sandwich on his desk.*

Tremaine looked up, distracted by an impatiently jiggling foot. "Is something wrong, Dr. Fisk?"

Fisk stared back at him. "I was wondering," he said, "just how necessary it is for us to sit through this nonessential material. Couldn't we—"

"I would hardly call it nonessential, Doctor," Tremaine said tightly.

"What would you call it, essential? I mean, tuna-fish sandwiches, for God's sake. Tell us, was there mayonnaise on them? I can't stand the suspense."

"Your point?" Tremaine said.

Fisk gnashed his teeth, or something very close to it. "My *point* is that we're here to supply personal perspectives, aren't we? Well, for God's sake, why can't we simply skip over the background information and get on with the story of the *expedition?*"

Gerald Pratt took the pipe from his mouth and uttered his first words of the day. "Hear, hear," he said pleasantly enough.

"No," Anna said firmly. "I wish to hear everything." She turned her head stiffly to fix Tremaine with a meaningful glare.

"Oh, me too," Shirley said with that crooked, taunting smile. "I wouldn't want to miss a single, teeny word."

"The question is moot," Tremaine said grumpily. He hadn't liked that look of Anna's. "My understanding with Javelin requires that nothing be omitted . . . other than those events of which I and I alone have knowledge, of course."

"Such as?" Anna said promptly.

Tremaine ignored her. "Now, if I may continue? Thank you. What you've heard up to now has been essentially a setting of the stage, a preface. At this point the book shifts to a first-person narrative—my own voice, naturally—and the tragic personal story of the expedition per se begins." He smiled thinly. "I trust Dr. Fisk will be pleased."

He waited, but Fisk chose not to respond, staring mumpishly into the fire instead.

Tremaine began to read again.

*Had I any inkling of the trouble to come, I would have chosen very differently from among my graduate students for the crew. But who could tell then that Jocelyn Yount's limpid blue eyes were windows to a wanton and amoral personality that would eventually create so much animosity and bitterness among us? The first sign—*

"Whoa," Shirley said. "What was that again? About my sister's personality?"

Tremaine paused briefly before answering. Here, of course, was where things would begin to get difficult. Once again he wondered uneasily just how good an idea this "co-opting process" was. There was a great deal to be said against it, in his view; not least that it had been thought up by a lawyer.

"Miz Yount," he said soothingly, understandingly, "I'm extremely sorry if this causes you distress, but surely you realize that I must be honest in my opinions, my perceptions." He could, he reasoned, delete the "wanton" without any great loss, if necessary. He had been a little doubtful about it in the first place, truth to tell. But on the "amoral" he would stand firm. Literary integrity demanded it.

"Well, yeah, sure," Shirley said. "Nobody's saying you shouldn't be honest, but that just isn't true, what you said. My sister was something else; she was an angel on earth, a—"

Anna barked a single note of laughter. "Some angel."

Ah, good. He had Anna on his side on this one. As expected. His master plan for the week depended on playing them off against each other in different combinations.

Shirley stared at Anna, angry and off balance. "What are you talking about? You're crazy!" She turned back to Tremaine. "Hey, what's going on here? What are you trying to do?"

"I'm not trying to do anything, Miz Yount—"

"Will you call me Shirley, for Christ's sake?" Her increase in self-assertion over the last several days had not made her personality any the more attractive.

"—Shirley, except to tell the story as I saw it unfold. Sometimes, I'm afraid, it's necessary to put aside our personal feelings in the interest—"

"My sister was not amoral, Jack! My s—"

"The hell she wasn't!"

This ringing corroboration came, amazingly, from Elliott Fisk—Elliott, who had been eleven in 1960.

Shirley rounded on him, her face reddening. "What the hell do you know about it, you little turd?"

"I know what I know," Fisk said mysteriously, uncowed by Shirley's toothy hostility. "I know she was ruining my uncle's life."

"*She* was ruining *Steve's* life? Ha-HAH! Really! Jesus!"

"Oh, yes?" Fisk's thin voice rose spitefully. "Oh, yes? Well, I hate to tell you this—*Miz* Yount—but it's all in his diary. All the one-night stands she had with anybody who—"

"What are you talking about? What are you talking about?" Shirley tore her big glasses off and jabbed them at Fisk. "You listen to me, you slimy, sick-minded . . . slimy . . ."

"That's enough now," Tremaine said, employing a trick he had of relaxing his vocal cords so that his voice seemed to swell. His voice of authority. "Organlike," *Television Radio Age* had once called it. "I fully understand," he said, tempering command with compassion. "In a difficult situation like this our emotions sometimes—"

He stopped with Fisk's words still echoing in his mind. He looked directly at the dentist.

"Ah, diary?"

"Well, journal."

"Journal? Steven kept a journal?" Why had Tremaine not known of this?

"To the last morning of his life," Fisk said, with every appearance of satisfaction. "They found it in his room back in Gustavus. It went to my father with the rest of his things." He paused to study Tremaine's face and smiled meanly. "I didn't think you knew about it. Oh, it's just filled with information. On all sorts of things."

Tremaine shifted his feet. Just what was being driven at here? He didn't care for this journal business at all. Or the tone of Fisk's voice. Or that smirk.

"And you've seen this journal?" he asked.

Fisk wordlessly held up a flat blue-bound notebook.

"I think we better get a few things straight here." This from Shirley, who had gotten her second wind. "First, I'm not going to sit still while my sister gets bad-mouthed by anybody." She glowered at Tremaine, at Fisk, at Anna. "Second," and here the baleful gaze returned to impale Fisk again, "Jocelyn didn't ruin Steve's life; it was the other way around. From the day she was stupid enough to fall in love with that pretentious, self-righteous creep—"

"Oh, now, just a—just a minute." Fisk, blinking rapidly, pushed his wire-rimmed glasses up on his nose. "I won't have this. When your sister met Steve she was just a lousy waitress, and you know it. Had she even finished college? Was she headed anywhere? It was Steve who—"

"Now, now," began Tremaine, organlike. "I believe we're getting off the sub—"

"Ha-HAH!" It was not a sound that even Tremaine could talk through.

"It was Steve who what?" Shirley cried. "Who told her that the great Steven Fisk couldn't waste his time on a lousy waitress? Who made her finish up her stupid degree and then go to graduate school on top of it? So she was killing herself taking classes full time and *still* working in a goddamn Chinese restaurant, humping dishes every night to support herself, while he sat around on his ass, on a scholarship? Tell me, did he ever try to help her out—"

"This is ridiculous!" Fisk burst out, his arms spread. By

now they were making their cases to the rest of the group, as if pleading before a jury. "Somebody tell me, is there supposed to be something wrong with motivating a person to go back to school? I mean, here's somebody who was a waitress since she was fifteen, right? No motivation, no drive. She drops out of college after three years and goes *back* to being a waitress. What kind of life was she headed for? But then she meets Steve—"

"Just what the hell is wrong with being a waitress?" Shirley interrupted, her coarse cheeks pink. "I want to know. She was *happy*, she didn't want to be a scientist—a botanist, for Christ's sake—"

At a movement near the top of the stairs to the right of the fireplace, Tremaine turned his head. "Ah, Dr. Oliver," he said hurriedly. "Thank you for coming."

Gideon hesitated. "Uh, if this isn't a good time . . ."

"No, no, come in. We were just waiting for you. There's a chair over there for you." He smiled. "Try not to trip over Dr. Judd's legs."

Gideon came in reluctantly, feeling like an intruder. He'd inadvertently overheard the argument and had been in the act of trying to back inconspicuously down the stairs when Tremaine had spotted him.

He was welcomed by the botanist with smooth assurance and introduced all around. Chairs scraped on the wooden floor as the six people rearranged themselves to fit him into the semicircle in front of the hearth. The movement seemed to clear the air. Eyes shifted to the large paper bag he'd brought with him and placed on one of the low, round side tables.

"I'm afraid I don't have very much to tell you," he said. Briefly he went over as much as he and Owen had agreed they should know.

"The bones you found yesterday are almost certainly

from the 1960 survey party. What we have are the near-complete skeleton of a right foot, a segment of a jawbone, and part of a right femur—a thigh bone."

"We know what 'femur' means," Elliott Fisk grumbled.

"They belong to one or more males in their mid-twenties," Gideon went on. "That's about all I can tell right now."

"And did you find any more today?" Tremaine asked.

"Yes," Gideon said offhandedly. "Part of a cranium."

He watched Tremaine, who brushed impassively at a bit of lint on his crisply pressed trousers.

"Males?" Shirley asked. "Then there aren't any . . . any remains of my sister?"

He shook his head. "I'm sorry, no. Everything so far seems to be male. The rangers will be doing some more searching near Tirku in the next few days; they might turn up some more." They would be doing it by themselves. His only pair of heavy shoes would take a week to dry.

He waited for more questions. They watched him noncommittally. Where was the "burning interest" Tremaine had talked about? Or was it Tremaine himself who was so eager to know exactly what he'd found out? He glanced at him again, but Tremaine merely returned the look with a faint, meaningless smile.

Gideon fidgeted in his chair. He was uncomfortable with the residue of tension still in the atmosphere, uncomfortable with the macabre situation he found himself in—talking so matter-of-factly to next of kin about their relatives' mandibles and crania. And uncomfortable with his role in things so far. He had, in effect, practically accused Tremaine of murder, but Tremaine knew nothing about it. A secret accusation. Gideon was anxious for things to be out on the table. Tomorrow, he hoped; maybe even this evening. But that would be up to Owen.

It was Gerald Pratt who broke the silence. He pointed

with the stem of his pipe at the paper bag Gideon had brought. "What's in the sack?"

"These are some items of clothing and equipment we found today. The chief park ranger asked me to show them to you to see if you could identify them."

Pratt put the pipe back in his mouth, leaned back, and crossed one skinny, sharp-shinned leg over the other. "Well, let 'er rip."

"By all means," said Tremaine. Was it Gideon's imagination, or did he suddenly look shifty?

The bag rustled noisily while Gideon got it open, and now for the first time they all showed what seemed to be genuine curiosity, if not quite "burning" interest. The ragged strip of plaid cloth was not recognized by anyone, although Walter Judd thought that Jocelyn Yount might have had such a shirt. But neither Anna nor Tremaine was willing to confirm this, and after a minute Judd began doubting it too, finally talking himself out of the notion. Gideon put the material back in the sack.

"Shouldn't that be kept in a plastic bag?" Fisk asked disapprovingly.

"Not while it's wet. Putting it in a plastic bag is the last thing you'd want to do."

Fisk's lips compressed. He wasn't so sure about that.

Gideon took the eyeglass frames from the sack and laid them on the table where they could be seen. They were from an inexpensive pair of sunglasses, in the wraparound style that had been popular in the sixties, and had now been twisted back into an approximation of their original shape. "Ban-Sun" was stamped on the inside of one of the aluminum temple pieces.

"You know, that looks familiar," Judd said, tapping his lower lip with a finger.

"Everything looks familiar to you," Anna said. "Maybe you should go back to sleep."

Judd chuckled as happily as if she'd complimented him. "No, now wait, just wait a minute." He appealed to Tremaine. "Don't you remember one of those boys wearing a pair like that? I think it was James Pratt. I'm almost sure it was. Or was it Steve?"

Tremaine frowned. "I do remember something . . ."

"Were they—" Gerald Pratt's voice caught in his throat. He swallowed. "With orange lenses?" he asked Judd. "Jimmy always said to wear orange sunglasses. Said they filtered the ultraviolet rays or something."

"You know, I think that's right," Judd said slowly.

Tremaine snapped his fingers. "By God, you *are* right. I remember now. Wraparound orange sunglasses; ugly things." He looked at Gideon. "You think these might be James's?"

Gideon didn't answer. With his tongue between his teeth, he was busy probing with a ballpoint pen at the collapsed browpiece of the glasses, a thin, straight band of metal folded into a U-shaped trough and then crimped to hold the missing plastic lens. After a few seconds he managed to get the point between the crimped edges and push out onto his palm the tiny, shiny particle that had caught his eye. He looked at it briefly, then turned his hand over so that it dropped onto the white Formica surface of the little table in front of him. A scrap of broken plastic no bigger than a fingernail paring. Gleaming. Transparent.

Tangerine-colored.

A murmur went around the group, a soft "ah" of appreciation.

"Those Jimmy's then?" Pratt asked huskily. He had gotten out of his chair to come tentatively closer.

"It looks as if they are," Gideon said gently. He held the frames out to him on the palm of his hand.

Pratt pulled momentarily back as if they might sting

him, then came forward again, taking them gingerly from Gideon, turning them over, staring at them, trying to find God knows what. The muscles in his throat worked.

"Just turned twenty-five," he said thickly. "My baby brother, you know."

Abruptly he thrust the frames back at Gideon. With his other hand he stuck his pipe into his mouth and took two quick, furious puffs, blowing out rather than sucking in. Glowing sparks of tobacco popped from the metal bowl.

"Would I get to keep 'em?" he asked. "After you people've finished with 'em?"

"I think so," Gideon said. Empathy had made his own throat tight. "I can't see why not."

"Good, then." He wiped the back of his hand across his nose, shrugged, and went back to his chair, chewing on the pipe. The shoulders of his bright blue coveralls hunched slackly away from his body as he sat down, as if he had shrunk inside them.

"Well, then," Gideon said into the awkward silence, "one more thing."

As soon as he took the broken ice ax from the sack, Anna spoke out sharply.

"It's one of ours. An Alpiner."

Judd nodded gravely. "Right you are. I remember."

"Were they all exactly the same?" Gideon asked. "Is there any way to distinguish one from another?"

"After thirty years," Tremaine snapped, "you expect us to remember who wrapped red tape around the handle and who used yellow? Not that there's any tape left on this one. Really, is there some purpose to this?"

"I'm just trying to come up with anything that might be useful in identifying the remains. If we knew for sure whose ice ax that was, it could help."

"Well, it seems as if you'll have to figure it out on your own," Tremaine said impatiently. He closed the loose-leaf binder in front of him, tucked it under his arm, and stood up with the brittle agility of a man who worked hard at aging gracefully. "Thank you for coming, Dr. Oliver. And now, if there's nothing else, the fire is dead, the Icebreaker Lounge is open for business, and I, for one, am in dire need of the comfort of a Rob Roy." With a nod he was gone, his rich voice seeming to hang in the air behind him.

Tremaine's voice was all his own. Like the larger-than-life stars of Hollywood's golden era—Cary Grant, Katharine Hepburn, John Wayne—he had created a way of speaking that was to be found in no one else on the planet. Lush but nasal, British but American, elegant but intimate.

About what you'd expect, was Gideon's grumpy and uncharitable thought, if you crossed John Gielgud with W. C. Fields.

# 8

Five-Squad. Lau."

"Mr. Lau? The SAC would like to see you, please."

With his shoulder hunched to prop the telephone receiver against his ear, John continued to fill out a quarterly progress report. Christ, the bureau put you through a lot of paperwork. Which was saying something, coming from a man who had put in four years in the NATO Security Directorate.

"Now?" he said, writing.

"Well, no, naturally not," Charlie Appletree's secretary purred, "not if you have something more important to do."

"Yeah, well, you see, my paper clips have gotten kind of tangled up and I was counting on separating them this afternoon. And you know how the telephone cord gets all twisted around itself? I was planning—"

Melva switched to her gravel voice, one of many. "All right, Lau. Get your ass up here right now." Melva was a buxom, apple-cheeked woman in her fifties who had been Appletree's secretary for twenty-two years. Sassing whoever she pleased was one of her undisputed perks. "Or do you want me to come down there and drag you up by the—"

"No, ma'am," John said. "Right away, ma'am."

Smiling, he headed for the stairwell and climbed to the seventh floor. Appletree's office was an airy, properly impressive corner room in various shades of tan, with two big windows looking down rain-wet Madison Street toward the Seattle waterfront. There was a slate-gray sliver of Puget Sound visible between the buildings if you leaned in the right direction and looked hard. The other two windows, the ones overlooking the enormous peeling painting of Canadian geese in flight on the side of the old Warshall's sporting-goods building, and beyond that the tacky storefronts of First Avenue, were discreetly shuttered by beige venetian blinds.

The huge kidney-shaped desk—a table really, with no drawers—held a blotter, a small vase of fresh daisies, a picture of Appletree's wife and children, and a pen-and-pencil set on a marble base. There wasn't a paper on the oiled walnut top and there never was, a fact that always impressed visitors. John, however, was aware that the inconspicuous door to the left of the desk did not open into a small room with a cot, as was popularly believed, but into a comfortable office with an old desk that was every bit as cluttered as John's was. *This* big room, with its American flag, its wall-mounted FBI seal, and its authoritative serenity, was strictly for guests; a reception room, so to speak.

Appletree was at the desk speaking into a dictating machine, his jacket off, immaculate white shirtsleeves turned back onto hairless forearms in wide, crisply perfect folds. When John came in he gestured toward the grouping of upholstered chairs around a coffee table in the corner.

Atop the table was a small, dark-brown bust with a lean, long-nosed head. On his first visit to the office, John, nervously looking for something to talk about, had picked it up and examined it.

"You're looking at my hero," Appletree had said. "Know who it is?"

"Lincoln? Before he had a beard?"

"Machiavelli."

John still didn't know whether it was or it wasn't. He'd found a picture of Machiavelli somewhere and concluded that Appletree might have been telling the truth.

The SAC came over to join him and fell into one of the chairs, rubbing the top of his crew cut with the flat of his hand. It sounded like a scrubbing brush on tile.

"Well, your pal did it again."

"My pal?" Not that he couldn't sense what was coming.

"Oliver. He screwed things up again."

"In one day?"

Appletree put his hands in his pockets, stretched out his legs, and leaned the back of his head against the high back of his chair, looking up at the ceiling. "Amazing, isn't it."

"What do you mean, screwed up?"

"As in 'complicated.'" He tilted his head back to level and looked at John. "He says those bones show evidence of homicide."

John stared at him. "Murder by avalanche?"

"Murder by pickax. Ice ax, rather. You have any idea what an ice ax is?"

John shook his head. "So then the bones aren't from those scientists who got caught in the avalanche?"

"Wrong. They are."

"I don't get it."

"Join the crowd, John."

Melva came in holding a mug in each hand: tea for the SAC and coffee for John.

"So glad you were able to make it, Mr. Lau," she said pleasantly.

"I believe John takes cream, Melva," Appletree said, "and sugar too. Right, John?"

It was like Appletree to remember that kind of personal detail, even with seventy agents working for him. John smiled. The SAC probably kept a file on everyone in that little office next door and reviewed it before anybody came in.

Appletree took a couple of sips from his mug and set it on the coffee table. "Now, the thing is, there's some confusion over just who's going to handle the case."

"How come? Doesn't the Park Service have, what do you call it, proprietary jurisdiction?"

"Well, yes, technically, but the chief ranger's asked the bureau to come in and run things. It's federal land, so it's a legitimate request. The guy's really shorthanded because all his seasonal help are gone. And, frankly, I don't think he's too keen on running a homicide investigation."

"Okay, so what's the problem? There's an FBI office in Juneau, isn't there?"

"Yes, but there's only one resident agent, and he's close to filing on a big drug case. He just can't spare the time. Anchorage says they can't either. Even the state police say they don't have people to help out."

"I'm getting the impression nobody's too anxious to take this on."

"Well, think about it. Corpus delicti consists of some rags and a few old bones dug out from under an avalanche along with a broken ice ax. Hotshot professor comes along and *alleges* it adds up to murder. But he can't say who's been murdered. Case file not opened—not even thought about—until almost thirty years after the fact. Talk about cold leads. It's no wonder they don't want to waste any manpower on it. How'd *you* like to have a case like that dumped in your lap?"

"No, thanks."

Appletree's lipless but disarmingly youthful grin suddenly split his face. "Well, you've got it." He rubbed the top of his head again, looking pleased with himself.

"*Me*? What the hell do I have to do with Alaska?"

"Actually, it's very logical. In the first place, in 1960, at the time this happened—if it happened—the Juneau office reported to Seattle, so it would have legitimately been our baby from the start. If anyone had known about it."

"Oh, yeah, that's really logical."

"Second, this was a U-Dub expedition. Whoever those bones belong to, he was from here, not from there. So's the number-one suspect."

"We've actually got a suspect? Terrific. What is he, ninety years old now?"

"I'll tell you about that later. Third, you've worked with Oliver before. You're the one who got him involved."

"Now we're getting down to it. This is a disciplinary assignment, right, boss?"

Appletree laughed. "You're working on the Tackney Mutual file, aren't you? Why don't you turn that over to Mintner and get on this instead? Glacier Bay's only three hours by air. You could start tomorrow morning. Well, couldn't you?"

"Yes, sir, I guess so."

"Good. Give it a shot, see what you can do. If you're not getting anywhere at all by, say, Friday, we can quietly drop it." His expression sobered. "Look, John, if you'd really rather not—"

John shook his head, smiling. "I'll take it."

He was, in fact, pleased, as he was sure Appletree knew. Tackney Mutual was a fire-insurance underwriting firm involved in a massive, complex case of interstate insurance fraud. John had spent the last three days at his desk, analyzing endless columns of mind-numbing claim-report breakdowns. Just the kind of case that made him grind his teeth. A straightforward homicide was a lot more down his alley. Not that "straightforward" seemed to be the word here.

"I thought you would," Appletree said. He tore a slip of paper from a pad and gave it to John. "The chief park ranger's name is Owen Parker. Give him a call at this number and let him know you're coming."

"Will do."

"And we've started a case file on it. They're making copies of the serials for you downstairs. Probably ready by now."

"Okay, I'll check with clerical as soon as we're done."

"Clerical! Good heavens, man, we don't have *clerks.* We have," he said solemnly, "support staff."

"Right, I keep forgetting. Do I report to Anchorage on this or what?"

"No, we treat this as if we're the OO."

"The OO?"

Appletree shook his head in amiable wonder. "John, you're amazing. How do you manage to function so effectively in this bureaucratic maze? Do you really not know what 'OO' means?"

John ran a finger around the inside of his shirt collar. "Well—"

"The OO is the originating office," Appletree said, picking up a small pitcher of real cream that Melva had deposited on the table, "the office with the primary responsibility for a case."

"I'll try to remember."

"Do. For one thing it saves time; two syllables instead of whatever. And, of course," he added with a smile, "if we went around saying things like 'originating office,' everybody would know what we were talking about. And we certainly wouldn't want that, would we?"

He poised the creamer over John's mug. "Let's see, if I remember right, you like it heavy on the cream."

Why was it, Gideon had sometimes wondered, that his students got so possessive about their chairs? Even when seating at the first class meeting was random or arbitrary, they headed right for the same places the next time and forever after. Try to rearrange things and there were groans of frustration and despair.

The phenomenon, he now noted, was not limited to the classroom. By this, the third predinner cocktail hour since their arrival, the seating arrangement in the Icebreaker Lounge was fixed and apparently immutable. There were Tremaine and his admirers in possession of the bar. There were Anna Henckel, Walter Judd, and Gerald Pratt at their corner window table. There were the customary groupings of trainees. When Julie and Gideon had come in at five-thirty, half an hour into things, their table, directly before the fireplace with its newly laid log fire, was waiting for them as if it had been reserved.

They downed hot apple ciders while Gideon brought her up to date. He had just come back from the bar with seconds when Owen Parker came in, got a 7-Up, and headed their way. It was the first time they'd seen him in the cocktail lounge. He was in uniform, the only ranger who was. But then he was the only one on duty.

He pulled over a chair from the next table and dropped solidly into it. "So. I just got off the phone with the FBI. The guy who's going to be running things gave me a call."

"And?" Gideon asked.

"And he'll be out here tomorrow morning."

"Fast work," Julie said.

"These guys don't mess around," said Owen. He slowly poured 7-Up from the can into his ice-filled glass. "Oh, he had a message for you," he said to Gideon. "He said: 'Tell Doc the next time he comes up with something, would he please make it Arizona, not Alaska?'"

"Doc?" Gideon looked at Julie, then back at Owen. Only one person called him "Doc." He put down his glass mug. "You're kidding me. John Lau?"

"That's right," Owen said doubtfully. "What's the matter, is there a problem with the guy?"

Gideon laughed. "No, John's terrific, first-rate. He's an old friend."

"What's he got against Alaska?"

"He just likes it hot," Julie said.

"And dry," Gideon put in. "The world's only Hawaiian who can't stand humid weather."

"Hot and dry," Owen said. "He must love it in Seattle."

"Can't stand it," Gideon said. He stirred his cider with the rolled strip of cinnamon bark in it and licked the end of the bark. "But what's a Seattle agent doing in this? Isn't there a field office in Juneau?"

"It's a long story," Owen said. "Listen, you want to drive out to the airport with me to pick him up tomorrow morning? You can explain about the bones better than I can."

"Sure, what time?"

"I'll pick you up at twenty to eight. I arranged for a charter flight to meet his plane in Juneau at seven-thirty. He'll be here about eight."

"Can I come too?" Julie asked. "It'll be fun to see John."

"I thought you were heading out to the glaciers again tomorrow morning," Gideon said.

"Oh," Julie said, "that's right. Rats. I keep thinking I'm on vacation too."

*"I beg your pardon."* The voice was imperious, arresting, and unmistakable.

M. Audley Tremaine looked down upon them, erect and lordly. One hand was in the side pocket of his jacket. Gideon noticed that he had changed from the brown houndstooth-check sport coat he'd been wearing earlier to a bottle-green velvet jacket. If there were still such things as smoking jackets, this had to be one. The ascot had been tastefully changed to match it.

"I would like you to know," he said coldly, addressing Owen, "that I do not appreciate the way matters have been handled thus far, and I have every intention of informing your superiors."

Owen bristled. "Matters?"

"The hole in the skull. The ice ax. The whole damned thing." He had had that Rob Roy, Gideon realized, maybe two. He wasn't sloppy—far from it—but there was a telltale, sullen glitter in his eyes.

"Exactly what is it that you don't appreciate, sir?" Owen asked evenly.

"I don't appreciate being the last one to know. I lon't appreciate being the subject of innuendo and the object of macabre curiosity to every damned park ranger in the place. I don't appreciate this . . . gentleman"—a frigid glance at Gideon—"coming in to us and *lying*. Through his teeth. And all the while bathing us in that wide-eyed sincerity and compassion."

Gideon began to say something, but checked himself. What Tremaine had said was true. All right, he hadn't exactly lied to them, but he'd sure omitted a few things, and he wasn't too happy with it either.

"It was my decision," Owen said shortly. "I did what I thought was appropriate."

*"Your* decision," Tremaine repeated, the rich voice oozing contempt. "And your next decision? Am I to be

arrested for murder?" He held his slim hands out, as if for handcuffing. "Don't shoot, officer."

"Professor Tremaine," Owen said, his copper-brown face stony, "nobody's arresting you. The FBI will be—"

"The FBI. Dear me, is it as important as that? Do you suppose I'll make the ten-most-wanted list?"

"Look, Professor, nobody's accusing anyone, and nobody's arresting anyone. Why don't you just enjoy your dinner tonight and we'll worry about sorting things out tomorrow."

"Oh, we'll sort things out tomorrow, all right," Tremaine said hotly. "You'll be lucky to have a job as a janitor by the end of tomorrow." He glared at Owen for another moment, then turned abruptly, literally on his heel, and strode from the room.

"Whew," Julie said. "How did he find all that out?"

"I'd guess," Gideon said, "that someone overheard us on the boat and came back and passed the word around." He shrugged. "You can't blame them. It's pretty exciting stuff."

Owen turned to look over his shoulder toward the knot of young rangers who had been surrounding Tremaine earlier. Under his gaze they shifted and glanced sheepishly away. The hum of conversation picked up. Gideon realized belatedly that it had died down while people had listened in on Tremaine's tirade.

"Yeah, I'd say you were right," Owen said, turning back. "There weren't any doors on the galley, and we weren't thinking about being quiet. At least I sure wasn't." He leaned his elbows on the table and hunched over his glass. "What the hell. Your friend John's going to love this."

"Don't worry," Julie said. "John's a sweetie."

"I'm happy to hear it." Owen drained his 7-Up, crunched an ice cube between his teeth, and smiled. "I'm a sweetie too."

# 9

John tossed his shoulder bag into the back seat of the green Park Service car, ducked to get through the door, and slid in. "But what are you saying *did* happen, Doc? That Tremaine killed this guy with this ice ax, and a few minutes later this avalanche just happened to come along and conveniently bury everything?" He pulled the door closed after him.

"And conveniently kill the only two witnesses?" Owen put in, turning the key in the ignition.

"And conveniently *not* kill Tremaine?" added John. "Just bury him up to his eyeballs in the ice for two days?"

Gideon pulled his own door closed and settled himself in the front passenger seat. "What are you ganging up on me for? You're the ones who're supposed to figure all the hard stuff out. What do I know? I'm just a simple bone man."

John muttered something, finished off the last of his

candy bar, licked his fingers, and stuck the wrapper in the pocket of his denim jacket.

His plane, a single-engine two-seater with "Kwakiutl Airlines" stenciled on the doors, had been early. When Owen and Gideon had arrived at the lonely cedar-board longhouse that was the Gustavus/Glacier Bay Airport terminal building, the big FBI agent had been sprawled on a wooden bench, sipping from a cardboard cup of coffee from one vending machine and munching a Butterfinger bar from the other.

"No breakfast," had been his wistful greeting.

"I figured you wouldn't get a chance to eat," Owen had said. "I asked them to have something for us at the lodge when we get there."

John had brightened immediately, but it hadn't stopped him from getting another cup of coffee and a second Butterfinger. Gideon and Owen had gotten coffee too, and for fifteen minutes they had sat in the otherwise deserted waiting room talking over the case, trying and rejecting one murder scenario after another.

The only thing they'd agreed on was that the murder was probably unpremeditated. Why would Tremaine or anybody else have planned to kill someone out on Tirku Glacier, with the others right there and nobody else within fifty miles? Why not wait until they were all back in Gustavus, where there'd be a couple of hundred other people to serve as potential suspects too? As it turned out, the avalanche *did* just happen to come along and bury everything, but there had been no way to foresee that.

No, it had been unpremeditated, spur of the moment, a crime of passion; perhaps the outcome of a fight. The logic of the situation pointed to that. And—more important, in Gideon's mind—so did the damaged mandible.

Now Owen twisted the steering wheel, backed away from the terminal, and swung out of the parking lot. The airport in Gustavus was only eleven miles from the lodge, but it seemed as if it were on another continent. Southeastern Alaska, as Owen had told Gideon on the way out, was a land of microclimates. There were no towering hemlocks or spruce around Gustavus, no pleasant green hummocks of mossy undergrowth. Here there was just a drab, level, tundralike plain, windswept and gloomy, alongside the gray waters of Icy Strait. No wonder they had put the airport here. No mountains to fly in over, no trees to get tangled up in, and not much in the way of bulldozing to get the place flat in the first place.

Owen edged the car onto the gravel road and turned right, toward the lodge. It was the only direction the road went. They drove past two rustic A-frames, the only structures in sight besides the terminal. The one on the left housed a smoked-salmon business, the other an arts-and-crafts shop. Both were closed. Between them a brave, brightly colored wooden sign announced "Puffin Mall. Hours 5–6 P.M. every day, June–September." That was when the daily Alaska Airlines flight from Juneau made its turnaround stop.

"All right, try this on," John said. "What if we jumped on the idea that Tremaine's the killer a little too fast? What makes us so sure it's him?"

"Well, he's the only one who came out of it alive," Gideon said. "And he sure was in a hurry to get off the subject of that ice ax yesterday."

"That doesn't mean he killed anyone."

"I don't know. Even if he didn't, he must have seen what happened. He was right there."

"So?"

"So why didn't he ever say anything about it? It's been thirty years. He's talked about the avalanche in public hundreds of times."

"Maybe he was protecting somebody."

"Protecting somebody's memory?"

"Sure, why not? Or maybe he was saving it for this book he's writing, waiting until he could cash it in for big bucks."

"It's possible," Gideon said. He doubted it, but John was right to keep his mind open.

"What the hell," John said, "I'll be talking to him soon enough, see what he has to say. To the others too. Look, I think it'll work a lot better if we keep this whole business about the hole in the skull to ourselves for another day or so, okay?"

Gideon and Owen exchanged a look.

Owen spoke. "Uh, I'm afraid we have a small problem there."

John leaned back resignedly. "Oh, boy," he said, "don't tell me."

"Sorry, my fault," Gideon said, and went on quickly. "I don't suppose you've had a chance to put together any kind of a file on the case yet? Newspaper articles . . . ?"

"There isn't much," John said, leaning across the back seat to slide open a zippered pouch in his bag, "but I brought out copies of what I have." He held up a thin sheaf of papers with a buff-colored cardboard cover and an Acco fastener at the side.

Gideon took it and turned to the first page. "*Skagway Herald,* July 27, 1960" was written in longhand across the top. The headline beneath was "Avalanche Near Glacier Bay. Scientific Research Team Feared Lost." He read on with interest.

"About this breakfast," John said to Owen. "I hope we're talking real food here—eggs, bacon, that kind of thing?"

"Whatever you want," Owen said over his shoulder. "We'll be there in ten minutes; 8:45 at the latest."

"Good, I just might make it," John said, leaning comfortably back. Then, abruptly, he sat up straight, swiveling his head to stare at a rapidly receding dark shape in the roadside foliage. "What the hell was *that?*"

"Bear," Owen said casually. "Brown, I think. Maybe black. Hard to tell the difference this time of year."

"Jesus Christ," John muttered, settling back and closing his eyes, "where did they send me?"

Shirley Yount banged her coffee cup into its saucer. "It's twenty minutes after eight. Maybe somebody ought to go knock on his door."

This was said with more relish than impatience. Like the others, she was eager to get at Tremaine, who had been on the run from them since the electrifying news of thirty-year-old foul play on Tirku had buzzed so excitedly around the bar the night before. Tremaine had not appeared for dinner, and now here he was, going on half an hour late for their daily breakfast meeting.

"He knows what time it is. He is choosing to avoid us," said Anna Henckel, who believed in stating the obvious.

"I wonder why," Elliott Fisk said dryly, slicing a one-by-two-inch rectangle from his cinnamon roll and facing carefully away from Shirley, lest she think he was speaking to her.

"Well, he's going to have to come out and face us sooner or later," Walter Judd said with a happy grin. He buttered another couple of biscuits to go with his three-egg, fresh-salmon omelet. "And when he does, he's going to have a few questions to answer."

"He sure is," Pratt agreed equably, working steadily on a plate of steak and eggs.

"If I knew his room number I'd go get him myself," Fisk grumbled.

Anna glanced at him, eyebrows lifted fractionally. "Room 50."

"Oh?" Fisk paused in his dissection of the bun. "Yes, well, I'll give him fifteen more minutes. Until 8:45."

Doris Boileau placed the small paper-wrapped bar of Camay on the bathroom counter, put a larger one on the recessed shelf of the shower stall, and took a final practiced look around. Satisfied, she closed the door to the room behind her and checked her watch. Only a little after eight-thirty and here she was already done with Room 48, way ahead of schedule. It certainly was a help when people got up and about their business early.

She took off one of her plastic gloves, glanced cautiously about, and had a restorative bite from the glazed cinnamon bun she'd been hauling around on her cart. She stuffed it all the way in with a pinky, then washed it down with a couple of swallows of heavily sweetened tea from a pint-sized insulated cup, while having another prudent look around. Mr. Granle didn't care for them snacking on the job, and she was in no mood to stir him up, especially after the snit he'd gotten into yesterday when she couldn't find her passkey at the end of her shift.

And all over nothing. Hadn't the key turned up this morning in the bottom of the linen cart? Really, it could have happened to anyone.

She put her glove back on and pushed the cart along the wooden walkway to Room 50, chewing reflectively. The extra four hundred dollars she was earning this week was going to come in handy. For the dozenth time she cast luxuriously about in her mind for spending alternatives. Maybe a trip to visit Flo in Victoria next February when she couldn't stand the gray days anymore. Maybe even a shopping trip to Seattle, if she could find somebody to share expenses with. But not with Nadine again. No, that was more than a soul could be expected to bear.

She knocked briskly at the door to Room 50. "Service!"

she shouted, but she was already inserting the key in the lock. M. Audley Tremaine would be long gone, having breakfast with his group. Just once, she thought wishfully, it'd be nice if he *wasn't* gone, just so she could say she'd gotten to meet him, maybe even get his autograph. Of course she'd tell Nadine she'd met him anyway, but that wasn't the same thing. And it wasn't the same thing just peeking at him from a distance, the way she'd managed to do a few times; not that it wasn't exciting. She turned the key.

As she was to tell it for the rest of her life, it was her sixth sense, which she'd inherited directly from her Grandmother Strankman—a mysterious tingling across her cheeks, just below her eyes—that told her something was wrong even before she got the door all the way open. This, Doris ardently believed. Actually it was a combination of things, none of them consciously noticed at first, and none of them mysterious, but all of them different from the way things had been on previous mornings.

First, the drapes were still closed, the room dim. Second, the bed had been made up. Now why would he do that? And third, there was the smell. God knows, she had encountered plenty of peculiar smells after two decades of opening hotel-room doors first thing in the morning, but this was different; not a smell so much as a thickness in the air, cloying and gamy.

She stood in the doorway for a few seconds. "Professor Tremaine?" she called uncertainly.

No answer. Now she noticed the pint bottle of brandy on the near nightstand, and the empty glass next to it, caught in the shaft of light from the open door. Next to it was another glass with—my Lord, with a set of dentures soaking in pale blue liquid. M. Audley Tremaine with false teeth? She stared at it, shocked and embarrassed. The morning light illuminated rows of bright bubbles, clinging like beads of quicksilver to the crevices between the teeth.

"Professor Tremaine?" she called again.

She entered tentatively. From the partially open bathroom door light flooded onto the burlap-covered partition between bathroom and bedroom. She walked slowly toward the door, breathing shallowly through her mouth, her heart sinking with each step. Her ears hummed.

"Professor?"

Trembling and ready to bolt, she pushed the bathroom door all the way open. Her teeth were bared, her breath stopped in her throat. There were used towels tossed all over the shower door, paper wrappers from the drinking glasses crumpled and dropped onto the counter, a blow dryer with its cord neatly coiled. The hum was coming from the ceiling fan.

No M. Audley Tremaine.

She exhaled sharply, dizzy with relief, and switched off the fan. Just what had she expected to find, for God's sake? M. Audley Tremaine, crumpled in a heap on the floor in front of the toilet, the way Sheila had once found that poor old man when she was working at the Prospector in Ketchikan? Heart attack while at his stool was the official verdict. What a thing.

"Well, now, let's just get a little light in here," she said aloud, pert and businesslike. She rubbed her plastic-gloved hands together to prove she was herself again. "And air."

She rounded the burlap-covered partition, heading for the windows. Doris Boileau was a hefty woman, and when she moved forcefully she built up considerable momentum. By the time she realized that the shadowed, hanging mass she was about to brush against was not a bundle of clothes draped over the partition, it was too late to stop. Her right shoulder plowed into it, sending it swinging slowly away from her. Her eyes clamped themselves shut, but not before she had seen those dangling, naked feet, white and horrible. She stood paralyzed and empty-minded, her flesh crawling. Noiselessly the body swung back with nightmare slowness to bump against her, weirdly heavy, its silk bathrobe smooth and cool. She began to edge backwards, her eyes still pressed shut, the skin of her scalp cold and jumping. Don't look. Don't think. Just—

A man's voice sounded behind her. "What's—"

Doris screamed. Her eyes popped open. The eyeballs rolled up out of sight. She lifted her heavy arms with unlikely grace and fainted.

Luckily for Elliott Fisk, he was able to leap nimbly out of the way at the last moment.

"Listen to this," Gideon said as the car pulled into the lodge parking area. "'National Monument officials have now confirmed reports that the fragmentary human remains recently discovered at the terminus of Tirku Glacier are those of members of a botanical research party killed in a 1960 avalanche.' And then— 'A skeletal-identification expert has subsequently identified the bones as those of Fisk and James Pratt.'"

"When was this?" Owen said, turning the car onto the lodge driveway.

Gideon looked at the photocopy again. "September 8, 1964. You didn't know about it?"

"Nope, way before my time."

"Well, I need to find out more about this, Owen. I'd love to see what this guy came up with, match my findings to his. And I'd like to see the bones themselves, if they're still available. Maybe they'd help us figure out which of the new fragments are Fisk's and which are Pratt's."

"What would that do for us?" Owen pulled the car to a stop in the small parking space to the left of the main building and turned to face Gideon, one elbow over the back of the seat.

"For starters, it would tell us who got murdered."

John stirred and stretched. "Doc," he said sleepily, "those remains would have gone to the next of kin a long time ago. You have any idea what it takes to get an exhumation order? Assuming they weren't cremated."

Gideon sagged. "That's right. Damn. John, don't you have any more information on this? The name of the expert?"

John shook his head. "Just what's in the article. Hey, Owen, which way's the dining room?"

They climbed out of the car and headed toward the main building. The sky was the same sullen gray it had been over Gustavus, but the air of Bartlett Cove was softer, milder; rich with the clean, damp-earth smell of ferns.

"What about you, Owen?" Gideon said. "There must be a record of this somewhere in your files. Photographs of the bones, maybe, or measurements."

"Which files would those be?"

"I don't know; the official park files, I guess."

The ranger put his head back and laughed. "I wouldn't count on it. In 1964 this place wasn't even a national park, just a monument and preserve. Hell, Alaska was barely a state. I don't think they were too big on files at the time. But let me ask Arthur. If anybody knows about files, Arthur's the man."

They mounted the wooden steps to the deck surrounding the building. "Owen, something's bothering me," Gideon said. "Here's an expedition lost on a glacier in 1960. Four years later, in 1964, a bunch of bones fall out of the terminus. And then some more from the same group pop out twenty-five years after that. How can that be? Why wouldn't they all be carried to the snout at the same speed, the speed the glacier's advancing? Flowing, I mean."

Owen stopped with his hand on the front-door handle. "You don't know too much about glaciers, do you?"

Gideon sighed.

"Doc knows about everything," John said.

"Not glaciers," Gideon said.

"Well, nobody knows that much about glaciers, when you come down to it," Owen said kindly, "but the rate of flow *inside* isn't necessarily the same as it is on top, or even the same from one part of a glacier to another. And when you're talking about what's happening in crevasses, nobody knows *anything*. All I can tell you is that a twenty-five-year spread isn't that amazing. There's an ice field on Mount Blanc—"

"Owen! Thank God you're back!"

They turned to see the lodge manager running nimbly over the deck toward them. Mr. Granle was a willowy and fragile man of thirty, whom Gideon had thus far not known to speak above a whisper or move with anything but discreet restraint.

"Owen, he's dead!" Mr. Granle shrieked. "He killed himself! Come quick!" He turned and started back the way he'd come.

"Who's dead?" Owen shouted after him. "Who—" He looked briefly at John and Gideon. His amiable face dropped. "Oh, shit."

The three of them took off after Mr. Granle at a run.

# 10

The guest units of Glacier Bay Lodge were small, attached, shake-roofed cottages that fanned out from the main building and were connected to it by a network of wooden walkways that rambled through the greenery and provided secure footing above ground that was sodden in summer and icy in winter. Mr. Granle scrambled over these with unexpected speed, like a spider skittering through its web; left from the main building, down a short flight of steps, right along the next section of walkway, up a few steps, then left again. Some distance behind him the three larger men sprinted, the walkway vibrating under their pounding feet.

"Dammit!" John shouted as the manager vanished behind a corner, "hold up!"

Mr. Granle bobbed back into view. "It's here!" he piped.

"In there," he said, as they reached him. Trembling, pale, he pointed to an open doorway ten feet farther on. A housecleaning cart stood innocently in front of it. Mr. Granle licked bloodless lips. "Do you mind if I don't—"

They rushed past him and into Room 50: John first, then Owen, then—hesitantly—Gideon, wondering uneasily if he shouldn't have waited back at the main building. What business did he have in here?

The room was a duplicate of his own. Double bed to the left, desk to the right, a table and a few chairs near the windows at the back. A large woman in a maid's smock lay groaning, her eyes closed, propped against the wall under the windows. At the right rear was the bathroom, outside of which was a sink and small open closet for hanging clothes. This area was separated from the main part of the room by a sturdy, burlap-covered partition with two clothes hooks in it at shoulder height. Tremaine's body was on the room side of the partition, suspended from a cord stretched up and over the top and attached to one of the hooks on the other side. At the hook itself stood Elliott Fisk, staring at them, motionless, his hands raised to the cord.

"What are you doing?" John said sharply.

Fisk blinked rapidly. "Doing? What am I doing?"

"Please take your hands off that, sir."

"What? Of course." His hands leapt from the hook as if they'd been slapped. "I was just trying to . . . it didn't seem right to just leave him . . ." He backed away, reaching behind him to brace himself on the sink counter.

"Don't touch anything," John snapped.

Fisk jerked his hand back; clutched it in his other hand the way a child does to keep himself from touching something he isn't supposed to. "Touch? No, of course not."

"Who are you?" John asked.

"Elliott Fisk." He pointed distractedly at Gideon. "He knows me."

John didn't bother to confirm it. "What are you doing in here?"

Owen caught Gideon's eye briefly. What's going on? the look asked. John's treating this like a murder, not a suicide. Gideon gave him back an eyebrow shrug. He was wondering the same thing.

"Doing? I came to get Dr. Tremaine. He was late. You can ask the others. They—"

The maid gave a louder moan, one with her heart in it, and rocked her head back and forth. Her eyes were still closed.

The sound seemed to steady Fisk. Under his beard his little mouth firmed. "Look here, why shouldn't I touch anything? It's simple human decency to get him down off that hook. Just who are you, anyway?"

"Mr. Lau is with the FBI," Owen said, looking a lot more official in his snappy uniform than John did in his washed-out blue denims.

The maid groaned again. A stocky, stretched-out leg quivered. The heel of her blue jogging sneaker thrummed on the carpet.

"Do you mind if I help this poor woman?" Fisk demanded. He didn't wait for an answer but boldly bent to her and began chafing the back of her hand. "There, there." Startled, she stared confusedly at him.

"It's all right," he told her earnestly, "I'm a dentist." Such was the state of her mind that she appeared to be reassured. Fisk chafed some more. "Well now," he said with empty professional cheer, "do we think we can get up?"

"I'll give it a try," she said weakly.

With Gideon's and Fisk's help she got to her feet, then tottered from the room, leaning heavily on Fisk's unsubstantial but freely offered arm and keeping her face averted from the corpse. Once outside, judging from the sounds that came in from the walkway, she was received into the solicitous embrace of Mr. Granle and led tenderly away with much cooing and sympathy. John walked to the door and closed it without touching the knob. The three men studied the body silently.

Tremaine was wearing only a burgundy-silk bathrobe, tied at the waist. Open-backed leather slippers lay near his feet, one right-side up, the other overturned. A small, hard-bodied dressing case, also on its side, lay a few inches away. Tremaine's toes rested on the carpet, his heels just above it.

Owen waved vaguely at the dead man's feet and murmured something that caught in his throat. He tried again. "Rope must have stretched," he said thickly.

"Yup," John said. He was thinking, his hands on his hips, his feet spread.

"This is the first—" Owen began. "I mean, you'll probably think it's funny, but I've never—I mean, I've seen dead people before, but never a—" He realized he was running on and stopped. He rubbed the back of a forefinger across his upper lip.

Gideon looked at him sympathetically. He knew how the ranger felt. Asphyxiated people are terrible to look at, and Tremaine was no exception: thickened tongue pushed out obscenely, dried blood around the nostrils, protruding eyes, lips and ears a weird blue-gray, fingers clenched like talons.

At least Owen didn't look as if he were about to throw up, which was more than Gideon could say about his own first experience in similar circumstances. He had done it into a stainless-steel sink in San Francisco's Hall of Justice, which, while demonstrating a certain degree of fastidiousness, had done little to increase the coroner's confidence in him.

"Uhh," Owen said, and on second thought Gideon moved a step away.

Not that he wasn't a little queasy himself. It wasn't the physical horrors that got to him so much these days, but the pathetic little concomitants of death that were always there, one way or another. While Owen's eyes were jumpily fixed on Tremaine's dreadful face, Gideon's were on the dead man's throat. Not on the naked, purple crease in which the cord had buried itself, but on the loose flesh beneath his chin; the old-man's wattles of M. Audley Tremaine—in life so carefully hidden by those tasteful, elegant ascots—now bared for anyone to see, fold on fold, layered against his bony, naked, elderly chest.

"Doc," John said, "you have any way of telling how long he's been dead?"

"Me? No, you need a pathologist."

John turned to Owen. "How do we get a pathologist?"

"We have to ask the state troopers to send somebody up from Juneau."

"How fast can he get here?"

"In an hour, if he comes by seaplane. They can land in the cove. That's if somebody's available."

"An hour," John said. "Doc, the longer he stays dead the harder it is for anybody to tell anything; you know that. You're the closest thing to a pathologist we've got right now. Can't you come up with a guess? I'm not gonna hold you to it. What about rigor mortis or something?"

Gideon hesitated. "Well, yes, it looks as if rigor's set in, all right . . ."

"Sure," Owen said. He was making a resolute effort to sound less qualmish. "The hands. They're all clenched."

"No," Gideon said, "that's different. The tendons in the wrist shorten after death. But . . ." He gingerly reached out a hand toward Tremaine's blue-clad forearm and pushed gently. The entire arm moved stiffly, with resistance, perhaps an inch. Gideon stepped back, barely restraining an unprofessional grimace.

"Well, there's large-muscle stiffening of the shoulder and arm, so I'd say it's fully set in," he said. "If I remember right, that takes about twelve hours."

"I don't get it," Owen said. "Don't your muscles flex when you get rigor mortis? Don't you sort of curl up? Don't you—what the hell *is* rigor mortis, anyway?"

"The muscles don't flex," Gideon said, "they stiffen. From a decrease in the concentration of adenosine-triphosphate in the fiber. Which is caused by the postmortem conversion of glycogen to lactic and phosphoric acid."

"If you don't want to know, don't ask," John told Owen. "So what are you saying, Doc, that he's been dead twelve hours? Since nine o'clock last night?"

"Since ten, anyway. At least since then."

"And you saw him alive when?"

"During the cocktail hour," Owen said. "He came over to rake us over the coals. That was a little before six, wasn't it, Gideon?"

"About ten to."

"Right," John said with satisfaction. He raised the flap of a breast pocket and pulled out a little notebook. "Time of death," he said as he wrote, "between 5:50 P.M. and 10:00 P.M."

Gideon shrugged uneasily. He was out of his element. "Look, John, there are a lot of factors that can hasten or retard rigor; things I don't know anything about. Temperature . . . hell, I don't even know what all the factors are."

"Stop worrying, will you? I told you I wouldn't hold you to it." He had walked to the window while speaking and was examining the snap lock on the frame. "Locked on the inside," he said, "but that doesn't mean anything. It's the kind that locks itself when you close it."

He came back to the body, looked at it a few seconds longer. "Listen, Owen, will you give the state troopers a call and ask them to send their man out right away? And a crime-scene investigation crew while they're at it. Tell them what we've got here."

"Crime?" Owen said. "You think this is murder?"

John looked at both of them. "I wouldn't be surprised, folks."

"Jesus," Owen muttered, "Arthur's just gonna love this." He headed for the door. "Okay, I'll do it right now." He exhaled softly. "Then I better tell Arthur."

"Don't touch the knob," John said. "Just pull it open. I didn't shut it all the way. And, Owen?" He hesitated. "I didn't mean to take over like I did. I'm here because you asked for help on an old murder. This"—he jerked a thumb over his shoulder at Tremaine's body—"is another case. You've got proprietary jurisdiction. If you want me to back off, just say so. It's your baby if you want it."

Owen stared at him. "You gotta be kidding," he said.

John laughed. "Okay, look, I tell you, one thing you could do is have this room sealed till the state people get here."

"Uh, sealed?"

"Well, secured. Just have one of your law-enforcement types stand outside the front door. Somebody with a sidearm. And somebody outside by the back window too. I wouldn't want anybody getting in while the room's empty."

"Empty? You're not staying here?"

"Here?" John said, surprised. "Hell, no, what about that bacon and eggs?"

"Aahh," John said, sloshing his English muffin through the glutinous orange residue of one of his sunny-side-up eggs, "this is great. The bacon's got a little fat on it for once." He poured another glob of ketchup into the depression he had made for that purpose in his hashed-brown potatoes and shoveled another forkful into his mouth.

John's transparent pleasure in food usually stimulated Gideon's appetite too. Not this time, however. He looked away from the happily chewing FBI man, focusing instead on the big Tlingit totem carving on the wall of the dining room. He had ordered only orange juice and toast, and he was having a hard time with the toast.

John masticated contentedly, washed down the potatoes with a slug of coffee, then went after more bacon.

"What makes you think it was a murder?" Gideon asked.

John stopped with his fork in the air. "You really don't know?"

Gideon didn't have a clue and said so.

The bacon was deposited into John's mouth and thoughtfully chewed. "When I tell you, you're gonna argue with me."

"I won't argue with you. Why would I want to argue with you?"

"Yeah, you will. Look, Doc, you know how sometimes when you're explaining something to me about bones—like when you look at some little piece an inch long and say, 'This guy was five-foot-nine, and right-handed, and weighed a hundred and sixty-two-and-a-half pounds, and—'"

Modesty came to the fore. "Come on, John."

"'—and had a pimple on the left side of his ass'? And I say, 'How can you tell all that from a goddamn pinky bone?' Remember what you always say?"

"No."

"You say, 'This may take a small leap of faith.'"

"It does sound familiar," Gideon allowed.

"Well," John said, "this is gonna take a small leap of faith." He leaned forward. "You ready for this?"

His eyes were sparkling. It wasn't often that he got to do

the edifying, and when the opportunity came he relished it.

Gideon smiled. "I'm ready."

"The false teeth," John said.

"The what?"

"The false teeth."

"What false teeth?" Gideon didn't remember any teeth at all; just that awful purple tongue filling Tremaine's mouth.

"In the glass," John said.

"What glass?"

John made an irritated sound. "On the goddamn nightstand—" He held up a peremptory hand. "Doc, if you say, 'What nightstand?' I swear to God . . ."

"What nightstand?"

"You're amazing, you know that? How the hell did you ever get to be a famous scientist? You never notice anything."

"Beats the hell out of me," Gideon said with a sigh. The last couple of days hadn't been doing much for his self-esteem. "I guess we notice different things. Maybe that's why we make such a good team."

"Yeah," said John grumpily, and then when he realized Gideon meant it, more energetically, "Well, yeah, right. Anyway, the thing is, Tremaine's teeth weren't in his mouth; they were sitting in a glass of denture cleanser. That's what made me wonder."

"You mean, why would someone who plans to kill himself go to the trouble of putting his teeth in a glass of cleanser?"

"Well, that too. But the main thing is"—John mopped up the last of his egg with the last of his muffin—"is that suicides usually do it with their teeth in."

"Really."

"Sure. And if they wear glasses, they generally take 'em off. If they're ladies, they make sure to put on a little makeup." The muffin was popped into his mouth and disposed of. He looked sideways at Gideon. "Doc, you really don't know this stuff," he said with mild incredulity. "I would've thought a big-time anthropologist—"

"John," Gideon said with a sigh, "just do me a favor and—"

John waved his hand amicably. "Well, the point is, people worry about how they're gonna look when they're found. I'm not talking about the crazies that blow themselves up, or set fire to themselves, or slice themselves up with a power saw. But people who hang themselves, or take pills, or sit out in the car with the windows closed and the carbon monoxide pouring in—they like to look nice. Generally speaking."

Gideon nodded. "You're probably right."

"Sure, I am. The minute I walked in there I didn't like it. Would you figure a guy like Tremaine to let himself be found wearing a bathrobe with nothing under it? Wouldn't you figure he'd put on silk pajamas, maybe an ascot?"

"Yes, I guess I would."

"But there were those yellow silk pajamas laid out on the bed. Why would he lay them out, then not put them on, if—" John's eyes narrowed. "You did see those pajamas, didn't you, Doc? . . . Doc?"

Gideon crossly drank some orange juice.

"Unbelievable," John said. "Hey, are you gonna eat that or not?"

Gideon shoved his untouched toast over to him. John opened a packet of strawberry jam and lathered half a slice. "There was one other little thing," he said. "One of the passkeys was missing last night at the end of the afternoon shift. Turned up this morning in the bottom of the laundry cart. What do you think about that?"

"I think you're right. We have a murder. Another murder."

"Yeah, I think so." John pointed toward the sky. Another Kwakiutl Airlines plane, this one pontoon-equipped, was tilting down over the cove. "Well, here come the pros; maybe they'll be able to come up with something better than false teeth in a glass." He swallowed the toast and stood up. "I better go down to the pier and meet them. You want to come along, or do you have things to do?"

"I have things to do," Gideon said.

# 11

Well, not really. All he had to do was to continue his analysis of the skeletal fragments. There was nothing about this that couldn't wait, but he preferred to give the pathologist plenty of breathing room. Forensic pathologists were a generally amiable—even jolly—breed, but when Gideon hung around watching them ply their trade, they tended to get crabby and make rude remarks about skeleton detectives.

Owen had gotten him a more convenient place to work: the "contact station," a ranger post that had recently been built to provide information to lodge guests. This was located about two hundred feet from the main building, overlooking Bartlett Cove at the foot of a long pier from which tour boats operated in the summer. A small, neat, wooden building, it had been closed since Labor Day, and it made a good place for him; bright, clean, and uncluttered, still smelling of fresh paint and newly carpentered wood, with plenty of waist-high counter space that allowed him to work standing up, something he preferred.

The perforated cranial fragment was in a safe at park headquarters, but the other bones were here, and his equipment had arrived from the university in Port Angeles. Gideon set up shop on the main counter, under an intimidating wall display of mounted Alaskan crabs. He whistled softly as he unpacked. The smooth, expensive tools of steel and wood were always a delight to handle, always cleared his mind—even of images like Tremaine's dead face and exposed, dewlapped throat. Precise and finely machined the tools might be, but they were marvelously low-tech, uncomplicated things all the same: measuring calipers, jointed boards, gleaming, six-foot-long telescoping rulers. They would have looked fine in a 1930s mad-scientist movie. Even the names would have fit right in. "Bring me the goniometer, Igor." "Do not be frightened, my dear; I am merely going to put the head spanner on you."

But soothing as they were to work with, there wasn't much they could tell him. Gideon spent an hour measuring, then checked his measurements. He determined the transverse and vertical breadths of the head of the femur and its subtrochanteric diameters; he computed the various angles, heights, lengths, and thicknesses of the mandible and the tarsals; he patiently measured the five metatarsals and the other foot bones. He made a dubious estimate of total height from the partial femur. (This was getting into "fudge-factor country," as John called it.)

And when he finished it all, he knew what he had known before: The bones had come from one or more sturdily built males in their mid-twenties and within an inch or so either way of six feet. Almost certainly James Pratt and/or Steven Fisk.

The difference now was that, if need arose, he could

justify his conclusions with figures, something that always pleased policemen and prosecuting attorneys. The funny part was that all the measuring really added nothing new. Most of the impressive-sounding calculations—the platymeric index, the claviculo-humeral ratio, the various robusticity indices—were recent approximations of time-honored subjective judgments, and not the other way around at all. When a choice had to be made, was there an experienced practitioner who wouldn't go with the testimony of eyes and fingertips over that of calipers and calculators? Not likely. Or of goniometers either. This was a dark secret that he and other professors guarded from the tender ears of their graduate students, who would, if they stuck with it long enough, eventually find it out for themselves.

Well, at least he could do something about preserving the fragments, now that they were dry. He was looking for a container to mix the acetone and Duco that Owen had gotten for him, when John appeared on the wooden porch of the building, a giant Styrofoam cup in either hand. Gideon pulled open the door for him.

"Hiya, Doc. Figured you could use some coffee."

"I sure can, thanks." He lifted off the plastic lid and took a grateful swig. "Where'd you find coffee this time of the morning?"

"Restaurant kitchen. They keep a pot going in there."

Gideon laughed. When there was a kitchen around, John usually didn't take long to make a friend in it. He took another swallow. "How's Dr. Wu coming?"

John growled. "He booted me out. Dr. Burton W. Wu. Kind of a touchy little bastard. Like you."

"Me?" Gideon said, surprised. "Touchy?"

"Yeah, like when you come in to look at some bones and you don't let anybody tell you anything about anything. You have to figure it all out yourself."

"That's not being touchy. That's trying to keep myself honest. You know that."

"Yeah, I know, but I'm not used to it from a medical examiner. I was in there examining the scene, you know? Being really careful not to disturb evidence, not getting in anybody's way. But finally this guy turns around and grins with these sharp little teeth and tells me to get the hell out of the room because he's trying to work and I'm bugging him. Jesus Christ," he muttered, "prima donnas all over the place. Everybody's gotta have everything just the way they want it or they have a temper tantrum."

He put his unopened coffee on the counter and dropped into a chair. "What the hell," he said with a sigh, never one to sulk very long. "How's the coffee?"

Gideon took another taste, rolling it judiciously on his tongue. "Well, now that you mention it, it's a little heavy on the cream. And I prefer half-and-half to the nondairy stuff. And in the future it'd be nice to get something to stir it with. Also—"

John looked sharply at him, began to speak, and then burst out laughing, a sunny peal that folded the skin around his eyes into a network of happy crinkles. As usual, Gideon couldn't help laughing along.

"Anyway," John said, stretching his legs out and getting his heels up on a carton on the floor, "I took off and told the little bugger where he could find me. Now, fill me in on what's been going on around here. What are these meetings Tremaine was having? Who're these people he was meeting with?"

"There's not too much I can tell." Gideon pulled over an armchair and told John what he knew. He explained what Tibbett had told him and described his own meeting with the group with all the detail he could remember. John jotted down a few notes. It took no more than fifteen minutes.

"Okay, Doc, that'll be helpful." His notebook went into a breast pocket of his jacket. "Now tell me what's going on with the bones."

They got up and went to the counter. The fragments were neatly arranged on butcher paper. "Here they are," Gideon said, "but there isn't anything new to tell. Owen's sending a couple of his rangers back out there today and tomorrow, and maybe they'll come up with some more, but right now, all—" His attention was caught by movement outside, glimpsed through the side window. "Looks like the little bugger's found you."

The diminutive figure of Burton Wu was striding rapidly down the path from the lodge, purposeful and splayfooted. Splay-kneed, really; every small step swung him off to one side or the other with a roller skater's waddle. A moment later he appeared around the corner of the building, walked in, and looked at the two men sourly. Then he went directly to the counter. It took him seven steps to cover the eight feet.

"Bones, huh?"

"Yes," Gideon said, "they're from—"

"You got some more of that coffee around here, chief?"

"Sorry, no," Gideon said.

John held out his cup. "Here, I haven't touched it."

"Thanks." Wu took it, pulled the cover off, and sipped. He made a face. "Cold. And way too much sugar. You know what that stuff does to you?"

All the same he kept it, taking rapid, minuscule sips and continuing to make faces. He looked at the bone fragments without interest for eight or ten seconds, then spoke to John. "Well, that's no suicide in there. It's homicide, all right. No doubt about it."

"That's what I thought," John said, looking distinctly self-complacent.

"You were lucky, chief," Wu told him. "That false-teeth

crap doesn't prove a thing. Save it for the shrinks." The pathologist had a small man's way of making everything sound like a challenge. His speech was crisp and blunt, leavened only slightly by echoes of the quick, singing vowels of Canton. Parents from China, Gideon guessed, and himself raised in Los Angeles or San Francisco.

"Is that right?" John said crossly.

John's ancestry was Cantonese too. From an anthropologist's perspective they made an interesting contrast, a textbook demonstration of the difference made by a single generation's interbreeding with the vigorous native stock of Hawaii. At ten inches taller, eight inches broader, and almost a hundred muscular pounds heavier than Wu, John loomed over him.

Not that the waspish Dr. Wu was intimidated. "Yeah, that's right," he said, narrow chin thrust up and out. "And the missing key doesn't prove a goddamn thing either. Fortunately, we've got some scientific things to go on." He rubbed his hands briskly together. "Now, the first thing I noticed was indications of postmortem hypostasis superior *and* inferior to the ligature; diffused but mostly a dorsal distribution."

"No kidding." John was an excellent cop, but like many excellent cops he had a block against scientific terminology. Or not a block so much as a self-erected barrier; the innate skepticism of the man of action for the man of words.

Wu looked at him. "Hypostasis," he said. "Livor mortis. Lividity."

"Settling of the blood, you mean?"

"Right, right," Wu said impatiently. "Blood and body fluids."

"Due to gravity after you die."

"Yeah, yeah, sure."

"And the ligature is the cord around his neck, is that right?"

"Of course, ligature. All of which means he couldn't have died in that position."

Gideon had no prejudice against scientific words, but until Wu spelled it out, he hadn't seen what he was driving at, either. "I see," he said slowly. "You mean, the blood would have settled below the ligature if he'd been hanging there when he died. So if there was some lividity *above* it, on the dorsal aspect"—for John's benefit he patted the back of his own neck—"then Tremaine must have been lying on his back for a while after he died; long enough for some of the fluid to settle there."

"Not long; less than an hour," Wu said. "The lab boys—" He turned abruptly to John. "Who is this guy?"

"Dr. Gideon Oliver. It's okay. He's working with the bureau."

Wu shrugged. "It's your case. Anyway, that's point one. Second, I did a little palpation of the throat area; not much, because I didn't want to screw anything up before the autopsy. But I think I could feel a fracture of the left—well, there are these sort of extensions of cartilage that tend to get broken when you strangle somebody with your hands, but not when you get hanged."

"The laryngeal cornua," Gideon said.

Wu looked him over again. "Who'd you say this guy's supposed to be?"

"I'm Gideon Oliver, Dr. Wu. I'm a physical anthropologist."

"He's the Skeleton Detective," John offered helpfully.

Gideon managed not to wince.

"Never heard of him," Wu said, "but it so happens he's right. The left superior cornu. Maybe the inferior too. And the third thing is, the rope's not right. Neither is the burlap on top of the partition."

"What do you mean, not right?" John asked.

"The fraying runs the wrong way. Say a guy wants to hang himself. He ties a rope to a hook on a partition, okay? He runs it over the top of the partition, then ties it around his neck, stands on an overnight case, and kicks the case out from under him. He drops a few inches and *ghaagh!*—the rope strangles him. Well, when that rope gets pulled over the top and down, the rope itself is going to fray in the *opposite* direction . . ." He peered up at John. "You got any idea what I'm talking about?"

"Yeah," John said peevishly, "I think so. The scraping on the rope is gonna be in the direction of the knot around the hook. And the burlap on the partition is gonna get scraped in the opposite direction when the rope pulls over it."

"Give this guy a banana," Wu said. "Well, in there, the fibers show signs of friction, all right, but in the wrong direction—which has got to mean someone tied the rope around his neck and *then* hoisted it up and over the partition. No doubt about it. Any questions?"

"Any idea where the rope came from?" John asked after a moment.

"Not a rope. Two thick bootlaces doubled and tied together. Looks like they came from a pair of hiking boots in the closet."

"What about time of death?"

"Well, rigor's just beginning to recede; small muscles are starting to unstiffen. So I'd say, oh, maybe—"

"Six to ten last night?"

"Right. How'd you know that?"

"Doc here looked at the body."

Wu glared at Gideon. "Skeleton Detective," he muttered. "Jesus Christ."

Gideon shrugged apologetically.

"I figure it'd be closer to ten than six," John said.

"You do, huh?" Wu said, unimpressed. "Why's that?"

"The false teeth. They were already in the glass for the night."

Wu's eyes rolled up. "Do you believe this?" he asked the ceiling. He finished the coffee, followed it with a final unappreciative grimace, and set the cup on a corner of a table which held a cautionary display of ruined cans, pots, and other food containers that had been savaged by bears. "I need to find someplace quiet and write up my report. The lab boys should be finished up with their tweezers inside of half an hour." He opened the door and stepped out onto the porch. "You got a problem with our taking the stiff out with us, then? You get a full report in three days."

"No problem," John said. "Well, I think I'll go on up to Tremaine's room and see how they're doing."

Wu looked disapprovingly up at him. "Try not to bother them, will you?" He rammed the door closed and headed decisively up the hill toward the lodge.

John looked at Gideon. "Friendly little guy, isn't he?"

Gideon smiled. "A little testy, but he seems to know what he's doing. I guess we really do have ourselves a murder here."

"I guess we do. You want to come up with me and see what's happening?"

"No, thanks," Gideon said. Not if Tremaine's unstiffening body was still there, he didn't.

"Okay. What do they do for lunch here?"

"They put out a buffet in the dining room from twelve to one-thirty."

"I want to get in a couple of interviews before then. How about meeting me there at one?"

"You're on," Gideon said.

# 12

For fifteen minutes, comfortably occupying the largest armchair in the upstairs lounge, Walter Judd had snuffled, chortled, and suspender-snapped his way through John's questions. No, he hadn't seen Audley after the cocktail hour last night. Yes, he himself had gone directly to his room after dinner and remained there all night. No, there wasn't anyone who could confirm that; just what was Mr. Lau insinuating? (Chuckle, rumble, snap, snap.) Yes, his room was next to Tremaine's, but no, he hadn't heard anything unusual, or anything at all for that matter.

Now, at John's latest question he stopped with his thumb hooked in a suspender strap. "Would you mind repeating that?"

"Sure. Who do you think killed Tremaine?"

"Now *there's* a question. My, my. Must I really answer that?"

"No, sir," John said affably, "but I thought you'd want to help."

Judd slowly eased the band back. "Well, I just might. May I assume anything I tell you is confidential?"

"No," John said, "you can't." He had learned a long time ago that nine times out of ten, once someone got as far as asking him that question—paid informers excepted—the information was already as good as given, regardless of his answer. Refusing confidentiality at the outset made life simpler and saved grief all around.

Judd chuckled softly. "You certainly don't give a man a lot of room. Well, I don't imagine I'm telling you anything you don't already know if I say that the Illustrious Deceased had a somewhat, ah, shall we say, tarnished reputation when it came to using other people's ideas. Without attribution, I need hardly add."

"You don't sound as if you liked him very much."

"And who do you know who did?" Judd smiled. "Anyone of normal intelligence, I mean. And not counting his legion of adoring television fans." The smile broadened. "Two mutually exclusive categories, I should think."

"Go ahead and tell me about his using other people's ideas."

"For example: A few years after the expedition, he published a very well received monograph on postglacial Rosacea dryas colonization. Anna Henckel claimed, quite probably with cause, that most of the ideas were stolen from her own unpublished work."

"And Dr. Henckel resented this?"

Judd gave him an amused look. "A bit," he said drily. "To be frank, Anna still resents him quite bitterly. The other night in the bar, she was beating us about the head and shoulders with Audley's mismanagement of the Tirku survey." He shook his bearish head wonderingly. "I mean to say, it's been *thirty* years."

"Us?"

"Gerald Pratt and me, though I don't think she ever quite got through to poor Gerald. One often doesn't."

"What was she saying?"

Judd blew out his lips and fluttered them like a horse. "God knows. She had some ancient memo, some self-serving document written by an obscure federal minion and mercifully lost in the files all these years, I suspect. Frankly, I wasn't paying much attention. Audley *did* botch things, of course, but after all this time, who cares? Unless, of course, he was going to gloss them over in his precious book and blame the problems on certain other people—which I wouldn't have put past him—in which case I, too, was prepared to set him straight. Oh, yes."

The botanist began chortling again. "If you were a botanist you'd have heard of the famous—the infamous—scene between Anna and Audley at the ASPT conference in 1969. Or 1968, was it? No, 1969; the year it was in Phoenix."

John waited patiently.

Judd's small eyes twinkled with remembered pleasure. "This was after an acrimonious exchange of letters in the *Journal of Phytogeography* that followed the publication of Audley's monograph. Anna had spat accusations and Audley had waffled, both true to form. Well, while Audley was speaking at a plenary session, Anna stood up in the audience and challenged him. And he refused to acknowledge her."

He leaned forward, eager and happy. "Whereupon the fearsome Henckel simply stood there and stared him down until he more or less wilted to a halt." He rubbed his hands together. "Then she said—and I do mean *said:* 'You, sir, have the balls of a fish!' Upon which she stamped grandly out, thumping that staff of hers, her great black Dracula cape billowing."

His body began to jiggle with mirth. "Not being a piscine anatomist I can't vouch for how much sense it makes biologically, but I can tell you it brought down the house. Without fear of contradiction I may say that it has entered the annals of botanical legend." He laid his head comfortably back and laughed without sound, eyes closed, shoulders shaking. It occurred to John that he was always making noise—sniffling, wheezing, snorting—except when he laughed. That he did silently.

The botanist was built like a turnip. His excess weight was all above the waist, mostly in that high, swollen belly. Below, he was chunky and solid, even at sixty. No spreading, sagging butt, no jellied thighs. A powerful man for all the fat, John thought; wide-shouldered, massive, thick-armed.

"Tell me," John said, "did Tremaine ever steal any of your ideas?"

Judd clutched at his heart. "Egad, I'm a suspect!" His shoulders started jiggling again. "Sorry, Mr. Lau, I'm flattered, but I'm afraid I never impressed Audley enough for him to covet any of my ideas. More's the pity, more's the pity." The jiggling slowly subsided. He batted a finger back and forth across pursed lips. "Although I suppose I *should* mention in this regard that there was some trouble between Audley and . . . no, no, that couldn't have any relevance to this."

John waited for him to go on. Outside of the movies, had he ever heard anyone say "egad" before?

"Really, no, it couldn't," Judd said. "I don't know what I was thinking of."

"You never know," John said. "Why don't you just tell me?"

"Well, it was one of Audley's graduate students: Steven Fisk. Steve seemed to think that Audley had appropriated some of his data, too. I seem to remember some grumbling about it from time to time, but it never came to anything. Of course he was Audley's student, and professors are *expected* to steal from their students, aren't they? In any case, Steve's been dead for all this time now, so . . ." He spread his palms and shrugged. "Well, you see, it just doesn't apply. *Sed hoc nihil ad rem.*"

"Uh-huh," John said, not willing to give him the satisfaction of asking him what it meant. "I understand you just missed getting caught in the avalanche yourself. You were sick that day?"

"I was *attacked*, sir. By a vicious specimen of *Culex pipiens*." Again he closed his eyes and shook his bulky shoulders, consumed with his odd, silent hilarity. "The things that lay men low."

John recrossed his legs and quietly sighed. He didn't think much of this heavy-footed posturing. He wasn't sure if the botanist was putting him down, or putting him on, or if maybe this was just some kind of standard routine he went in for. Whichever, it didn't make him like the man any better, or trust him, either.

"So what is that, some kind of bug?" he asked.

"Indeed, a mosquito of particularly nasty disposition. Apparently I'd been bitten several days before, and the bite had gotten infected without my realizing it. True, I wasn't feeling my best, but I flew out to Tirku with the others, determined to do my part. But when our exalted leader caught a glimpse of my wrist he said no. Despite my protestations, I was forced to remain down below on the beach, at the edge of the lateral moraine, while the others trekked across the glacier to the survey area."

"You wanted to go with them?"

"Certainly. In the strongest imaginable way, but Audley was adamant."

"The airplane had already gone back? Is that why you had to stay on the beach?"

"That's right. It was a seaplane. It was coming back for us later."

"So you were on the beach when the avalanche hit?"

"Yes, wallowing in bitterness and self-pity." He pursed his lips. "Of course, as it turned out, I suppose you could say I was lucky."

"I suppose you could. What did you do when it happened?"

Judd seemed startled. "Do? What was there to do?" For the first time he treated a question as something other than a rich, juicy joke.

"You heard it, didn't you?"

"I *saw* it. In a general sense, I mean," he added hurriedly. "I saw it sliding down the mountain. It was terrifying, unbelievable." He sobered still more. "I didn't actually see it strike them, of course."

"Did you go up and try to help them? Find them?"

It seemed to take a few seconds for the question to get through. Judd sat like a plaster Buddha, his smile frozen, his hands clasped motionless over his belly. Even his wheeze was suspended. The only sound was a soft thud from the stone fireplace. Someone had lit a fire hours before, but it had been allowed to go out. A few blackened remnants of logs still smoldered.

"*Find* them?" Judd said at last. He gave an incredulous snort. "I don't believe you have any idea of the colossal—of the— It was unbelievable, stupendous. And I was desperately ill. I—"

"Ill? I thought you wanted to go with them."

"Well, I did, yes. But that had been hours before. They'd already done their reconnaissance and were on their way back when it happened. By that time I was feverish, weak . . ."

"So it turned out Tremaine was right about the bite."

"Well, yes," Judd said grudgingly, "you could say that.

Anyway, the first search plane arrived in less than an hour. What was there for me to do besides stay where I was and wait?"

John could think of a few things, but kept his thoughts to himself. "Afterwards," he said, "did you get medical care for those bites?"

"I can't remember," Judd said. He seemed offended at the question. "Wait a minute, yes I do. I was treated at the hospital in Juneau. I was put on antibiotics for ten days. I'm sure there's a record. And now I think I have a right to know why you're asking these questions. If there's any relevance to Audley's death I fail to see it."

"I'm not just looking into Tremaine's death, Dr. Judd. As I think you know, there's reason to think there was another murder—"

"*Another* . . ."

"—almost thirty years ago. We—"

Judd whistled softly. "Of course, of course. What with poor Audley, I'd almost forgotten. You're investigating James Pratt's death too, aren't you?"

John looked at him, his interest quickening. All *he* knew was that there was a piece of a male skull that had had an ice ax put through it. Gideon had said it could be Pratt's or it could be Steven Fisk's. Two possibilities, take your choice.

"What makes you think that was Pratt's skull?" he asked.

"Well, whose else would it be?"

"What about Steve Fisk?"

"Steve Fisk?" Judd seemed honestly surprised at the idea. "I suppose it's possible, but . . ."

John waited.

"I don't like to pass on gossip," Judd said with an unconvincing show of reluctance, "and I hesitate to speak ill of the dead . . ."

Aside from M. Audley Tremaine, John thought. "Go ahead, Dr. Judd."

"Very well. Were you aware that Steve was engaged to Jocelyn Yount, the female graduate student who was with us?"

John nodded.

"Well, Jocelyn was—how shall I put it?—a rather odd young lady. She was bright but extremely passive, compliant, almost childlike. No self-discipline, no judgment—and not constitutionally inclined toward, er, celibacy, if you get my drift."

Judd reached down to tug his ankle onto his knee and wedge it forcibly into place. He leaned forward conspiratorially and leered, male to male. "What it added up to," he said, lowering his voice, "was that Jocelyn Yount was hardly the world's most difficult lay, if you'll pardon my Latin." He made a snuffling noise. His small eyes twinkled. "I do not speak from personal experience, I hasten to add."

"You were telling me why you think that's Pratt's skull," John said.

Judd chewed his lower lip for a moment. "I think it was the weekend before the avalanche. Steve flew back to Juneau for the day for something or other—supplies, I suppose. The rest of us took most of the day off and James talked Jocelyn into going off on a picnic, which didn't take much talking. Anyway, Steve got back to Gustavus before they did, and when they finally got in, you'd have had to be blind not to see what they'd been up to. Well, Steve had had this sort of trouble with Jocelyn before, and he just blew up, literally flung himself on James like a panther. Chairs flying, Jocelyn screaming—oh, it was quite a show. You can ask Audley—oops." He rolled back his head and chuckled warmly. "Well, that might be a little difficult, but you can ask Anna. She was there too."

"Who got the best of it?" John asked.

"Oh, Steve, quite definitely. They were both powerful men, you understand, but James was in the wrong and knew it. Besides, he was caught by surprise. This wild animal just leaped on him. He wound up on his back with Steve straddling his chest, pummeling away like a madman—"

"Were there any injuries?" John asked, remembering what Gideon had told him about the mandible. "To Pratt's jaw? Or Fisk's jaw, for that matter?"

"Injuries?" Judd made chewing motions, presumably to help him remember. "Well, there was a little blood, I think. James had a split lip, a few scrapes, no more than that. Why do you ask?"

"Go ahead," John said. "What happened then?"

"Somehow Audley cooled things down before anyone got killed, but Steve took himself pretty seriously, you see, and this was a real blow to his ego, his manhood, whatever. And the fact that Jocelyn truly couldn't see what all the fuss was about didn't make him any happier. Audley insisted on a truce, and Jocelyn got a fatherly lecture, too, but it was all very touchy, very uncomfortable, from then on."

He went back to snapping his suspender strap gently, thoughtfully. "Well, when I heard yesterday that someone had apparently been murdered, I assumed . . . well, obviously."

"Assumed what, Dr. Judd?"

"Well, I can't say that I reasoned it through very carefully. I suppose I assumed there must have been another confrontation out there on the ice before the avalanche struck, and that Steve—well—killed James."

"Why not the other way around? Pratt must have had it in for Fisk too."

"Oh, well, I suppose so, but James was a quiet, sober

sort. He knew he had that licking coming and he took it like a man. Steve was more of a brawler by nature; thin-skinned, belligerent, quarrelsome . . ."

Judd's fingers drummed thoughtfully on either side of his abdomen while he searched for more adjectives. For a man who hesitated to speak ill of the dead he was pretty good at it, once he got going.

"It doesn't sound as if you liked him too much yourself," John said.

The fingers stopped their tapping. "Ah, liked him myself?"

I hit some kind of nerve there, John thought. He's thinking hard. "Did you and Fisk have a problem?"

Judd tipped back his head and chortled. "Why should there have been a problem? He was Audley's student, not mine, and Audley was welcome to him."

John waited for him to go on. Judd was hiding something, waffling, embroidering the facts. Something.

"Oh, I suppose you could say I didn't care for his ways too much, but no, there was no problem, none at all. Steve and I got along just fine."

Something.

"I make no secret of it," Anna Henckel said forthrightly. "Professor Tremaine was no friend of mine; there was little about him I respected." She hesitated, not something she did often, John imagined. "But I am sorry he was murdered in that way."

Did that mean she'd have preferred some other way? Dr. Henckel didn't show much in the way of grief for the dead Tremaine. No more than Judd had. She had made an impressive entrance in her "Dracula cape"—not black these days, but bottle green—a dramatic, full-length, collared cape held together at the neck by a heavy chain. She had set the staff she carried in a corner and had taken the one unpadded wooden chair in the upstairs lounge. Since then she had sat with the cape around her shoulders, stiff and distant, as restrained as Judd had been wriggly. Occasionally she took a puff from a cigarillo, held between the tips of her thumb and middle finger, European-fashion.

"What was it about him you didn't like?" he asked.

"Because you are a policeman is no reason to dissimulate," Anna replied sharply.

These weren't exactly your everyday interviews. He'd been at it only an hour and already he'd run into an "egad" and a "dissimulate." What next?

"I'm aware," she went on, "that you've already talked with Walter. Do not ask me to believe he passed up the opportunity to prattle about my long-standing differences with Professor Tremaine."

"I think maybe he did say something about it, now that you mention it," John allowed.

Anna studied him expressionlessly. If that was her you-sir-have-the-balls-of-a-fish look, no wonder Tremaine had wilted.

"I'd like to hear your version," he said.

"It's very simple, Mr. Lau. I did not dislike him. I was . . . disappointed in him. As a young man he had had enormous potential; a truly original mind, capable of the highest level of synthetic thinking. He had already done great work in the 1950s. He might have become . . ." For a moment the aloof gray eyes gleamed, but she cut herself off with a tired wave. "However, he threw it all away."

"To become a TV star?"

"No, that was later. That followed, perhaps inevitably. No, he threw it away by taking the easy course, not the scientist's way. He was lazy and he was dishonest," she said flatly. "He plagiarized the ideas of others, Mr. Lau. No, that isn't the right word. He *stole* the ideas of others."

"Including yours."

"Most definitely. In 1966 he wrote a monograph, in its time a significant contribution, in which his 'new' approach to the nondirectional complexities of primary-plant succession were taken directly from an unfinished paper on which I had been working for more than a year."

"Rough."

The lounge was warm but she pulled the collar of the cape a little closer around her. "Afterwards I made the most strenuous objections, quite publicly, and he baldly denied my accusations. That's all there was to it."

"You never got any satisfaction?"

One gray eyebrow rose. "Prior to last night, you mean?"

John didn't smile. "Prior to last night."

"Once in print he went so far as to say that it was conceivable we had gotten the same idea at the same time, but that he had simply been fortunate to publish first. Like Darwin and Wallace, you know? That was not enough for me."

"Sorry, I know who Darwin was," John said. "I'm afraid I never heard of Wallace."

She smiled for the first time. Not with humor, but not with malice either. "That is precisely my point."

"It must have been pretty hard to take."

"Mr. Lau," she said wearily, "if I had wanted to kill him over it, I assure you I would have done it many, many years ago, not now. Believe me, I put all this behind me when I left the hallowed halls of ivy for the far more civilized world of commerce."

"That was when?"

"In 1970. I've been with Amore Cosmetics ever since. I'm now their director of research and development."

"Have you had much contact with Tremaine since then?"

"None at all. It was a chapter in my life I was happy to close. Nothing until his publisher contacted me about this book of his."

"You must have had to take a week's leave to come here."

"Yes, a week's vacation."

"Why?"

"I beg your pardon?"

"Why use up a week's vacation for this if you put it behind you long ago? Why not just let him write whatever he wanted to?"

She stared silently out the window for a moment. "Audley was incapable of perceiving his own inadequacies, Mr. Lau. I have no doubt whatever that his book would have blamed his misdirection of the expedition on others. Especially on me, as the assistant director. I couldn't allow that."

"You think he misdirected the expedition?"

She gave a dry bark of laughter and looked levelly at him again. "Yes, I think he misdirected the expedition. I make no secret of that either."

"I understand you have some kind of report on that."

"*I* have?" She looked genuinely puzzled.

"You were showing it to some of the others in the bar."

"Oh, that, yes. Not a report, but a Park Service memorandum: the results of a pro forma investigation concerned with the tragedy. Sketchy as it is, there is no doubt about Audley's culpability."

"I'd like to see it, please."

"As I recall, I gave the copy I have with me to Mr. Pratt. But I can tell you what it said, Mr. Lau. Simply this: They should never have been on the glacier that day. There had been increasing earth tremors, even small avalanches, and what did any of us know about ice travel? I advised against it, the Park Service advised against it. But no, he knew better. And as a result of his obstinacy and Walter's incompetence, three young people died."

Two, John thought. One was already dead when the avalanche hit, assuming Gideon was right. Which he was, of course.

"Or rather two," Anna murmured, in tune with him. "I understand someone seems to have been killed with an ice ax before the avalanche struck. Can you tell me which one it was?"

"I don't know which one it was. I hear there was some bad feeling among the crew."

"Oh, yes, there was considerable bad feeling."

"Over what?"

"Over Jocelyn Yount, primarily." The dry, scaly corners of her mouth turned down. "She was a woman of scant discretion and few morals. To her, anything wearing trousers . . . surely Walter didn't fail to go into this?"

"No, ma'am. He told me her fiancé and James Pratt fought over her, that Fisk physically attacked Pratt."

"That is true."

"Would you care to make a guess about what happened out there on the ice?"

"No. Is there anything else?"

"Dr. Henckel, you said Jocelyn Yount was the primary cause of bad feeling. Does that mean there were other causes?"

"I see no relevance to what you are investigating, but at the end, of course, we were all somewhat irritated with Walter."

"Why was that?"

She eyed him. "You don't know why it was they had to go back into the field that final day, the day of the avalanche?"

"No, ma'am."

"Ah," she said with a pale smile. "So Dr. Judd left a few things out of his account after all."

"Maybe he forgot."

Again the shadowed smile. "I don't think so."

"Suppose you tell me then."

She pulled the high collar closer about her neck. "Mr. Lau, our fieldwork had already been completed. We were to leave for home the next day. Our equipment was packed. And then it was found that Walter had bungled his sampling. An immediate, unscheduled field trip was required to regather the contaminated data. We had to put off our departure. Naturally, this was a source of annoyance and some bad feeling."

John played a hunch. "Between Steve Fisk and Dr. Judd in particular?"

If the question surprised her she didn't show it. "Yes, it was Steven who discovered Walter's slovenliness and called it to our attention. Being Steven, he was not overly charitable in his manner of doing it. Walter held his tongue at the time—what could he say?—but I imagine that—being Walter—there was some sulking and resentment later, in the privacy of his room."

Bingo. Judd had been covering something up, all right. Dissimulating like hell.

"You needn't look so keen, Mr. Lau. Steven may have been murdered, but Walter didn't do it. He may be a weak man, an ineffectual man, but he is not a bad man. Besides, I saw him when he was brought out, and I assure you he was in no condition to do anyone violence; his infection was very real."

Was it? Or had he somehow faked those bites? Had he remained behind on the beach for only an hour or two, then gone sneaking after Steve Fisk, disgraced and enraged, to bury that ice ax in his skull? And now, thirty years later, had he throttled Tremaine to keep him from revealing it in his book? No, that didn't add up. How could you "sneak" across a glacier? How could Judd have managed to escape the avalanche himself and get back to the beach? And why would Tremaine have kept quiet about it all these years? For that matter—whoever had really swung that ax—why *had* Tremaine kept quiet? Because he'd done it himself, as Gideon had thought? Maybe, but now his own murder raised questions about that.

John scribbled a few notes, reminders of things to look into. "You yourself weren't with them that day."

"No. I remained at our headquarters in Gustavus."

"The headquarters were in Gustavus? Not here?"

"There was no 'here.' This lodge was not built until 1965. No, we rented a house in Gustavus, and it was there that I stayed, redoing our frequency distributions and dot maps. This was at Audley's express instruction."

"Uh-huh." There didn't seem to be much point in continuing in that direction. "A few minutes ago you said Jocelyn went after everything in pants. Did that include Tremaine? Were there any problems there?"

"Females," she said stiffly, "were not one of Audley's problems."

John glanced up from his notebook. "Are you saying he was gay, ma'am?"

"No, Mr. Lau," she said quietly, looking out the window. "I have no knowledge of or interest in his sex life. I only know that women were not central to him. A woman can tell such things. I was young then myself, remember, and would have known if his attitude toward me had included anything more than—" She jerked her head angrily and ground out the stub of her cigarillo. "Why are we discussing these things? If you have no questions more pertinent than these, I would like to go now."

"Yes, ma'am, you can go. Thanks for your cooperation."

He watched her descend the open stairwell, erect and

regal, thumping her polished wooden staff as she went. Step, *thunk,* step, *thunk,* step, *thunk.*

John dropped his notebook into his shirt pocket. Deep stuff here, he thought.

# 13

By the time Gideon had mixed the Duco-and-acetone solution, coated the fragments, and set them out to dry, it was 12:20. He locked up the contact station and went seeking fresh air to clear the sharp fumes from his lungs. He walked out to the end of the wooden pier that began a few paces away and jutted two hundred feet into Bartlett Cove. Here and there the silver flank of a salmon would break the rippled surface of the water momentarily and disappear again, almost before the eye had registered it, leaving a small splash like an afterimage. Above, dark wisps of cloud drifted like flecks of ash under a luminous, oyster-gray cloud sheet. He leaned his elbows on the railing and stared down at the dark water.

Murder. No mere intellectual exercise this time, no decades-old shards of bone posing a dusty forensic puzzle. Flesh-and-blood murder. So had the other been, of course, but what a difference time made. Tremaine had been alive yesterday; Gideon had talked to him. And no more than three hours afterward someone had stolen a passkey to his room and strangled him—had pressed brutal thumbs into the fragile, elderly windpipe, holding them there until Tremaine's face turned purple from the desperate need for air, and his tongue stuck out, and his mouth frothed, and his eyes popped. And the left superior cornu of his larynx snapped.

The killer had left him lying on his back while he—or she—rummaged through the closet, looking for something of Tremaine's to make it look like a credible suicide. He had found the boots, removed the laces, wrapped them around Tremaine's neck, hoisted the body into position—that couldn't have been an easy job—and knotted the laces around the hook. Then, for a little extra verisimilitude, the overnight case–*cum*–gallows stool had been provided. The killer had left, perhaps immediately, perhaps waiting until late at night, through either the window or the door, locking it behind him.

Had there been an argument? Had Tremaine threatened to reveal something that someone wanted hidden? Had someone . . . Still looking at the water, Gideon shook his head. Too early for answers. Too early for the questions. There was nothing to go on yet.

*Who* the "someone" was, was easier. The possibilities, after all, were limited. It had to have been one of the five people Tremaine was working with. Who else was there with any connection to him?

The dark underclouds were thickening, the day growing colder. Tiny whitecaps were forming even in the protected cove. Two or three hundred feet down the wild shoreline, across a shallow, rock-strewn inlet, the breeze ruffled the neck fur of a mother bear and cub browsing choosily among the blueberry bushes. Gideon zipped his windbreaker up to his neck, but still the wind chilled him.

He turned to head back and saw someone peering into the window of the contact station, face pressed against the glass, hand to his forehead to block the reflections. When the figure moved, Gideon recognized him.

"Arthur!" he called.

Tibbett turned around. "Gideon! I was just looking for you." He hurried to meet Gideon, his pale face doughy with misgiving. A cardboard box was clamped under one arm. "Is it definitely true? He was murdered?"

"I'm afraid so."

"Awful. The vultures have already begun to gather," he said with distaste. He blew out his cheeks, walking hunch-shouldered with Gideon back toward the head of the pier. "I've just had a call from the *Anchorage Daily News*, wanting to know if a press conference has been scheduled yet."

"You'll probably have to hold one eventually, Arthur. Tremaine was a nationally known figure."

"You don't really think so!" Tibbett's head jiggled back and forth in disapproval, but beneath the surface Gideon sensed a dawning excitement; the glittering exhilaration of involvement with murdered celebrities. Gideon had seen it before, in cops, coroners, even priests. Why not an assistant park superintendent?

They had reached the head of the pier. Arthur stopped and looked at him with mild reproof. "Owen told me about the other murder—the old one, the skull. You might have told *me*, you know."

"Well, I didn't want to bother you," Gideon said lamely. "I wasn't really positive at first."

"But you're positive now?"

"Yes."

"Do you know, I don't think there's ever been a murder in this park before. And now, here we are with two in two days." He started a nervous giggle, but broke it off. "You know what I mean. Oh, I almost forgot. This is for you." He extended the box.

Gideon took out a white kitchen scale. "For me?" he said, confused.

"You said you needed an accurate scale. You wanted to do some kind of regression equation on the bones."

"Oh, yes, that's right." He'd forgotten all about it. It had been mentioned originally only to soothe Arthur's anxieties. There *was* a way to use bone weights to find out whether a set of bones had come from the same person, but you needed the right bones, and Gideon didn't have them. Of course, with Owen's rangers out searching for more, there was a possibility that they'd turn up, and then a scale would come in handy. But not this scale.

"Actually, Arthur, I'd need something a little more accurate. This—"

"*Accurate?*" Arthur cried. "Good heavens, man, this is a *Cusinart!*"

"Well, I know, and I'm sure it's a good one. But it's a spring scale. I need a—what do you call it—a beam scale, a counter scale."

"You don't mean the old-fashioned kind where you put little weights on one side?"

"Right, and something that will weigh in grams and centigrams."

"I'll see what I can do," Arthur said. He was put out. The box was snatched back. "I'm afraid I have more bad news for you," he said grumpily. "We've been unable to come up with the records you wanted. If such things ever existed."

"Records?"

"Of the recovery of those bones in 1964; the ones that came out of the glacier. Owen told me you were interested."

Gideon had forgotten all about that too. First-thing-in-the-morning corpses had a way of clearing the mind.

"Damn, they could have been useful. You don't have any files on it at all?"

"We don't have *any* files from 1964. On anything."

"Maybe your office in Washington, D.C.—"

Arthur shook his head. "I called. Nothing."

"But there was a skeletal-identification expert involved. He must have submitted a report somewhere."

"No doubt, but it's a little difficult when we don't even have a name to go on."

Gideon nodded. "Well, thanks for trying, anyway."

Arthur took pity on him. "I still have Owen working on it for you. Maybe he'll turn something up."

"Maybe."

"You never know," Arthur said more cheerfully, his mind turning elsewhere; to his coming press conference, perhaps. "You just never know."

It didn't take Owen long to turn something up. By the time Gideon got back to his room to wash up, there was a note under the door.

> *Gideon—*
>
> *Found your skeletal-identification expert for you. Professor Kenneth Worriner, University of Alaska Anthropology Department. Retired, still lives in Juneau. Telephone number 586–3774.*
>
> *We aim to please.*
>
> *Owen*

Glacier Bay Lodge, which advertised itself as Alaska's premier wilderness resort, took the "wilderness" part seriously. Communication with the outside world wasn't easy. There were no television sets, no radios, no telephones in the rooms. There was a single pay phone on the veranda, but it required a calling credit card, which Gideon was unable to find in his wallet. (Did he own one? He made a mental note to ask Julie.) The only other telephone was in the manager's office, where the shaken Mr. Granle had taken refuge behind his locked door.

He answered Gideon's knock, understandably apprehensive, and when he saw it was Gideon he shrank back. The message on his drawn face was as clear as if he'd spoken: *My God, what's happened now?*

"It's all right," Gideon said quickly. "I just wanted to use your phone."

Mr. Granle motioned to it and edged out of his office as Gideon came in, giving Gideon plenty of room. He closed the door softly behind him.

Gideon dialed the number, a little uneasy about calling Worriner now that he was doing it. Say Worriner had been in his forties in 1964; he'd be in his seventies now. If he'd been in his fifties, he'd be in his eighties. How welcome would this call be? How much would he remember? How much would he care?

The telephone was answered on the third ring. The voice was thin, pinched. "Hello?"

In his eighties, Gideon thought. Well into them. "Professor Worriner?"

A noticeable hesitation. "Yes." No one had called him professor in a while.

"My name is Gideon Oliver, sir. I'm a physical anthropologist too. I'm up at Glacier Bay, and I'm working on some human skeletal fragments—"

"Please hold on, I better turn down the TV." The telephone clunked down. The old man's speech had been a little slurred. Dentures not in? A stroke? Was Worriner up to this? Gideon shifted uncomfortably.

Worriner returned after what seemed like a long time. "Yes?"

"I'm working on some skeletal fragments up here, sir, and—"

"Excuse me. Is this going to take a while?"

"Well, a few minutes, I suppose. It's about—"

Gideon heard a querulous sigh. "Hold on, I better turn down the soup." The telephone was put down again, more softly. A murmured, regretful "almost ready, too," was just audible.

Gideon shifted again in the overpadded chair. He was keeping Worriner from his meal, something octogenarians didn't usually take lightly. This wasn't going very well.

After a good ninety seconds Worriner returned. "Yes, hello?"

"Sir, if this isn't a convenient time, I can—"

"No, it's quite all right." He paused. "I'm sorry if I sounded uncordial."

"Not at all. The bones I'm working on seem to be from the same party that you worked on in 1964, and—"

"Gideon Oliver, did you say?"

"That's right."

"I know you by reputation, of course." It was his first show of interest. "It's a pleasure to talk to you."

"Thank you." Gideon wished intensely that he could say the same thing, but he'd never heard of Kenneth Worriner. He almost said it anyway, but settled for safety's sake on, "It's a pleasure to talk to you, sir."

"And you say you've found some more skeletal material from the Tirku survey?"

"That's right," Gideon said, relieved. At least Worriner remembered.

A chair scraped. Worriner grunted as he sat down. "Well, that's very remarkable. What do you have? Where did you find it? Have you been able to make an identification?" His dry voice, vacant and listless a few moments before, was crackling. "Listen, have you seen a copy of my report? Did you find any evidence of—"

Gideon needn't have worried. When, after all, had he ever met an old physical anthropologist who'd lost his enthusiasm for the field? Mention bones and they came alive, whatever shape they were in. Gideon had high hopes of becoming such an old anthropologist himself one day.

"I'd like very much to see a copy of your report," he said. "That's why I'm calling. Things have gotten more complicated, Professor. It looks as if there was a homicide involved."

"Please, call me Kenneth, will you? A *homicide?* Do you mean to say you've found signs of presumptively lethal antemortem trauma not attributable to the avalanche?"

Gideon smiled. That would have been a mouthful even for a man with his dentures in. "That's right, Kenneth; a one-inch perforation along the right squamous suture, at the parietal notch. Definitely lethal, definitely antemortem."

"Have you identified the skull? As I recall, there were two people involved, weren't there? No, three; two men and a woman. Is that right? It's been a long time."

"That's exactly right."

"Ah, you have no idea how much I'd like to come up and see what you have, Gideon. Unfortunately, I don't travel much anymore. I use a walker these days, you see, and people at airports seem to be in such a hurry—well, that's neither here nor there. Why am I nattering on? Of course I'll send you a copy of my report. And would you mind letting me know how things turn out?"

"What I'd really like is to come down to Juneau tomorrow and meet you, if that's possible. You could have a look at the fragments yourself; I'd appreciate your opinion."

There was a startled pause. "You mean come here with the bones? To my house?"

"If it's convenient."

"Convenient? My dear man, I'd be delighted. I may be a bit rusty, you understand."

"I'll take my chances. I don't suppose there are any photographs in the report? I thought we could try matching the new fragments against them. Maybe there are some pieces of the same bones."

"Photographs?" Worriner laughed. "Yes, there are photographs, but I'll do better than that."

"You mean you have casts? That's terrific. We—"

"Gideon, I have the *bones*."

# 14

Gideon's appetite had caught up with him. He swallowed a mouthful of cold poached salmon and mayonnaise, followed it with a hearty helping of coleslaw and half a small boiled potato, and bit into a sourdough roll. Then he pulled over a nearby chair, propped his feet on it, fixed the plate more firmly on his lap, and settled down to serious eating.

On the other side of the small table, in much the same posture, John, whose appetite never needed to do any catching up, was working on his own heaped plate. They had brought their food from the buffet to John's room, preferring to keep their distance from the members of Tremaine's party, who were at lunch in the dining room.

"Food's good here," John said. On his plate were three pieces of fried chicken, two wedges of salami pizza, and a jelly donut.

"You know Marti's going to ask me if you ate lots of

monounsaturates and complex carbohydrates," Gideon said. "And fiber. What am I supposed to tell her?"

John's wife Marti attacked the hopeless task of reforming her husband's eating habits with a resolute affability that was remarkable in the face of continual defeat. For his part, John resisted with equal good humor.

"Tell her I did," he said around a mouthful of pizza. "It'll make her feel good." He washed it down with a swig of Sprite. "So what do you think, Doc? Do scientists really go around knocking each other off over who got which idea first?" He had just finished telling Gideon about his sessions with Walter Judd and Anna Henckel.

Gideon swallowed some grapefruit juice while he thought about it. "When I was within a couple of months of finishing my dissertation, I heard that somebody at the University of Chicago was doing one on the same subject. Believe me, if it'd been true, and if murder had been the only way to keep him from coming out with it first—well, I wouldn't have wanted to put any money on his survival chances."

"Come on, seriously."

Gideon eased the edge of his fork through some more of the pale, tender salmon. "I don't know, John. I don't know anything about Henckel, but, generally speaking, scientists take those things pretty seriously."

"Like Darwin and Wallace," John said knowingly.

Gideon looked at him, impressed. "Yes. But I can't see her waiting all this time."

John shrugged. "Well, maybe seeing him again brought it all back. I think she had a thing for him, you know? Something she wouldn't even admit to herself. A person's judgment gets screwed up when that happens."

"Maybe," Gideon said. "Do you actually believe this, or are you just throwing around ideas?"

"Just throwing around ideas. Our boy Judd's got a pretty

good motive too. Did you know he is up for some high mucky-muck state job? An appointment by the governor?"

Gideon shook his head.

"Well, he is. Imagine if all this stuff got raked up in Tremaine's book. First the guy messes up his work so bad they have to go out and do it over again. Then he sits around nursing a mosquito bite, for Christ's sake, while they're all getting creamed in an avalanche—which they wouldn't be, if not for his screw-up—and he doesn't even try to help them."

"You think the governor might think twice about appointing him?"

"I know if I was Judd I'd be worrying about it." He began shifting things on the table, looking for something. "Damn, didn't I get any ketchup?"

"For *pizza?*"

"What, are you kidding me? For the chicken. Ah," he said, and tore open a packet that had been under the edge of his tray. He made a puddle of it on the rim of his plate, stuck in a piece of chicken thigh, and heartily bit in. "Two interviews, two suspects," he mused, chewing. "By the time I talk to the other three I'll probably have five."

Gideon nodded. "It just about has to be one of the people he was meeting with, doesn't it? No one else here had any connection with him. That we know of," he said as an afterthought.

"Yeah. Of course it's *possible* someone came in from the outside, did it, and took off again, but pretty unlikely. They'd have had to come by plane, either to Gustavus or straight to Bartlett Cove by seaplane. Pretty hard to do that without being noticed."

"And pretty hard to wander inconspicuously around the lodge looking for Tremaine's room when there are only a few guests and everybody knows everybody else by sight."

"That's right. I got initial statements from all of them,

you know. Nobody saw any strangers. Nobody saw any anybodies. They all had dinner together—expecting Tremaine, who never showed—and then around seven they started going to their rooms. So they said. Shirley Yount read in front of the fire till eight-thirty, then she went to her room too. Nobody came out again till this morning."

"Well, one person did."

"True."

They addressed their food for a while, looking out the window at a forest of young alder and hemlock. A couple of the turkey-sized, speckled birds that hung around the woods meandered vacantly among the trees. Blue grouse, Julie had said they were. The day had gotten so gloomy the lights were on in the room.

"Doesn't the sun ever shine around here?" John said.

Gideon laughed. "You've only been here four hours."

"It's as bad as Seattle," John muttered, swabbing up a glob of ketchup with a thickly battered, unidentifiable piece of chicken (assuming there was any chicken under the deep-fried coating). He chewed with placid enjoyment, his muscular jaws working slowly. "They're sending out another agent to work with me. He'll be out on today's plane. Julian Minor. Remember him?"

"Wasn't he with you on the Lake Quinault killings?"

"That's the one."

Gideon recalled a middle-aged black man, competent and methodical, with rimless glasses, neat, grizzled hair, and the chubby, tidy, pin-striped appearance of a contented tax accountant. And a prim, anachronistic vocabulary straight out of the age of celluloid collars: "Be that as it may . . ." "I take your point . . ." "Thus and so . . ."

"I remember him," Gideon said.

"Well, he sure remembers you."

"Did he ever forgive me?"

"What's to forgive? Just because you left him cooking a

putrid piece of cadaver in a pot on a stove for three hours?"

"Two hours," Gideon said.

Other than that, John's description was accurate. A rotting human hip joint had been found in a river, and Gideon had had to boil the shreds of flesh off the bones with an antiformin and sodium-hydroxide solution. But he'd had to go somewhere, and somehow poor Julian Minor, with his white shirt cuffs folded neatly back, had gotten stuck with the task of periodically stirring the greasy mess with a long wooden spoon. Like a witch in *Macbeth*. He had given Gideon a lot of room after that.

"Well, there won't be any cooking chores this time," Gideon said. "Did the people from the crime lab finish up?"

"Oh, yeah, they're gone. So's the body. Dr. Wu too. You want to guess what they looked for and didn't find?"

"Fingerprints?" Gideon said after a moment.

"Good guess. Oh, there were plenty of latents on the walls and towel racks and stuff; they probably go back weeks."

"Years."

"Fingerprints don't last years. Didn't you know that?"

Gideon glowered at him.

"Anyhow," John said cheerfully, "the front doorknob was wiped off—nothing on it but the maid's prints—and the handle on the closet, and Tremaine's boots, and a few other things. The killer was careful." He finished the piece of chicken and wiped his fingers with a napkin. "Guess what else they didn't find."

Gideon shook his head. "I have no idea."

"Tremaine's book," John said. "The manuscript."

Gideon put down the piece of roll he was buttering. "Maybe he kept it in the hotel safe."

"Nope, I checked."

"Well, there must be other copies somewhere, John. He wouldn't have just one. Maybe he left one at home. Maybe his publisher has a draft."

"No good." John told him about two telephone calls he'd made to Los Angeles. He'd spoken to Valerie Kaufman, Tremaine's editor at Javelin Press, and to Talia Lundquist, his agent. Both said they didn't have copies of the manuscript and hadn't ever seen it. More than that, neither of them knew exactly what was in it.

John shook his head. "Do you buy that? Javelin was paying him half a million bucks without knowing what the book was about?"

"I don't think it's that unusual, John, especially with a celebrity author."

"You're kidding. Is that the way it is when *you* write something?"

Gideon laughed. Having published one extremely esoteric graduate textbook and several dozen scholarly articles and monographs, he knew little about half-million-dollar advances. Or any other kind of advances.

"Not in my kind of writing," he said. "The *American Journal of Physical Anthropology* lures its contributors with glory, not gold. And I have to send in detailed abstracts first. But I'd think someone like Tremaine would be in a different league. Anything he wrote would be as near to a guaranteed best-seller as you could come."

"Yeah. Well, Javelin knows it's about the expedition and that there's some sensational stuff that hasn't ever come out before." He took out his notebook and flipped it open. "'Dissension and jealousy among crew, open conflict . . .'" He glanced up. "'. . . and murder.'"

Gideon put down his fork. "Murder? So they do know—"

John shook his head. "All they know is that there was a murder. That was all he told them."

Not who had been murdered, or by whom, or how, or why. Those little matters he'd preferred to keep to himself. But it had been enough for Javelin. Now, of course, with Tremaine dead—sensationally dead—they were desperate for a copy themselves.

"There has to be one somewhere," Gideon said. "I can't believe he wouldn't have a backup copy."

"If he did, no one's seen it. From what I hear he was a little paranoid about copies."

There was an agitated barrage of knocks on the door. "Inspector! Inspector!"

John looked at Gideon. "Jesus, what now?"

"It sounds like Elliott Fisk," Gideon said.

It was. "I want to report a crime," the dentist blurted as John yanked the door open.

"What happened?"

"My diary's been stolen! Well, not my diary, my journal. Well, not *my* journal—"

John stepped back from the door. "Why don't you come in and sit down, Dr. Fisk?"

"I don't want to sit down," Fisk said petulantly, but he came in anyway and took the chair John had been using to prop up his feet. He glanced at Gideon and looked with distaste at the half-eaten lunches. "I want you to *do* something," he told John. "It was my uncle's journal."

"Your uncle was Steven Fisk?" John turned the other chair backwards and sat down, forearms crossed on top of the back.

"Yes, of course."

"And this was a personal journal he kept?"

"Yes, yes, of course." He was wiggling with impatience. "At the time of the expedition. It went to my father with his belongings when he died. My father was his brother."

"Uh-huh. What makes you think it was stolen?"

"I don't *think* it was stolen; it *was* stolen. A blue,

diary-type notebook. I had it with me in the dining room this morning when I was having breakfast with the others. I left it on my chair when I went to get Professor Tremaine. That was when . . ." His eyelids flickered. "Well, you remember."

John nodded.

"When I realized I'd left it and came back later it wasn't there."

"Did you check with—"

"I *checked* with the help. They hadn't seen it. And with the others. They all *claimed* they hadn't seen it."

"Are you sure you had it with you? Did you look in your room?"

"I *had* it with me. I brought it for the session we were supposed to have." He shook his head decisively. "Oh, it was stolen, all right."

"Uh-huh. Who would want to steal your uncle's journal?"

"Shirley Yount," Elliott replied promptly.

"And just why would Shirley Yount want to do that, sir?"

"Don't patronize me, Inspector," Fisk snapped.

"Sorry," John said amiably. "Why do you think she took it? And I'm not an inspector."

"Because she was afraid of what was in it, naturally. She's afraid my uncle told the truth about her unspeakable sister. And he did. Oh, he certainly did."

"Her sister was Jocelyn Yount? Steven's fiancée?"

John knew more than he was telling Fisk; he just liked to hear things more than once. Gideon had already told him about the angry exchange he'd walked in on between Fisk and Shirley Yount the day before.

"Yes, and she was like a stone around his neck. Steve deserved better than her. He was a brilliant student." Behind his beard, pale lips stretched in a catty smile. "Which Tremaine realized only too well. Steve did all the work, and the great Tremaine did all the publishing—with no credit, of course. That's all in the journal too. Oh, yes. *With* verification. You should have seen Tremaine's face—"

"What's this got to do with Shirley Yount, Dr. Fisk?"

Fisk bridled at being interrupted. "I was about to tell you before you got me off the track. Her sister was a tart. Can I be any plainer than that?"

"Did you know Jocelyn Yount yourself, Doctor?"

"Well, no, I didn't actually know her. But it's all in the journal."

"And you think Shirley stole it to protect the memory of her sister?"

Fisk turned to Gideon with a little moue of exasperation. At least, Gideon thought it was a moue. "Didn't I just say that?"

"I suppose you did," John said with a quiet smile. "How would she know what was in the journal?"

"Everyone knew. I told them about it yesterday afternoon. It came up during the meeting."

"If they knew about it, and if they were with you in the dining room this morning—they were, weren't they . . . ?"

"*Yes,*" Fisk said with an imploring look heavenward. "My God, how many times do I have to repeat this? I wish you'd write it down if you can't remember."

"Then how do you know it was Shirley?" John said in the same calm voice. "Why not one of the others?"

Gideon marveled at his equanimity. John did not have a quick temper, exactly, but neither was he the most restrained of men, at least not in the many heated, arm-waving discussions he had had with Gideon over the years. This was business, though, and that clearly made it different. Besides, John had spent over an hour with Dr. Wu that morning; Elliott Fisk was child's play in comparison.

All the same, Gideon thought, if it were me I would have kicked the guy by now.

"It was Shirley Yount," Fisk maintained. "Now are you going to do something about it, or are we going to sit here talking about it all day?"

"We'll do something about it, sir. I appreciate your telling me about it. I'll be in touch."

Fisk looked at Gideon again. "I gather I'm being dismissed."

John laughed good-naturedly and opened the door for him, then came back and picked up the last of the chicken pieces.

"John," Gideon said. "I think you're actually mellowing."

"That's the way they teach us to do it at the academy." He gnawed contentedly at the wing bone, searching out and finding the last resistant scraps of meat with his teeth. He was sitting on the base of his spine, with his feet back up on the other chair. "But inside I'm a mass of seething tensions."

"I can see that. It's terrifying." Gideon finished the last of the salmon, slid the plate away, and popped up the lid on his coffee. "Do you think someone really stole his journal?"

"Someone, yeah. Maybe even Shirley. But not to protect her sister's memory. I can't see that. Why should she care what Steve Fisk wrote in his journal all that time ago?" With the nail of a pinky he went after a shred of chicken between his lower incisors. "Why should anyone, for that matter?"

"I don't know. I'm betting it's got something to do with the murder, though."

"Could be. Whoever killed Tremaine—"

"Not that murder; the one in 1960."

"How do you come up with that?"

"Well, think about it: Yesterday we figure out that someone was murdered on that glacier—"

"*You* figure out. It makes me nervous when you get modest."

"—and inside of a few hours the only remaining person who was there gets strangled, and his description of it disappears. Then this morning the only other contemporaneous account of the survey that we know about disappears too. It can't be coincidence. There has to be a relationship." The Law of Interconnected Monkey Business, his old professor and friend Abe Goldstein called it.

"Maybe, maybe not. Twenty-nine years is a long time ago. Maybe Tremaine got killed for some reason we don't know anything about; he didn't seem to have any problem ticking people off. And maybe Fisk's journal got ripped off for a completely different reason. Let's keep our options open." He broke his donut in two and examined the interior, evidently finding it to his satisfaction.

"Let me ask you about something else, Doc. Maybe we can whittle down our suspects a little. Would a woman have been able to pull Tremaine's body into position like that? Actually lift him up off the floor and tie the thongs to the hook?"

Gideon leaned back in his chair, considering. "Well, those are two pretty hefty women you're thinking about. Anna Henckel must weigh a hundred and sixty; Shirley more. Tremaine was only a hundred and thirty-five or so. You'd get a lot of leverage from pulling the thongs over the top of the partition and then wrapping them around the hook as you went. And the body wouldn't have been hanging free, it would've been propped against the partition. That would have helped."

"So you're saying yeah?"

"I'm saying yeah."

John rocked slowly back and forth on the rear legs of his chair. "You know, it's sad. A few years ago we could have ruled the ladies out right off. Women didn't strangle people. Poison, sure. Guns, you better believe it. But no strangling, no knives, no torture, no mutilation. Boy," he said with a world-weary sigh, "times have changed. Well, what about Fisk? He's not exactly hefty. Would he be able to lift Tremaine?"

"I think so, John. It looks as if we'll have to stay with five suspects for the moment."

"What's with this 'we,' Doc? We're just having a conversation, that's all. This is *my* job, not 'our' job."

"Of course it's your job. You're the one who started talking about 'we.' What do I know about solving murders?"

"Yeah, sure, you're just a simple bone man, right?" John looked at him doubtfully. "Doc, I want your word that you're gonna concentrate on the bones. You solve that murder, I'll solve this murder. That'll make us both happy. My boss too."

"Fine."

"I mean it. And I want to know what you're doing every step of the way. I'm in charge, understand?"

"I said fine."

"That doesn't include going around doing your own little interviews with Judd or Henckel, or anyone else. Or messing around with—"

"John, I'm not a complete idiot."

John's feet came off the chair. "Yeah, you are! When it comes to this, you are! Look, I know you. You think you know everything about everything. You stick your nose into things, you get involved where you don't have any business, you make life hard for everybody. My goddamn boss was right about you." He was chopping at the air with both hands, more like the John that Gideon knew. "Well, do me a favor and stay out of this one, dammit!" There was a long pulsing silence while he stared angrily at Gideon.

Gideon studied his friend in return. "On the other hand," he said judiciously, "it could be that you haven't mellowed."

John's irritation hung on a second longer, then wavered and slid away like shards of glass from a broken mirror. He blew out his pent-up breath, leaned back in his chair again, and laughed. "Doc, Doc, somebody here is a killer. I don't want you making him mad, I don't—ah, hell, I don't want to see you get hurt, that's all I'm worried about."

Gideon clapped him on the forearm. "I know it, John. I never thought anything else. I'll concentrate on the bones, I promise. What do you mean, your boss was right about me?"

"Never mind, you don't want to know." He looked at his watch and stood up. "Things to do. Meet you and Julie for dinner?"

"Uh, I don't think we'll be here."

"You're not gonna be in Glacier Bay?"

"No, I was planning to catch the six o'clock plane into Juneau. If I can convince Julie to play hooky for a day, I'll take her with me. We'll be back on tomorrow's flight."

"What's in Juneau?" John asked suspiciously.

"The anthropologist who worked on those bones in 1964. I want to compare notes with him."

"Mm," John said. "I guess that makes sense."

"Would there be any problem with my taking the fragments along with me? That'd be a help."

John sat down again. "I don't know, Doc, that could be a problem. That's evidentiary material, especially that piece of skull. Tell you the truth, I'm not even too keen about it just being in the Park Service safe up here. I'd be happier if it was in an FBI evidence room somewhere."

"Well, isn't there an FBI office in Juneau? I could drop it off for you."

"That's not exactly kosher."

"I know, but we're not exactly in Seattle, with agents and couriers all over the place."

John paused, then made a decision. "Okay. Take it with you and leave it at the resident agency office. Federal building, ninth floor. I'll let 'em know you're coming."

"Good, I will."

John stood up again and stretched, then leveled a finger at Gideon. "Lose it, you die."

"Thanks for your confidence," Gideon said.

"Just don't screw up. Hey, are you planning to eat that brownie or not?"

"Damn right I am," Gideon said, and snatched it off the plate before John could make his grab.

Shirley Yount stopped them on the boardwalk outside by standing squarely in their way, hands on hips, elbows akimbo, feet planted. A formidable figure.

"I understand that little fart says I stole his diary."

"Yes. ma'am, you could say that," John said.

She glared at John, very nearly eye to eye. "Well, I didn't," she said.

# 15

The daily turnaround flight between Juneau and Gustavus is surely one of the most spectacular jet flights in America. Going southeast, toward Juneau, you leave the flat Gustavus plain, with Glacier Bay tilting on your left, rise quickly over Icy Strait and the huddled green Chilkat Mountains, and wing out over the Inside Passage. Below, in the muted blue water, are the thousand forested, uninhabited islands of the Alexander Archipelago, and a few miles to the east the rearing, gleaming white chain of the Boundary Range. Beyond them, in British Columbia, appears the even grander, whiter mass of the great Coast Range, stretching out of sight to the north and south. Toward the end of the flight, the vast Juneau ice field comes into view (larger than the state of Rhode Island, the pilot informs you over the public-address system), and, finally, as the plane wheels and drops toward Juneau Airport, the colossal, frozen river that is Mendenhall Glacier, impressive even after Glacier Bay.

All this in twelve minutes' air time, in a 727 that never gets more than four thousand feet off the ground and seems to float between the two airports like a dirigible with wings. Few passengers do anything during the twelve minutes but stare out the windows, struck dumb. But Julie and Gideon hadn't even glanced up, hadn't stopped talking.

They hadn't stopped talking since he'd met her boat at the pier at a little after four. Persuading her to play hooky for a day had taken all of thirty seconds. Trying to explain what was going on had taken the rest of the two hours, even with John's help on the drive to Gustavus. Small wonder. When she'd started off that morning the only mystery had been the pierced skull from 1960, and that had been mystery enough. But by the time Gideon saw her again nine hours later, Tremaine had been found dead; the manuscript had disappeared; Burton Wu had come, made his pronouncements, and gone; Elliott Fisk's journal had been stolen; and dark, old motives were popping to the surface like fizz in a glass of Alka-Seltzer.

It had been a hell of a day.

"So what's your working hypothesis?" Julie asked as the wheels touched down. "That Tremaine was killed to keep him quiet about the other murder?"

"Who has a working hypothesis?" Gideon pushed back into his seat against the strain of the backthrust as the plane touched down, and waited for the engine roar to quiet. "But if I had one, I guess that'd be it."

"But who would even know what happened out there, besides Tremaine? Everybody else was killed in—" She made one of her pitiful attempts at snapping her fingers. "I forgot. John thinks Dr. Judd might not really have been that sick, that he might have followed them out there and killed Steven Fisk himself and then gotten back out before the avalanche."

"No, that's just an outside possibility. I don't think he really believes it."

Julie unstrapped her seat belt as the plane rolled to a stop, and stood up.

"What do *you* think?"

"I don't think it's too likely either." He flicked open his seat belt, stretched, and stood up too. "What are we saying—"

Her hand went out. "Gideon—"

But she was too late. Straightening, he thumped his head on the overhead rack. "Damn!"

"It's just amazing," she said. "You do it every time. You never miss. Some physical anthropologist in five hundred years is probably going to go bonkers trying to figure out how your skull got so lumpy."

Wincing, Gideon rubbed his head. "Thank you for your concern," he grumbled, and looked at his hand. "No blood, anyway."

A flicker of worry crossed her face, like a shadow. "You're all right, aren't you?"

"Sure," he said with a quick smile, "I built up a callus there years ago." He reached up for their bags and squeezed her hand as they headed out of the near-empty plane. Julie squeezed back.

"Anyway," he said, "what would we be saying Judd did? Went sneaking over the glacier after them? You can't sneak over a glacier like Tirku, not without being seen. So, if not for a fortuitous avalanche, which he couldn't have predicted, there would have been three witnesses to the murder, or at least three people who saw him there."

Julie nodded. "That's so. And Tremaine himself was right there. Why would he keep quiet about it all these years? From what John said, there wasn't any love lost between the two of them."

They entered the terminal building ("Wipe your feet," the no-nonsense sign on the door told them), walked past the ten-foot-high stuffed polar bear that greets incoming passengers, and went out into the misty drizzle.

The fifteen-minute trip downtown was made in Juneau's version of an airport limousine, an old school bus painted blue, with MGT (for Mendenhall Glacier Transport) on the side. The route took them through the Mendenhall wetlands, a bleak silt plain left behind by the retreating glacier, then along Gastineau Channel, Juneau's sole avenue to the Inside Passage and the outside world. As with Glacier Bay—as with much of coastal Alaska—the only ways in or out of the state capital were by air and by water. The one highway out of Juneau led thirty-six miles to Auke Bay. And back.

As they walked the three blocks from the bus stop to the old Baranof Hotel on this dreary, drizzly late afternoon, Juneau looked like the isolated outpost it was, huddled uneasily in its narrow fjord at the foot of hulking Mount Juneau. Great snowfields clung to the mountain's steep flanks directly above them, seemingly ready to break free and come down on their heads at the next stiff breeze. Even the heavy sky seemed to press down on the little town; rain dripped from a layer of lowering clouds that smothered the tops of the surrounding mountains, closing in the fjord like a pewter lid.

The city itself was appropriately subdued in the face of this sullen, menacing Nature. The turn-of-the-century street lamps on Franklin Street glowed a gloomy yellow, the tourist shops that were the main tenants of the false-front, frontier-style wooden buildings were closed and dark, the street traffic minimal, the rainswept sidewalks nearly empty. Only the bars were open—the Red

Dog Saloon, the Sourdough, Mike's; open and rowdy, to judge from the sounds. An occasional group of two or three men, mostly in parkas and rubber boots, shoved their way through one set of swinging doors and wavered half a block to the next one.

"Never arrive in a strange place at night on an empty stomach" had been Abe Goldstein's first rule to his class on anthropological field technique. "In the dark and with a low blood-sugar level, new places don't look so hot."

Well, it wasn't quite dark, just midway through the long northern twilight, but it had been six hours since lunch, and Juneau, famed for its beauty, didn't look so hot.

"Except for the concrete sidewalks," Julie said, moving closer to him, "we could be in 1890." She sounded a little low on blood sugar too.

They had splurged on a reservation at the Baranof, Juneau's grand old dowager of a hotel, and their spirits lifted when they walked in. Burnished wood paneling, Art Deco light fixtures, gold-framed mirrors, oil paintings, a grand piano in the lobby.

Civilization. Out of 1890 and into 1935.

They checked in, went up to their room (with a Mozart horn concerto playing sweetly over the elevator speaker), washed up, and came back down to the Bubble Lounge for a drink. Their order for dry Manhattans, which seemed just the thing for 1935, was taken by a tuxedoed waiter who bowed when he received it.

Julie laughed. "I was just thinking. This is exactly the kind of place John hates, isn't it?"

"John hates any place where the waiters dress better than the customers."

The amber drinks, in cut-glass cocktail glasses, were placed carefully on the table with another bow.

"Getting back to Dr. Judd," Julie said thoughtfully. "Suppose we change the premise just a little."

"Fine. Did we have a premise?"

"What if Judd didn't kill him *before* the avalanche, but after?"

"After the avalanche?" Gideon looked up from his first swallow. It was all right, but it made him remember why dry Manhattans had gone out of fashion. "But Fisk would have been dead already."

"Why would he have been dead already? Tremaine was in the avalanche and he wasn't dead. Maybe Judd went up there, and he found Fisk unconscious or dying, and finished him off with the ax." She shook her head wonderingly. "What did I talk about before I met you?"

"After the avalanche," Gideon repeated slowly. "Now why didn't I think of that? Why didn't John?"

She grinned, pleased. "You didn't?"

"It never occurred to us. And it would answer a lot of questions. But—"

"Ah," she said sadly.

"Well, there'd still be the question of why Tremaine kept it to himself all this time."

"He wouldn't have known anything about it. He was probably unconscious. He fell into a crevasse, remember?"

For a moment Gideon almost thought she had something. "No. Why bother to kill Tremaine now if he hadn't seen anything?"

"Um. Yes, that's a problem. Maybe John can work that out."

"And just what was Tremaine going to write about that was so sensational if he didn't know about the murder? Come to think of it, he did know about the murder because he mentioned it to his publisher."

"Well," Julie said glumly, "I don't see that you and John have come up with anything better."

"You're sure right there," he agreed, and took another pull, beginning to unwind.

They went over the possibilities again: a jealous Steven Fisk as murderer, with James Pratt as victim; a brooding, vengeful Pratt as murderer, with Fisk as victim; a humiliated Judd as killer, with Fisk as victim—or maybe Pratt as victim. Just because no motive had come to light yet didn't mean there wasn't one. And of course, Tremaine as murderer, with either Fisk or Pratt as murderee.

"A nice how-de-do," he said.

"And don't forget about Jocelyn Yount," said Julie. "If she was as big as her sister she could have swung a pretty mean ax."

"That's true. And yes, she was big. But why would she want to kill anybody?"

"Because she was fed up. With a possessive, violent boyfriend on one side, and some creepy guy sniffing around her on the other, I wouldn't blame her. For being fed up, I mean."

"It's possible," Gideon said, for what felt like the fiftieth time that day. He rotated his glass slowly on the table. "We just need more data. We can't do any more with what we have."

"You'll get it," Julie said. "That's why we're here, right?"

"That, and because I thought we could use a little vacation. From our vacation." He was glad he'd asked her to come, glad to be off alone with her. He watched her sip her drink, watched her small, square, competent, sexy hands embrace the glass, looked at the moisture glistening on her lips.

"Uh-oh," Julie said.

"What?"

"I recognize that look."

"What look?" But of course she was right. "That's love," he told her.

"That is not love. I know love, and that isn't it."

"Sure it is. Well, partly, it is." He leaned closer. "Uh, I don't suppose I could interest you in some spousal activities before dinner?"

"Actually I was thinking of taking a shower before dinner."

"Gee, me too."

"I suppose," she said, "if we took one together it would save time."

"And water," Gideon pointed out.

"Oh, well," Julie said, pushing back her chair, "in that case . . ."

"I don't know how much time we saved," Julie said from the bathroom. She was still tinkering with her hair, which seemed somehow to have gotten wet under the shower spray.

"I know we sure didn't save any soap," Gideon said from the bedroom. "Or water, not that Juneau seems to have much of a water problem."

"Is it still raining?"

"I don't think so." He walked to the window. "Nope, it stopped. Wow, look at this."

She came to join him. "Wow," she agreed.

Their eighth-floor room looked out over the town and across Gastineau Channel. An enormous, midnight-blue cruise ship had just anchored; a sleek, stately five-decker with big, square, house-style windows instead of portholes. Four small launches were chugging steadily back and forth between ship and shore, depositing passengers onto the pier at the foot of Franklin Street.

And Juneau was springing to life to greet them, like a mechanical toy that someone had just plugged in. They could almost hear the gears creaking into action. Franklin Street was going into motion as the advance troops from the ship made their way up it, tentatively and somewhat suspiciously. (Were they arriving on empty stomachs?) Lights were blinking on in the shops ("Gold Nugget Jewelry," "Arctic Circle Gifts," "Alaska Trading Post"), sidewalk tables were being set up outside of restaurants, and all of downtown suddenly seemed to be crackling with noise and life.

Hokey, maybe, but cheerful and welcoming too. Even the mountain was starting to look friendly. They abandoned their plan to eat in the Baranof's sedate and elegant Gold Room and went back out into the now-bustling 1890s in search of typical Alaskan fare.

They wound up at the Armadillo Tex-Mex Cafe on South Franklin, a steamy, funky, homey place with plastic red-and-white tablecloths, waitresses in jeans and aprons, and a stuffed, seven-foot-high saguaro cactus near the door. John would have loved it, they agreed.

Over surprisingly good fajitas and beans (the owner turned out to be from Austin), they found themselves back on the same old subject without knowing how they got there.

"I don't think we should completely forget about Tremaine," Julie said. "Just because he got killed himself later on hardly proves he didn't do it."

"So John pointed out. But why would he want to murder Pratt or Fisk?"

"Pratt, I don't know. But didn't you say he was stealing Fisk's ideas? Maybe he thought if Steve was dead he could get away with it better."

"Except that I don't see him planning to do something like that out on the glacier, with the other two around. No, this had to be a spur-of-the-moment thing."

"Well, maybe it was. Maybe *Tremaine* did it after the avalanche. Maybe the other two were killed in it, and avalanche. Maybe the other two were killed in it, and Steven was hurt, and Tremaine saw his chance and sort of nudged him along."

"Into the great beyond," Gideon said. "Uh-uh. According to the newspaper, both of Tremaine's arms were broken. Plus a fractured skull and a broken leg and a few other little nuisances. He didn't hit anybody with an ice ax. Not after the avalanche."

"Rats," Julie said.

*Rats* was right. The pieces just wouldn't go together to make a coherent picture. He no longer believed that Tremaine had been the murderer, as satisfying as that idea had been. Maybe he'd been an accomplice. Very likely a witness. Surely he'd known something about it, and he'd been killed on account of it. The Law of Interconnected Monkey Business so decreed. Or if not decreed, strongly suggested. So far so good, but right there was where things came unraveled. If not Tremaine, the killer had to have been one of the other people on the glacier. But they had all died. So who cared enough to kill him over it almost thirty years later? Who besides him could even know what had happened?

Back to Judd? Judd, with his faked mosquito bite, lumbering after them over the glacier? Anna? Had Anna not spent the day on her frequency distributions after all, but hired her own plane, followed them out there . . . He shook his head. Every possibility was sillier than the one before. And more full of holes.

"I wish," he said with a sigh, "that we could figure out who that skull fragment belongs to. It makes it just a little hard to solve a murder when you don't know who the victim is."

"Will Professor Worriner be able to help, do you think?"

"I hope so. All we can do is compare the new material to the fragments he identified as Pratt's and Fisk's back in

1964. With luck, we'll be able to make some kind of positive match. Or positively exclude one of them, which would be just as good."

"You will," Julie said. "I have every confidence."

# 16

"Mr. Pratt, I'd like an answer." John was nearing the end of the morning's interviews. He was getting tired. Too much information, too many unconnected pieces. And maybe a little too much breakfast. All those complex carbohydrates were sleep-inducing. Not to mention Gerald Pratt.

Pratt was holding a match to his pipe, nodding to show an answer was somewhere along the way. In the meantime, he was sucking in great gulps of smoke and puffing them back out again like the old Camels sign on Times Square. Puh . . . puh . . . puh . . .

Was he stalling? How could you tell? The gaunt, raw-boned Pratt wasn't ever going to win any medals for speed. John glanced at Julian Minor in the chair at Pratt's left. Minor had his elbows on the arms of the chair, his hands resting lightly on his thighs, fingers splayed. Lips pursed, head bent, he was studying the perfect crescents at the ends of his flawlessly filed fingernails. One wing-tipped toe tapped noiselessly, discreetly, on the floor.

If Pratt didn't say something pretty soon, they were all going to fall asleep.

"Answer's no," Pratt said.

"No, what?" Jesus, what was the question?

"No, I never heard Jimmy'd had any trouble with this Steve Fisk. Never heard he had any trouble with anybody."

"He had some trouble with investors in Sea Resources."

Pratt puffed tranquilly. "That," he said, "was business."

So it had been. Julian Minor had done his usual meticulous check on everyone involved, alive or dead, and had found that James Pratt had been more than a simple graduate student in 1960. It had been the time of the first great cholesterol scare, and Pratt had been involved in a dubious scheme to harvest kelp and process it into tablets that were supposed to lower blood cholesterol. Pratt and his partners, deeply in debt, were in hot water with creditors and investors. At the time of the survey they were being sued and were about to be investigated by both the IRS and the King County Prosecuting Attorney. Two years after Pratt's death, his partners, who had provided the capital (Pratt had supplied the botanical expertise), had paid backbreaking fines and gone to prison for three years.

"Were you involved in Sea Resources yourself, Mr. Pratt?" John asked.

"Not me. Jimmy was the businessman in the family."

"I understand you fish for a living?" More of Julian's legwork.

"That's right. Out of Ketchikan." He rearranged his long frame in the chair, showing welcome signs of life. "Pink salmon, mostly. Sometimes a little chum. Got me a fiberglass work boat, thirty-four-footer, diesel powered, radio, radar, the whole shebang. Big power reel on the afterdeck with a couple of hydraulic gurdies. Rigged for gill netting and trolling both."

John understood about four words of this, and not just because the pipe had remained between Pratt's teeth the whole time. But at least now he knew the guy was capable of stringing together more than two sentences in a row when he was talking about something that interested him.

"No kidding," John said.

Pratt was encouraged by this show of interest. "Rigged to handle longline gear, comes to that," he added with quiet pride. "For halibut. Brought in a 440-pounder off of Hoonah last year. Name's *Inez.*" He removed the pipe. "The boat."

"Mr. Pratt," Minor said, restlessness spurring him to speech, "I'm given to understand you have the room next to Professor Tremaine's."

"That's right." He looked at the ceiling and ticked off names on his fingers. "Miz Yount, me, the professor, and Dr. Judd, all in a row. Don't know where the others are."

"Did you hear anything unusual in Professor Tremaine's room last night?"

"Unusual?"

"Did you hear *anything?*"

There was a long, long silence. "Well, I did hear some voices, now that I think about it."

John and Minor both sat up. "Angry voices?" Minor asked. "Arguing?"

"Just talking."

"No other sounds?"

"Not that I remember."

"Did you recognize them?"

"Well, sure, it was the professor."

"By the professor, you mean Tremaine?"

"Well, sure."

"Who else?"

"Just the professor."

"You said 'voices,'" John said.

Pratt took the pipe out of his mouth and blew smoke to one side. "Figure of speech. All I heard was the professor say hello. Must have said it to someone."

Minor frowned. "You heard him say hello? The word 'hello'?"

"You got it. I was just going to the toilet, you know, before I went to bed, and I heard his voice through the wall. Made me jump because I thought someone was talking to me."

"And nothing after the hello? No further sounds?"

Pratt shrugged. "That's when I flushed the toilet."

"What kind of hello?" John asked. "Loud, quiet, scared, friendly . . ."

"Just plain hello." Pratt sucked twice at the pipe while he sought further detail. "Pretty quiet, with kind of like a question mark at the end. You know, like, 'Hello, is somebody there?' Only all I heard him say was hello, because that's when I—"

"Flushed the toilet," John supplied.

"You got it."

"Did you hear anything before the hello?" John asked. "Any other sounds?"

"No . . . well, yes, I heard his shower. Is that what you mean by sounds?"

John thought this over. "You were able to hear a quiet hello over the sound of the shower? Maybe it wasn't so quiet."

Pratt shook his head with relative vigor. "No, I'm telling this wrong. I was lying on the bed and I heard the professor's shower go *off*. The pipes make this noise—clunk-clunk—and that sort of woke me up out of a doze, and I figured it was time to call it a day. So I went into the bathroom to take a pee and that's when I heard it: 'Hello?'"

"How long after the shower went off?"

"Maybe four, five minutes. Long enough to brush my teeth, wash my face, and take a pee."

"About what time was this?"

"Oh, maybe ten o'clock."

Ten o'clock, the probable time of death. "Is there anything else you remember?" John asked. "Sounds of a scuffle? Maybe a door closing?"

Pratt smiled. "Nope. Tell you the truth, I didn't know I remembered this much till you fellas started asking."

And that, despite further prodding by Minor, was all he had to say on the subject.

"So tell me, Mr. Pratt," John asked, "why are you here?"

"Mm?" Pratt looked at him with renewed interest, his arms crossed, one hand holding the pipe to his mouth. "'Fraid I don't follow what you're after."

John didn't know what he was after; only that Pratt was there in place of his sister, who had originally been invited by Javelin Press. And he just didn't seem the type to willingly spend a week sitting around indoors talking about a manuscript. Especially while the salmon were still running strong (which they were, according to Minor's thoroughgoing research). Javelin was picking up expenses, but that didn't make up for a week's lost income. And private fishermen didn't get paid-vacation time.

"As I understand it," John said, "the publishing company asked your sister, but you offered to come in her place. Why?"

"Didn't offer. Eunice asked me to."

"And why was that?"

"Well," Pratt said with a sigh, "Eunice isn't what she was. Just didn't think she was up to talking about Jimmy getting killed and all, so she asked me to come instead. So I did."

"You gave up a week's fishing to be here?"

"Yup."

"Why? What did you hope to accomplish?"

With the bit of his pipe Pratt slowly scratched his temple. "Danged if I know."

That seemed to end that, at least for the time being. "And what about your brother? What was *he* doing here?"

"My brother? I don't follow—"

"In 1960. Why was he on the expedition?"

"Oh. Something to do with his schoolwork, wasn't it?"

"Yes, certainly," Minor cut in impatiently, "but didn't it ever occur to you to wonder why he'd drop everything and agree to come way up here for the summer, when he was right in the middle of some major problems with his business?"

Pratt looked at him thoughtfully. "Nope."

"Well, why do you think he would?"

"Hard to say. Jimmy was sort of deep, you know? Even as a kid, he always liked to get away from things and think 'em through. I remember, where we grew up, in Sitka, there was this old tree house—old packing crate in a tree is what it was, must have been a million years old . . . well, what the hell." He reinserted the pipe.

"Did you know about his relationship with Jocelyn Yount?"

"Since I came up here, I heard about it. Don't know as I believe everything I hear."

"Would you say he had a bad temper?"

"I wouldn't say diddley-squat," Pratt said, not so much angrily as doggedly. "Now, look, mister, if you're trying to get me to say maybe my brother killed somebody way back then, you're gonna have a heck of a wait. Besides, he's the one who got killed, far as I can see."

"What makes you say that?" Minor asked.

"Those are his sunglasses they found, aren't they, all

busted up? That ought to prove something." What it proved he didn't say. "Hell, sure, he could get mad like anybody else, but he was a good-natured kid; bighearted. Blow steam off at you, and then five minutes later buy you a beer. Jimmy didn't kill anyone. No such thing."

He jammed his chin down on his chest, and his hands into the pockets of his brown jumpsuit. "Didn't sell anybody any bum stocks either," he finished in a mutter, but without rancor.

"You loved him a lot, didn't you?" John asked.

"Well, sure I loved him." He began to say more but stopped. He pinched his long, lumpy nose between thumb and forefinger.

Minor asked another question. "Do you think Dr. Henckel has a point when she says Professor Tremaine's to blame for taking your brother and the others out on the ice when there was danger of an avalanche?"

"Didn't know she said it."

"She had a Park Service report on it," John said. "She was showing it to you and Dr. Judd a few nights ago. I understand she gave it to you to read."

"She did?" Pratt's eyebrows drew together. "In the bar? Is that what that was?"

"You didn't read it?"

"I looked at it. Didn't see much point in reading it. That was all over and done with a long time ago."

"Do you still have it?" Minor asked.

"No, I probably threw it away. Maybe it's in my room. Be glad to look for it, if you want."

"Please do," Minor said. "So you don't hold Tremaine responsible for the death of your brother?"

The pipe had gone out. Pratt leaned over, using a small folding knife to scrape the sour-smelling dottle into an ashtray, taking his time. "Now look," he said reasonably, deliberately, keeping his eyes on his work. "I didn't kill

Tremaine, and my brother didn't kill this Fisk or anybody else. I don't hold with grudges, and neither did Jimmy. There's more important things in life."

"I'm glad to hear you say it," Minor said pleasantly.

Pratt nodded and gathered his long legs under him. "That it, then?"

"One more thing," John said. "Any objection to letting us into your room?"

"Guess not," Pratt said. Then a moment later: "What for?"

"I just want to test for myself the kind of sounds that come through from Tremaine's room."

"Sure." He dug in a zippered leg pouch for his key and handed it to John. "There you go. You can leave it at the desk."

"You can come with us. It'd probably be better if you did."

"No, thanks. You boys go ahead and do your job. I'll go and be first in the chow line."

John stood by Pratt's bed while Minor followed his instructions, working the shower next door in Tremaine's bathroom. As Pratt had told them, turning off the water produced a hollow double clank in the pipes, sufficient to awaken someone drowsing in Pratt's room. Neither the tap at the sink nor the toilet produced similar noises.

He got up, went into Pratt's bathroom, and knocked on the wall.

"Hello?" Minor said on the other side, his measured voice distinct.

"Fine!" John yelled. "Now try it from the bedroom." He heard the floor creak as Minor left the bathroom, but nothing more.

A few seconds later the floor creaked again and Minor

returned to Tremaine's bathroom. "Could you hear me?" he called through the wall.

"Not a thing," John called back.

"Which seems to mean," he told Minor a few moments later, as they clumped along the wooden walkway back to the main building, "that Tremaine'd just taken a shower when he heard a noise in his room—"

"Or maybe heard it while he was still in the shower, and turned the water off."

"No, because Pratt said four or five minutes went by after the shower got turned off."

"Assuming Pratt's telling the truth."

"True. Anyway, Tremaine calls out a hello and then—what?"

"Presumably he doesn't get an answer, he comes out of the bathroom, and he's killed by the intruder he's discovered."

"Doing what?"

"Looking for the manuscript, I suppose."

"Maybe," John said.

"What else?"

"I'm not sure, Julian. I need to think about this some more." They reached the lodge building and trotted up the short flight of steps. "Lunchtime."

"Shall we stop by the Icebreaker Lounge first?"

"Little early in the day, isn't it? Anyway, the bar doesn't open till five. I've got some vodka in my room if you can't make it till then."

"Very amusing, John. As a matter of fact I had something else in mind."

# 17

"But I don't know who those bones belonged to," Professor Worriner said simply. "I never did, except for one of them."

Gideon restrained his dismay. "But the article said you identified them as James Pratt's and Steven Fisk's. You mean the paper got it wrong?"

"I'm afraid they slightly misrepresented what I said. Tell me, have you found the popular press particularly reliable in such matters?" He smiled, his gentle gray eyes suddenly lighting up. "Let me see, don't I recall a recent reference to some of your remarks in one of the national tabloids . . . ?"

Gideon winced. Six months earlier he had given an abstruse all-university lecture ("Human Evolution: A Non-teleological Perspective") in which his thesis had been that, while the "logic" of evolution was comprehensible looking backwards, you couldn't use it to look ahead. Evolution—that is, adaptation—didn't "advance" or "progress"; it responded to the pressures of the moment. If there were a biological or reproductive advantage to being large, for example, humans would get larger. If there were an advantage to being small, they would get smaller. Somebody in the audience had raised his hand and asked a question: You mean we could all evolve into midgets? Yes, Gideon had said. Well, how long would something like that take, somebody else had wanted to know. It would depend, Gideon had told him. If, for some unimaginable reason, everyone over five feet tall stopped having children right now, today, six-footers could be biological oddities in a few generations; by 2050, say.

Somehow, *Inside Dope* had gotten hold of it. "Scientist Says We're Becoming Midgets!" the headline had screamed from the checkout stands. "By A.D. 2050 Humans Will Be Four-Foot Freaks, Claims U. of Washington Professor." With Gideon's picture. Copies were still making the rounds on campus. He'd be lucky if he lived it down by 2050.

"No, not wholly reliable," he said, laughing. "All right, just what *did* you say?"

"I said that one of the fragments, which consisted of a third of a mandible, including two teeth, had been conclusively identified as coming from Steven Fisk—"

"Identified from dental work?"

"Of course. How else are we poor anthropologists to make conclusive identifications? We had a time tracking down the dentist, I can tell you that." He broke a chocolate-chip cookie in half, then snapped one of the halves into two smaller pieces, placed one in his mouth, and chewed deliberately. The thin sheet of platysmal muscle at the front of his throat jumped. "There were several other fragments: the superior half of a right scapula, an almost complete left humerus, and a mid-shaft segment of a second left humerus. All were male."

"Two left humeri? So you knew for sure you had at least two people."

"Precisely. Two *men,* as I think you'll agree when you see the fragments. And inasmuch as there were only two males lost in the avalanche, and we already knew from the teeth that one was Steven Fisk, the other had to be James Pratt. Nothing too esoteric there."

"But, except for the mandible, you couldn't say which bones belonged to which man."

"No, not with certainty. Well, not even with uncertainty, if it comes to that. That is exactly what I put in my report, but the press was a little carried away."

"Only a little, really. You did determine that you had the remains of two people, and you knew who they were. You just couldn't apportion the fragments piece by piece." He shrugged. "Same problem I'm having."

"It's kind of you to put it that way, but it throws a monkey wrench in what you hoped to learn, doesn't it? Would you care for some more coffee? It's Viennese roast; decaffeinated, I'm afraid."

Kenneth Worriner was a tall, thin man of eighty-five; elegant and fragile, with skin like rice paper and hair as glossy and white as lamb's wool. With his courtly bearing, his prow of a nose, and his sunken cheeks he reminded Gideon of the pictures of Ramses II; or, more accurately, of the pictures of Ramses' mummy. His clothes were more up-to-date than the Nineteenth Dynasty, but not by that much: a full, droopy bow tie, white flannel trousers and vest (with chain), and a dark-blue flannel blazer with a carefully folded handkerchief in the breast pocket.

Here in the land of tractor caps and red suspenders, he seemed like an alien from another planet. In fact, as he had explained to Gideon, he was a Beacon Hill Bostonian who'd been educated at Harvard. He'd been in his twenty-eighth year of teaching at Wellesley—he was a teacher, he said emphatically, not a researcher—when a two-year appointment had opened up at the University of Alaska. Worriner, then sixty, had taken it for a change of scene and he had been the man on the spot in 1964 when Tirku had disgorged its first load of bones. He had also fallen in love with Alaska, and it was in this rugged country he'd settled when he retired from teaching.

But in his own living room—jacketed, cravated, delicately poised at a marquetry table—he might have been pouring coffee at his old eighteenth-century bay window overlooking Louisburg Square.

"That's fine, thanks," Gideon said when his cup was half full. Decaffeinated or not, Worriner liked his coffee strong to the point of bitterness. "That mandible fragment, Kenneth—which side was it, right or left?"

"The right. Just about the entire ascending ramus, and as far forward as the second bicuspid."

"Was the condyle broken off?"

"No, it was in good condition."

Gideon smacked his hands together. "Ah, great, we're finally going to find out a few things."

What they were going to find out was who had been murdered on Tirku Glacier in June 1960. The right ramus of the mandible was the right rear segment, the part that rises from the back corner of the jaw to the underside of the skull. It was precisely the part missing from the newly found mandible, the absence of which made it impossible to say whether the jaw and skull fragment came from the same person.

But now, with this ramus having been identified as Steven's, they would be able to say that and more. They would start by seeing whether the condyle on Worriner's piece fit positively into the mandibular fossa on the telltale skull fragment that Gideon had brought with him. Then they would match the broken front edge of Worriner's piece against the broken rear edge of the mutilated jaw fragment Gideon had also brought along.

If they got a fit at both ends—if all three pieces fit together like a jigsaw puzzle—then the man who'd had an ice ax driven into his head was Steven Fisk. With absolutely no possibility of doubt.

And if they didn't, then just as surely that man was *not* Steven Fisk, which meant he was James Pratt. Period.

He explained all this with growing excitement as Worriner led the way back to his study. The ex-professor left his aluminum walker in the living room and moved slowly, stoop-shouldered but straight-backed, pushing against the walls of the narrow hallway for support.

"Well, yes, your logic is reasonable enough," he said, but he sounded oddly subdued. "Go ahead and put your material on the table."

The old man's study was like any other academic's study: nondescript, mismatched file cabinets, some wooden, some metal; book-filled shelves wherever there was wall space; a couple of dusty, elderly typewriters; books and papers everywhere, even on the chair seats. And even, on a table of its own, the essential late-twentieth-century touch: a covered Compaq computer. Over everything hung the fusty, scholarly, stimulating smell of the printed page.

Gideon put his case on the scarred library table that had probably been cleared especially for his visit. He took out two irregularly shaped packages, thickly wrapped in newspaper, and used a pair of Worriner's scissors to cut the tape around them.

As he snipped he kept talking. There was the possibility that Worriner's ramus would fit the jaw but not the skull, or vice versa. That would be an interesting twist, because it would mean that the man with the broken jaw and the man with the broken head were two different people. Still, they would know who was who, which was a long way ahead of where they were now.

When he'd gotten the package open he laid out the two pieces of bone, brown and shiny with their new coats of preservative. "All right," he said enthusiastically, "let's have a look at that ramus of yours."

Worriner cleared his throat. "Well, er, Gideon . . . I'm afraid I don't exactly have it."

"You don't . . ." This time he couldn't quite hide his disappointment. "But you said—"

"Yes, I know. I *do* have the bones . . . All but that one."

He explained. Because the ramus had been positively identified, it had been sent to the next of kin: Steven Fisk's brother in Idaho. Surely Gideon saw the propriety of this? (The best Gideon could do was grunt, which Worriner accepted as affirmation.) But the rest of the remains, impossible to attribute definitely to either Pratt or Fisk, had been kept. Things being what they were in Alaska at the time, they had wound up in the physical anthropology laboratory collection and had been kindly delivered to Worriner's house that morning.

"I do have some pictures of the ramus," Worriner ventured timorously. "I think they're rather good."

They were. Ten clear black-and-white photographs taken from all the conventional angles and then some. The two men got down to work. What would have taken thirty seconds with the ramus itself took thirty minutes of measurement, comparison, and discussion, but when they were finished they had their answer. The ramus in the photographs, the perforated skull fragment, and the broken mandible all came from the same person. Steven Fisk. The jealous boyfriend was victim, not murderer.

Gideon sat back with a feeling of completion. With Worriner's considerable help he had done all that could reasonably be expected of an anthropologist. He had identified the remains. The rest was up to John Lau and the FBI. As John frequently and succinctly told him.

Still, he was naturally interested in seeing the other fragments that had come from the glacier in 1964, and Worriner was interested in showing him. Worriner opened a set of numbered, clasped envelopes and laid the pieces out in a row on the table.

There was a beaten-up piece of a right scapula that Worriner had identified as male, age twenty to twenty-five.

"That's just what I would have said," Gideon told him.

"Really?" Worriner said. "Well." He was unreservedly pleased.

Next was an almost complete left humerus, broken off just above the epicondyles so that only the elbow process was missing. Worriner had identified it as coming from a male, in the same age range, with medium to medium-heavy musculature. "A mesomorph," he said, using the archaic terminology.

Gideon nodded. Clear enough.

Next to this was a columnar segment about five inches long; a piece of another left humerus, from the middle of the shaft.

"As you remarked, this was quite crucial to the analysis," Worriner told him, "because it meant that there were at least two individuals represented, and both of them were adult males. As you see." He rolled the bone over, showing a well-defined, lumpy crest that ran almost the length of the piece.

Again Gideon nodded. The crest was the deltoid tuberosity, so named because it was the insertion point of the deltoid, the big muscle that formed the beefy mass of the shoulder. As with any other tendon-bone connection, the larger and more powerful the muscle, the rougher and more pronounced the bony insertion point. And the rougher and more pronounced the insertion point, the greater the likelihood that it was male.

Of course it was chancy to assign sex or anything else on the basis of a single criterion, but on this otherwise smooth piece of bone there wasn't anything else to go on. Except for the tuberosity, everything about it was borderline, just the kind of fragment an anthropologist hates: maybe male, maybe female. Fortunately, it was one heck of a deltoid tuberosity; nothing borderline about it.

As he told Worriner, he would have drawn the same conclusion. Adult male; there was nothing else to say about it.

Worriner looked highly gratified. He lowered himself into a disreputable old wooden swivel chair. "Well then. I hope coming here hasn't been a complete waste of time?"

No, Gideon told him, he'd learned just what he'd hoped to learn. When he arrived in Juneau he hadn't had a victim.

Now he had Steven Fisk.

Gideon walked from Worriner's hillside house to downtown Juneau by way of three flights of wooden street stairs and then took the elevator to the top floor of the federal building, a white, nine-story cube of concrete aggregate pierced by windows shaped like coffins. The FBI resident agency was in Room 957, and there, with a sense of relief, he delivered the bone fragments into the hands of the agent, receiving an itemized receipt in return. He then used the telephone in the office to call Glacier Bay and waited while Mr. Granle went to find John.

"Doc! How's it going?"

"Great. The bones are safely stored in the evidence room here—"

"Good."

"—and I can now tell you who the murdered man was."

He paused, the better to impart dramatic impact. "It was—"

"Steven Fisk," John said.

"—Steven . . . how the hell did you know?"

John's happy laugh burbled from the receiver. "I read it in a book."

"Damn, you spoiled my big scene," Gideon muttered. "What do you mean, you—"

"Gotta run. I'll pick you guys up at the airport at five. Tell you all about it then."

There was time for a late lunch at the Fiddlehead, just down the block on West Willoughby. There, in a country-kitchen atmosphere of knotty-pine paneling, flowered wallpaper, and the smell of baking bread, he sat at a butcher-block table wolfing down black bean soup with wedges of dark rye bread and wondered how John had come up with Steven Fisk. Well, at least it was a good thing they'd arrived at the same conclusion.

Restored, he caught the bus to the airport an hour before the flight for Gustavus. Twenty minutes later Julie arrived, having spent her truant afternoon on a bus tour of Juneau's major tourist attraction.

Mendenhall Glacier.

# 18

John didn't believe in keeping things mysterious. Before the borrowed green Park Service car had pulled out of the parking area at the Gustavus Airport he was handing a sheaf of papers to Gideon and Julie, who were in back.

"Tremaine's manuscript," he announced.

"You're kidding," Gideon said. "Where'd you find it? I figured it was on the bottom of the bay."

"It isn't the one that was stolen," Julian Minor explained from the driver's seat. "It's a copy, faxed from Los Angeles."

"There's a fax machine up here?" Julie asked.

"Faxed to Juneau, then flown here," John explained. "I got to thinking, maybe the guy used a word processor, and if he did there'd be a disk someplace, and maybe if our L.A. guys got into his safe deposit box they'd find it. And they did."

"Good thinking," Gideon said, opening the folder.

"I believe it was my idea, John," Minor said mildly.

"Hey, are we a team, or what? Turn to where the paper clip is, Doc. That's where he talks about it."

Gideon opened the folder and spread it so that both he and Julie could read.

> *Even now, writing in comfort and security during the twilight of my life, it stands out in my mind with a real and terrible clarity. Not the great cataclysm itself; not the endless day and night I lay, crushed and broken, locked in the freezing, blue-white embrace of the ice; not even the miraculous, dimly perceived appearance of my rescuers the next day, long after I had given up hope and longed only for oblivion from pain.*
>
> *No, what I need only close my eyes to call up in harrowing detail is an image rooted not in the great forces of nature, but in the equally ungovernable passions of men. In the blinking of an eye, everything—the sexual jealousies and antipathies of the last several days; the exasperation over Walter's costly errors; the natural tensions that arise in any isolated group which has been in too-intimate contact for too long under too-trying circumstances—all of it came to an explosive, tragic head over an incident so trivial as to be absurd.*
>
> *Until that moment the day had gone well, due, I think, to my one-more-fight-and-you-flunk warning before we started. James was affecting his brooding-genius mood: quiet, aloof, darkly contemplative—and wisely keeping his distance from both Steven and Jocelyn. For his part, Steven was doing his Zorro imitation: all handsome, flashing smiles, cavalier unconcern, and graceful bounds from boulder to boulder. Jocelyn was . . . well, Jocelyn was Jocelyn: vague, placid, and off somewhere in her own thought-free world. Thus far, our excursion had produced nothing more traumatic*

*than Walter's gallant but ultimately unsuccessful battle with a fierce mosquito, which had cost us the pleasures of his company.*

*The tragic incident to which I refer occurred a little before 2:00* P.M., *as we made our slow way back across the glacier, having successfully concluded our resampling in the area beyond its eastern lateral moraine. I should explain that our pace was slowed not by massive obstacles or yawning abysses (despite the pompous and officious warnings of the Park Service); on the contrary, we proceeded slowly because we were tired and warm—even on a glacier, the temperature in late July can reach the sixties—and because walking across the surface of Tirku is something like walking on a colossal natural garbage heap. No smooth, pristine ice field, this. One has constantly to pick one's way among the litter of "erratics"—boulders scraped from the flanks of the mountains above. It is all gritty black ice and debris, rocks and bumps, depressions and ruts.*

*In summer, things are at their worst because of the meltwater rivulets that cut shallow, meandering furrows into the grimy ice, necessitating numerous leaps (the streams are seldom wider than four feet) or tiresome deviations. It was at one of these rivulets that the trouble occurred; an inconsequential V-shaped channel two or three feet wide, with perhaps eight inches of water flowing along its bottom. Leaping it would have been an easy matter except that the far bank rose some four feet higher than the near one and overhung it like a protruding upper lip. Making it up that bank without getting our feet wet was the problem.*

*Steven, always ready to demonstrate his physical abilities, clambered up with the aid of his ice ax. Then he knelt while the rest of us, one at a time, extended our own axes to him, grasping the handle while he held firmly to the head, providing support while we scrambled up the bank. It was neither a dangerous nor a difficult maneuver. Jocelyn went first, then I did, both without incident. Then it was James's turn. Steven held out the handle. James grasped it, stretched one leg across the stream to prop his foot against the opposite bank, and began to haul himself up.*

*Whether by accident or design I cannot say—no one can say—but just as James's back foot came off the ice the ax slipped from Steven's hand. James dropped straight into the stream. There was no danger—the fall was a matter of a foot or two—and although getting wet during glacier travel is not generally a laughing matter, James had barely been moistened, having landed on his elbows and knees in only a few inches of water. In any case, hypothermia was hardly a problem with the temperature where it was and the plane due to pick us up in an hour.*

*"Sorry about that," Steven said, choking down his laughter.*

*James crouched on all fours, still holding the ice ax, his black hair tumbling over his forehead, glowering up at Steven from under dark eyebrows.*

*It was an uneasy moment, but I think we would have gotten through it had Jocelyn not giggled. An innocent, genuinely amused giggle to be sure; but understandably it stung James. He swiped hotly at Steven's legs with the wooden handle of the ice ax, Steven grabbed it, James tugged, and Steven went tumbling down the bank head-over-heels, missing the stream but landing squarely—and surely painfully—on the seat of his pants. He was on his feet at once, his face stiff with anger. James brandished the ice ax in warning, but I could see his heart wasn't in it. He was already regretting his impulsive act of a moment before. By nature a sulker and not a fighter, he'd been thoroughly cowed by Steven in their brief altercation a few days earlier and he hardly wanted another one.*

*Steven was another story. His eyes were glittering with pugnacity.*

*"That's enough!" I said forcefully. "Steven, stop there. James, put down the ax."*

*I might have been speaking to the wind, for all the good it did. Steven thrust the palms of both hands violently against James's upper chest, as bellicose young males do, and James staggered back a few steps. He lifted the ax again. "I'm warning you," he said in a strangled voice.*

*Steven sneered, or perhaps it was a snarl, and moved forward. I jumped down from the bank and made swiftly for them. "Gentlemen—!"*

*Too late. Steve's big fist smashed into James's face with a strange, flat sound. Blood spurted from his nose. His orange sunglasses hung briefly from one ear, then dropped to the ice. I managed to leap between them, grabbing for the ax, but one or the other—they both outweighed me by sixty pounds—sent me sprawling. Helplessly, disbelievingly, I watched James lash out with the ice ax. The flat of the heavy adze portion struck Steven full in the mouth, and the chin that was so square and strong a moment before was suddenly collapsed and formless, like the face of a plastic doll trodden on by a child. A dull, doglike whine came from Jocelyn. Steven's eyes rolled up under his lids and he fell forward, blindly wrapping his arms around James while he slid to his knees, his arms loosely around James's legs, his ruined mouth leaving a long, bright smear of blood on James's trousers.*

*Whether from jealousy or horror, murderous revenge or simple blood lust—certainly not from fear of the thickly moaning, virtually insensible Steven—James raised the ice ax with the unmistakable, appalling intention of bringing it down on the lolling head at his knees.*

*"James!" I cried, floundering to my feet, and launched myself at him. But the distance was too great, the time too short. Before my flailing arms could stop him, the awful weapon moved in its brief, flashing arc, deeply burying its point in Steven's head in a scene so horrible it is beyond my power, and my desire as well, to set it down in detail. Suffice it to say that the blow ended Steven's young life beyond any possibility of doubt.*

*Jocelyn and I stared at each other, unable to speak. Steven lay crumpled at James's feet, the awful pick still imbedded in its gruesome wound. Oddly, it was James at whom I could not bring myself to look.*

*"James—," I finally croaked, and then stopped, not knowing what I intended to say.*

*It was then that I felt the first vibrations in my legs and imagined that I was trembling. It would hardly have been surprising, considering what had just happened. But no, I told myself, I wasn't going to give way under the strain. It was up to me to remain cool and rational. I shifted my feet and willed the shuddering to stop. My boots crunched on the ice. The trembling continued.*

*"James," I said again, "I want you to—"*

*At that moment the sound struck: a metallic, shearing, impossible noise, as if a giant bridge were being wrenched apart behind me. Jocelyn's eyes, focused dazedly on me until then, sprang open as she stared slack-jawed over my shoulder. I whirled around just in time to see the immense, striated lobe of dirty-gray ice detach itself from the overhanging cornice atop Tlingit*

*Ridge three-quarters of a mile to the southeast, crack into three gigantic segments, and begin to slip down.*

*I was unable to tear my eyes away from the grim, apocalyptic vision. An ice avalanche is not like a snow avalanche. There is no long, graceful, white cascade into the valley below; no thick, creamy tendrils spewing clouds of white, powdery snow as they flow majestically downhill. Ninety million tons of ice falls very much like ninety million tons of rock, plummeting gracelessly in a titanic, closely packed mass, with a force beyond comprehension.*

*I was still staring when the ice beneath my boots dropped two feet, wobbling my knees, then rebounded, flinging me sideways into the air as if I were standing on a blanket flicked by some playful giant. I skittered drunkenly over the surface of the glacier, grabbing at boulders, feeling that I might be flung off the very planet itself if I didn't catch hold. Twisting, I landed heavily on my right shoulder. My arm must have gone dead instantly, but I was too shocked by what was happening around me to notice.*

*In all directions the rough surface of the ice was splitting into jagged crevasses, snapping and banging, and emitting puffs of white as it cracked open. Underneath, the ground pitched, tossing like a rubber raft on the open sea. With my left hand I held convulsively to an icy outcropping, dazed and unable to get up.*

*As if in a dream I saw Jocelyn sliding by me, spinning like a top on the seat of her pants, down a slope that hadn't been there a few seconds before, toward a crevasse that was even then splitting open to receive her like a dreadful mouth. I tried to reach for her but to my astonishment my arm wouldn't work, and I couldn't loosen the hold of my other hand or I would go sliding after her.*

*Desperately I kicked out for her with my feet. "Get hold of my legs!" I shouted (I could not hear my voice over the roar), but she only stared back, blank-eyed and dumb with shock or terror, and I had to watch, stupefied and powerless, as she slipped smoothly over the edge of the great crack and simply disappeared. A second later Steven's body slithered heavily down the same slope, the handle of the ice ax jutting up from his skull, bobbing hideously. Dogging her in death as in life, he too flopped over the brink a moment before the ice convulsed again, and the sides of the crevasse shifted, grinding back against each other with a ragged screech that sealed these two tragic lovers—what was left of them—together for eternity.*

*And while this was happening I could see James on the other side of the crevasse, desperately fighting for his balance on the shifting, splintering ice; falling, then stumbling to his feet, only to be knocked down again by the incredible upheaval. For an instant his panicked eyes locked with mine, and then he was lost to sight, driven headfirst, despite his frenzied scuttling, into a jumble of sharp black boulders and broken ice.*

*A sharp wind spattered my face from the direction of the avalanche and I lifted my head to see an almost spherical gray cloud already blotting out the mountains and expanding in every direction, like a motion picture of an atomic-bomb blast. Caught up in this exploding cloud, chunks of ice the size of trucks were hurtling toward me, bouncing in mesmerizing, slow parabolas of two and three hundred feet.*

*A second later the vanguard of the blast was on me, howling and strafing my face with freezing, burning grit. I shut my eyes to it just as a spate of ice spicules were driven into my face. I could feel them sticking out of my cheeks like nails. A sharp piece of ice or rock struck my knee and I screamed with pain. Something hit my wrist, and something far larger crashed and squealed along the ice a few yards away. The wind was terrific, screaming in my ears, rasping my bloodied face, tearing at my handhold.*

*I huddled behind the small outcropping as well as I could, but a piece of flying debris struck me in the temple with paralyzing force. Numbly, I watched my good hand loosen its grip, flutter tentatively, and drop to my side, palm up, fingers loosely curled. I seemed to be outside my own body now, looking down on myself with no more than a dispassionate curiosity. Feet first, unresisting, I slid slowly down a gentle incline toward the turquoise gash of a newly opened crevasse.*

*I resigned myself to meet my maker.*

"It does fit what you found, doesn't it?" Julie said, looking up. "The ice ax, the jaw injuries, everything."

Gideon finished the page and nodded. "All the skeletal evidence supports it. I'd have to guess this is pretty much the way it happened." To himself he admitted a keen sense of disappointment. No profound, complex motives had come to light, no unexpected twists; just another squalid, brutal homicide, prompted by nothing more than sex, and revenge, and the searing, momentary heat of rage. The usual.

"Not necessarily," Minor said, keeping his eyes carefully on the road. "What happened to Steven Fisk, yes; who did it to him, no."

"You mean maybe it was Tremaine who killed him? And then blamed it on James?"

"Exactly. Who is there to argue the point?"

"That could be," John agreed. "Steve was complaining about Tremaine ripping off his ideas. Maybe this was how Tremaine shut him up." He glanced over his shoulder at

Gideon. "I hear these scientist types can get a little uptight about that stuff."

"Maybe," Gideon said, "but I don't think it was Tremaine who swung the ax. He would have been forty or so at the time, and a small, fragile forty at that; he couldn't have been more than 135 pounds. Steven was a muscular twenty-five-year-old 200-pounder."

"I should think that an ice ax might compensate for any disparities," Minor put in.

"As far as the blow to the back of the skull goes, sure. But what about the one to the front of the jaw? Did Steven just stand there and let Tremaine belt him? From everything we've heard, he wasn't exactly a pacifist. And he had an ice ax of his own."

"Hum," Minor said.

"If Tremaine *didn't* do it," Julie said, "which he says he didn't, then why did he cover it up all these years?"

"That's in here," John said, taking back the manuscript and leafing through the pages. "Well, I can't find it, but he talks about how he knows he made some mistakes the way he ran the project, and the personal relations were lousy and all, and he deserves the blame for the whole thing because he was the director, and he was afraid that if people found out somebody actually got murdered, he'd never direct another project."

"So why is he suddenly willing to tell everything now?"

"That," John said, "isn't in here."

"It doesn't seem so hard to figure out," said Gideon. "Scandals and murders sell books, and Tremaine had a book to sell. None of this could hurt his botanical career anymore. If anything, it would have made him more popular than ever. He comes off looking pretty good, at least the way he tells it."

"Yeah, that's probably right, Doc."

"But wouldn't the police have come after him, once it

came out? For withholding evidence or something?" Julie asked.

"Maybe, maybe not," John said. "Anyway, what could they do to him? What would be the point?"

"Besides," Minor said drily, "anything they *did* do would hardly be harmful to sales."

Julie nodded. "Okay, but look: If he was going to tell all this anyway, why did he pretend he didn't remember the ice ax a few days ago? Why did he get so angry when the murder was discovered?" She held up a hand before anyone could answer. "Wait . . . he wanted the book to make a splash when it came out. He didn't want the story leaking out piece by piece before he was ready."

"Could we get back to now?" asked John, whose interest in the old murder had always been limited. "Can anybody tell me what's so important about this thing?" He slapped the manuscript. "What's the big deal? Why would anybody steal it? Why would somebody kill Tremaine over it? So what if it got published? Who'd give a damn?"

"Well," Julie said hesitantly, "one person—I'm just thinking out loud—one person who'd care would be Gerald Pratt. He wouldn't be too happy about his brother being labeled a murderer."

"I take your point," Minor said, "but in all honesty it hardly seems a credible motive for killing Tremaine."

"Besides," Gideon said, "how could Gerald know what was in the manuscript? About the murder, I mean."

"How could anybody know?" John asked. "Tremaine was the only one who got out of there alive." He shook his head. "So what reason would anybody have—"

Julie frowned. "John, can I have that manuscript back?" She quickly found the place she wanted "Listen. 'For an instant his panicked eyes locked with mine, and then he was lost to sight, driven headfirst, despite his frenzied scuttling, into a jumble of sharp black boulders and broken ice.'" She leaned forward, growing more excited. "That's James Pratt he's talking about. Tremaine saw Steven killed, right? He saw Jocelyn fall into a crevasse that closed up over her—but the last he saw of James he was still *alive.*"

John looked at her temperately. "So?"

"Well, I don't know exactly. But how do we know he was killed at all? How do we—"

"We know," Gideon said, "because we have skeletal remains from two males, and those are—necessarily—Steven Fisk and James Pratt. As far as the bones go, Jocelyn's the only one unaccounted for. Sorry."

Julie grumpily withdrew, as she sometimes did under such circumstances, sinking back into the seat and folding her arms. "Why do I always do this to myself?" she muttered to the window. "Why don't I just let all the big-time detectives solve it themselves?"

"Oh, yeah," John said with a laugh, "we're doing just great."

That effectively ended the conversation for the rest of the drive. When Minor pulled into the lodge parking lot and turned off the ignition, they continued to sit silently for a few moments, lost in their own thoughts, until John sighed loudly and pushed open his door.

"See you guys for dinner," he said. Then, without moving to get out, he added: "You know what I'm starting to think? That maybe we've been on the wrong track all along; maybe the two murders aren't even connected; maybe Tremaine was killed on account of something else in the book. Hell," he finished glumly, "maybe the damn book doesn't have anything to do with it."

"Could be," Julie said.

"Perhaps so," said Minor.

Maybe, Gideon thought, but only if somebody had just repealed the Law of Interconnected Monkey Business.

# 19

Due to the recent tragedy involving M. Audley Tremaine, things were understandably subdued at the lodge that evening. The Icebreaker Lounge had remained closed and dark during the cocktail hour, and now in the dining room the atmosphere, if not one of inconsolable grief, was appropriately restrained. Most of the search-and-rescue class were at their usual large table, eating heartily enough, but without the attendant verve and hilarity that usually characterized their meals. The death of Professor Tremaine had cast a pall of gloom on their customary animation. That, or the deletion of the cocktail hour.

The members of Tremaine's party were no longer sitting at a single table. If they had ever enjoyed each other's company, it was obvious that they didn't anymore. Gerald Pratt sat with Elliott Fisk, both of them silent, Fisk picking sourly at his food, Pratt shoveling it placidly in. Nearby, with her back pointedly toward Fisk, Shirley

Yount was at a table with Walter Judd, who was chugging and chortling away like a washing machine, but seemingly by rote, his mind elsewhere. Shirley made no pretense of listening. She looked mostly over his head, at the top of the wall behind him. Under the table her long, bony foot bobbed while she chewed.

Alone, her cape draped majestically over the back of her chair, her polished staff leaning against the wall, Anna Henckel sat in regal isolation, looking out over the darkening water of the cove as she ate.

And at a table at the far end of the room, in front of a wall that was carved and painted with owl-eyed totem figures to look like the side of a Tlingit longhouse, six newcomers—three women and three men—gobbled down their food and talked earnestly.

"John, who are those people?" Julie asked. She had seen them on the flight from Juneau a few hours before. They had kept to themselves in a knot in the smoking section and been met by Arthur Tibbett with the lodge bus.

"Reporters," John said, picking up a menu. "And a TV crew." He had just joined Gideon, Julie, and Minor. "The media's been pushing us for news, so we're going to have a press conference tomorrow at four o'clock."

"Do you want me to deal with the logistics?" Minor asked. "Orient them, show them around, arrange a meeting room, and so on and so forth?" He took off his rimless glasses and blew a speck of dust from them.

"If you can get them away from Arthur Tibbett, but I don't think you have a chance. Let him do it; he's like a kid with a new bike." He looked at Gideon. "Doc, can you be there? There'll be questions."

"Sure."

"Good. You can come too, Julie, if you want." He scanned the menu, folded it, and dropped it on the table. "I told Henckel and Pratt and the rest of them to come too.

I figured I'd let Tibbett run the show, since he's having such a good time."

Minor's pepper-and-salt eyebrows lifted briefly. "Do you think that's wise?" He began polishing his glasses with a handkerchief that looked as if it had never been unfolded before, let alone used.

"Sure, I don't have any problem with it. Besides, who says we have a choice? We don't have any right to keep the press away from them; and I figured an open meeting'd be the best way to handle it. I had a talk with them when they arrived, and they promised to stay away from Tremaine's people if I promised to have them at the press conference. At least this way we get to hear what they say."

Cheri, the chirpy, whip-thin waitress who had single-handedly been doing the serving all week, was at his elbow. "Have you decided, or do you want me to come back?"

John looked at the menu again. "What's the Prospector's Special?"

"Salisbury steak with bacon strips and mushroom gravy, buttered mashed potatoes, fried onion rings. Yum."

"Sounds good. Can I get French fries instead of mashed?"

"Sure."

"Great. Make it well done, okay? Lots of gravy. On the fries too. Thousand Island on the salad."

"I just hope Marti doesn't ask me what you ate," Julie said.

John looked at her over the top of the menu. "Are you gonna get on my case too? What'd *you* order?"

"Broiled halibut."

"Doc?"

"Same."

John growled something. "Julian?"

Minor replaced his glasses, adjusting the wire earpieces

one at a time over his ears. "Penne pasta with cauliflower and broccoli in sesame-seed sauce," he said.

John stared at him with something like awe. "Jesus Christ." He heaved a sigh of capitulation and handed the menu to Cheri. "Okay, okay, hold the gravy on the fries."

"You got it. Back in a sec with the salads."

She stooped at the folding table behind Gideon to shoulder the heaped tray of dirty dishes and silverware just cleared from the rangers' table. The tray looked as if it weighed as much as she did. Instinctively Gideon reached out to help her steady it, but she laughed him off.

"Never mind, honey, I'm used to it. I only look skinny. I got muscles on my muscles."

A lift, a momentary hitch like a weight lifter performing a clean-and-jerk, and up it went with a clank of settling dishes to rest firmly on the flat of her hand and her shoulder. She grinned at them, adjusted the load with a hunch of her shoulder, and scudded off.

"John," Minor said in his precise way, "when I asked if you were sure it was wise, I wasn't referring to the press conference in general; I was referring to the idea of allowing Tibbett to lead it"—he lowered his already quiet voice—"considering what we learned today."

"Yeah, I think it's okay, Julian." John scowled. "Hey, do they give you bread with dinner, or do you have to—"

"What did you learn today?" Gideon asked. "What's wrong with Tibbett running the press conference?"

Minor looked warily at John, who nodded. "He's on our side, Julian," John said. "So's she."

From a thin briefcase on his lap Minor extracted a few sheets of paper. He was as decorous and fastidious as Gideon remembered him: dark-blue banker's suit, meticulously knotted tie decorated with tiny fleurs-de-lys, blinding white shirt with mother-of-pearl cuff links. He passed the sheets to Gideon and Julie.

They glanced at a densely typed two-page memorandum done on a National Park Service form, its print faded to a barely legible gray from being photocopied so many times.

"Go ahead and read it," John said, and turned to call over his shoulder: "Hey, Cheri, does bread come with this?"

The first line of the memo was the date: September 24, 1960. Two months after the Tirku expedition. Their eyes were drawn to the lower part of the page, where several paragraphs had been heavily circled with a red felt-tip marker.

> *Although appellant admits that he "lost his temper" twice in dealings with Professor Tremaine, and that such behavior is inexcusable, he feels that it was the understandable result of Professor Tremaine's "abusive, belligerent, and unreasonable manner," and his refusal to heed safety advice of the most basic kind, e.g.:*
>
> *(a) Professor Tremaine's refusal to postpone or cancel his group's final day of activities in the vicinity of Tirku Glacier despite the increasing frequency of earth tremors in the region;*
>
> *(b) His insistence on taking a route directly across the northern tongue of Tirku, although it was in the path of a large, unstable hanging glacier. (Professor Tremaine's justification for this was that the half-mile walk over the ice would save his party an arduous three-mile trek around the tongue, through an area choked with postglacial vegetation.);*
>
> *(c) His "contemptuous disregard" of suggestions to carry ropes and/or other safety equipment, despite summer conditions that had left an extremely treacherous film of snow obscuring many crevasses.*

Gideon looked up. "You guys have been busy. This is the report Anna Henckel was showing to Pratt and Judd, isn't it?"

John nodded. "Right. Henckel didn't have it, Pratt didn't have it, so I figured the place to look was where she was showing it to him: the bar."

Minor politely demurred. "I do believe that was my suggestion, John."

"Julian, you gotta learn to be less territorial. Anyway, there it was, in one of the stacks of magazines."

"But what does it have to do with Tibbett?" Gideon asked.

"Finish reading it, Doc." He broke a roll from the basket the waitress had brought, buttered it, and leaned back, chewing reflectively.

Gideon and Julie continued with the memo.

> *Appellant stated that he believes his warnings to Professor Tremaine were borne out in the disastrous results of the Tirku expedition, an opinion in which this investigator concurs.*
>
> *However, while it is true that appellant's advice to Professor Tremaine was sound and would, if followed, have resulted in the saving of three lives, it is also true that Park Service personnel must use tact in dealing with members of the public. It is the view of this investigator that the complaint filed by Professor Tremaine on July 25 pertaining to appellant's "obstructive and officious manner" is justified. It is this investigator's further view that a more sensitive and diplomatic attitude on appellant's part would very likely have convinced Professor Tremaine of the need for more vigorous precautions and precluded the needless loss of three lives.*
>
> *Finding: Appellant's termination is sustained.*

"I still don't get it," Gideon said. "What does this have to do with Arthur?"

"I don't get it either," Julie said.

John sighed. "Will you people read the *beginning?*"

This time Gideon read aloud.

DATE: September 24, 1960
TO: Thomas Llewellyn, Assistant Director for Personnel
FROM: Edgar V. Luna, Appeals Mediator
SUBJECT: Appeal of Cornelius H. Tibbett from Termination

The purpose of this—

*"Tibbett?"* Julie said.

Gideon had passed right over it. Not that he was about to admit it to John.

"Bingo," John said, "Tibbett. Finally. Cornelius H. Tibbett was Arthur Tibbett's father. Tell them what you found out, Julian."

Julian folded his well-groomed hands on the table. "Upon losing his job, Cornelius Tibbett returned to New York with his wife and turned to drink, never holding a meaningful job for the rest of his life, which was unhappily brief. In 1962 he jumped in front of the Lexington Avenue IRT at Eighty-sixth Street."

"You're saying," said Julie after a pause, "that this gives Arthur a motive for killing Tremaine?"

"Damn right," John said. "Tremaine gets his father canned, which ruins his career and his life, and two years later the guy kills himself. And the way Arthur probably sees it—hell, the way I see it—is that it was Tremaine that was in the wrong every step of the way."

Julie shook her head. "But, John, Arthur was just a little boy. It was such a long time ago."

"Are you kidding?" John said, laughing. "Compared to the other things we've got to go on, 1962's recent."

"In point of fact," Minor told Julie, "Arthur Tibbett was twenty at the time his father was dismissed."

He continued explaining while they ate their meals. Arthur himself had just begun working for the Park Service as a seasonal ranger in 1960 and had been shattered by what had happened to his father. Throughout much of his subsequent career he'd been obsessed with the idea of someday returning to Glacier Bay in a position of authority; to restore the Tibbett honor, as it were. Two years ago the position of assistant superintendent became vacant. Arthur applied, did well on the examination, and got the job.

"All of this," Minor concluded, "is well known to his colleagues and superiors in Washington, D.C."

"But not to me," John said, "which is what bugs me. Never once did he say anything to me about having a grudge against Tremaine."

"Well, why should he?" Gideon asked. "He achieved his goal, he was satisfied. Why stir it up again? I'd probably have kept it to myself too."

"No, you wouldn't," John said crisply. "Not once Tremaine got killed, you wouldn't. Once that happened it was damn pertinent. You'd have come forward and told the investigating officers. You wouldn't have sat around waiting for us to dig it up by ourselves."

"No, you're right; I would have told you. Arthur should've told you. Still—"

Still what? Now that Gideon thought about it, Tibbett's virulent dislike for Tremaine had come through clearly enough that first evening at dinner. And after Tremaine had been killed, hadn't his mood perked up noticeably? Well, yes, but still—

"Look," John said, "I'm not accusing the guy. I just need

to have a little heart-to-heart with him, that's all. Get a few things straight."

"I'd like to wait on that until tomorrow, if it's all the same," Minor said. "I still have some telephone calls in to Washington on him."

Across the room, the members of Tremaine's group had been leaving one by one, darting glances at the FBI agents. Elliott Fisk remained behind and was now approaching the table.

"Sir?" John said to him.

Fisk held out a thick, flat notebook bound with blue imitation leather; the kind with a little fold-around flap that fitted into a slot on the front to keep the cover closed.

"The journal?" John said.

"I found it under a bird feeder near my door this afternoon. There's a bench next to it and I usually sit there for a few minutes before breakfast." He turned to Gideon. "To plan my day."

Plan his day? At the lodge? What was there to plan?

John took the journal and held it without opening it. "How do you think it got there?"

"Isn't it obvious?"

"You tell me."

"Shirley finished with it and decided to return it after all, for reasons of her own."

"She told you this?"

Fisk gave him a look of scathing incredulity. "Oh, certainly."

"Uh-huh," John said.

"Now, look. I assure you I did *not* accidentally leave it under the bird feeder yesterday morning. I had it with me at breakfast. Dr. Judd can vouch—"

"Okay, I believe you," John said. "Are any pages missing?"

"None."

"Can I hold on to this for now?"

"By all means, do. You'll find it quite interesting, I'm sure."

When Fisk had left, John pulled out the flap and riffled without interest through the pages. The last third were empty, the rest covered with a sloppy, slanting scrawl in blue ink. "The first entry's January 2, 1960. Last is"—more riffling—"July 25, the day before he got killed."

He closed the notebook and slid it to Minor. "Julian, will you have a look through it and see what you find?"

"My pleasure," Minor said. Gideon could smell his cedary cologne as the agent reached for the journal. The dark, neat hand hesitated over the notebook. "Perhaps we'd better go over it for fingerprints first."

"Nah," John said, "don't waste too much time on it. Just read it when you get a chance."

"You don't think there'll be anything important in it?" Julie asked.

John shook his head. "Not if it got returned."

They were on their second cups of coffee when John suddenly snapped his fingers. "Hey, I almost forgot! They found some more bones for you, Doc."

Gideon was caught in the act of putting his coffee cup to his mouth. He managed to avoid spilling any and set the cup back in its saucer. "Bones?"

Julie and John both burst out laughing.

Gideon looked at them, puzzled. "What's funny?"

"You," Julie said. "The way you say 'Bones?' If dogs could talk that's the way they'd say it. I think your ears actually prick."

Gideon shrugged. "I guess I like my work," he said, laughing too.

*"Chacun à son goût,"* said Minor, who hadn't joined in the hilarity.

"Owen's people spent the day on Tirku again," John

explained. "They brought back a box of stuff; mostly pretty ratty-looking. They're in the contact station."

"Are they human?"

"You're asking me?"

Gideon was out of his chair, fishing in his pocket for the key to the station. "I'm going to have a look. Anybody want to come along?"

"Sure," Julie said, standing up too.

"Sure," John said. "Come on, Julian, you'll learn something."

Minor hesitated. "I think I'd better use the time to go through the journal."

"No pots to stir this time," Gideon told him. "I promise."

Minor permitted himself a faint, not-unfriendly smile. "Be that as it may," he said.

# 20

Weasel," Gideon said, tossing a tiny vertebra into the wastepaper basket. "Marten, maybe."

More bones and bone fragments followed. "Goat . . . bird—seagull, probably . . . bear . . . um, elk . . ."

"There aren't any elk around here," Julie said.

"Okay, moose, if you're going to be like that. Cervidae, anyway . . . fox . . . bear . . . bear . . . goat . . . *ah!*"

He held up a flat, twisted piece of bone six or seven inches long and looking something like a dog's rawhide chew.

"Human?" Julie said.

John put one hand to his forehead and pointed at the bone with his other. "Scapula? Wait, wait, I mean, I mean—what the hell do I mean?" He scowled mightily. "Clavicle! Collarbone! Am I right?"

"On the button."

John beamed.

"Why, John," Julie said, "I'm impressed."

He nodded modestly toward Gideon. "Well, you know, I took that class from him in Saint Malo."

"Amazing," Gideon said. "I guess there must be something to this sleep-learning business after all."

"Hey, come on, I wasn't sleeping. I just like to get relaxed. It helps my concentration."

"He was snoring," Gideon told Julie. "Nobody could hear what I was saying. I had to ask the guy next to him to give him a nudge."

Unexpectedly, John broke into one of his brief, gleeful peals of joy. "You know what the guy answered?" he asked Julie. "He said, 'You put him to sleep, you wake him up.'"

"How would you know?" Gideon said. "You were asleep. Okay"—he held the bone out to John—"right or left?"

John spoke with convincing authority. "Right." Then, after a moment: "Left?"

"That narrows it down, all right. Well, they're easy to confuse. But it's a right. And it's adult male."

"I agree," John said soberly.

"I'm relieved to hear it." Gideon had switched on a gooseneck lamp over the counter. He was turning the clavicle over and over directly under the light, tilting it, fingering it, seeing what else it could tell him. Clavicles are not among the most informative of bones, and this one had no visible pathology, no sign of trauma, no unusual genetic variation.

But it did have epiphyses. "I'd put the age at about twenty-five, like everything else we've found. I think we can assume it's another piece of Pratt or Fisk."

He used a sliding caliper to measure the maximum length. "Pretty big," he murmured. "A shade under 172 millimeters."

"How do you tell a clavicle's male?" Julie wanted to know.

"Hey, ask *him,*" John said. He let himself down into the armchair near the counter and stretched comfortably out.

"Pretty much like any other bone," Gideon explained, sliding the caliper closed. "Size . . . robusticity . . . roughness. The bigger and rougher the clavicle, the bigger and more heavily muscled the person it came from. And the bigger and more muscular the person, the better the chance it's a male."

"But—" Julie chewed momentarily on the side of her lip. "I know we've had this discussion before, but—well, there are a lot of women around who are bigger and stronger than a lot of men, aren't there? There are women athletes, women weight lifters—"

"She's right, Doc," John said. "And don't forget about steroids. Women take steroids these days, too."

Gideon shook his head. "Steroids make bones thicker but not longer. In fact, they're as likely to stunt them as anything else. They make for premature ossification, so the bones stop growing before they should. Anyway, we're not talking about 'these days.' This is from 1960; there weren't too many women taking steroids in 1960."

"Yeah, he's right," John said to Julie. "Not a hell of a lot of female weight lifters then either."

"I wasn't thinking of weight lifters," Julie said. "I was thinking of Jocelyn Yount; six feet tall, athletic—and killed in the avalanche. Why not her?"

Gideon shook his head. "This clavicle's male. Take my word for it, people."

Julie looked at John. "Does he always get this defensive?"

"Yeah," John said. "Usually."

"Who's getting defensive?" Gideon asked. "You have to remember, I've had tons of experience with this stuff, I've looked at a zillion clavicles—"

"The last resort of the pedant," Julie said scornfully.

"Oh, hell, I wouldn't say that," John said equably. "I mean, how can you argue with 'Take my word for it, I've looked at a zillion clavicles'?"

Properly humbled, Gideon raised his hands in submission. "All right, I'm sorry. You're right. I admit, I can't *know* this is a male clavicle. Unless you have a pelvis, you can't be a hundred percent sure, but I'd still bet money on it. Look, it's true that there are a lot of women around who are taller than most men—"

"Jocelyn Yount, for example," Julie said, "and her sister Shirley too."

"My wife," John said. "Marti's practically as tall as I am."

"Right," Gideon said, nodding, "and maybe her legs are as long as yours, or her arms, or her ribs, but some things aren't as big."

"Her feet, for instance," Julie said. "No offense, John."

"I was thinking of her shoulders," Gideon said. "Women's shoulders are narrower than men's, and it's a question of genes, not exercise. You have to look a long, long time before you find a woman, no matter how big, whose shoulders are as broad as even the average guy's. I mean a *long* time. Maybe the female shot-putting champion of the Soviet Union has shoulders like this, but that's about it."

Julie and John looked confused. "Shoulders like what?" Julie asked. "What do shoulders have to do with anything?"

Gideon held up the bone. "Look. This clavicle's 172 millimeters long. That's a good three standard deviations above the female norm. Your chance of finding a woman with a clavicle like this is well under half of one percent."

"I still don't get it," John said. "You're saying how wide your shoulders are depends on how big your clavicle is?"

"The clavicle runs from the sternum—here, at the middle of the upper chest—over the top and out to the scapula, the shoulder blade. And what it does is act as a strut to keep that shoulder blade pushed out to the side and back. Long clavicles, wide shoulders; short clavicles, narrow shoulders."

"Is that right?"

"Sure. Without those little things our arms would be lying flat against the walls of our chests. We wouldn't be able to rotate them. They'd just be able to go pretty much back and forth, like a dog's front legs. Look at a dog's shoulders. Or a cow's, or a horse's."

"Yeah," John said, fingering the path of his own clavicle. "Wait a minute, a cow doesn't even have shoulders. I mean, not like a person."

"Aha," Gideon said.

"No clavicle?"

"No clavicle."

"Son of a gun." John grinned, pleased, as he always was, to pick up another arcane osteological tidbit.

"This is all very interesting," Julie said, "but you said a minute ago there was a half-of-one-percent chance—"

"I said less than a half-of-one-percent chance."

"—that a clavicle like this *could* come from a woman. That means you can't be absolutely positive—"

"I never said I was absolutely positive." Well, not in so many words. "Science is never absolutely positive," he added virtuously.

"Wait, she's right, Doc," John said, having trouble deciding which side he was on. "For all you know, this just happens to belong to a women's Olympic shot-putting champ. How do you know it doesn't?"

Gideon shrugged. "If this just happens to belong to a women's Olympic shot-putting champ," he said, "then I'm in big trouble."

But it couldn't and he wasn't. This was a male clavicle. He'd examined zillions of them.

* * *

On this particular morning even the aroma of newly brewed coffee failed to get a reaction from Julie. Gideon put the tray on the nightstand and sat on the edge of the bed. He pulled the cover a few inches down from her chin. She stirred, almost imperceptibly. With his fingertips he gently stroked the front of her smooth, bare shoulder.

"Now you," he said, "have extraordinarily lovely clavicles. Especially this one right here." He leaned over to kiss it.

"Coffee," she mumbled. Her eyes were still closed.

He kissed the tender recess just beneath her shoulder, touching it lightly with his tongue and thinking about working his way down.

"Coffee," she said.

He laughed, kissed her chin, and sat up. "I'm not overstimulating you, am I? Just let me know if I am."

It was what he deserved for forgetting priorities. He poured cups of coffee for both of them, and put hers in her hand once she'd managed to pull herself up almost to a sitting position.

She gulped, gave him a closed-mouthed, closed-eyed grin of pleasure, and took another swallow. "I've been wondering about Jocelyn Yount," she said suddenly, just when he thought she was drifting off again. "Maybe I've been dreaming about her. About the mystery of her bones."

"Have some more coffee."

"No, I'm awake." She forced her eyes tentatively open to prove it. "Where are they?"

"Where are Jocelyn Yount's bones?"

"Yes. You haven't found any, have you?"

"No, just male fragments."

"And neither did Dr. Worriner, did he?"

"That's true. Well, there are a few that can't be sexed, so we don't know."

"But everything that can be identified is male. Doesn't that strike you as odd? Why don't we have any of her bones?"

"Julie, there's nothing odd about it at all. It's amazing that we recovered anything from any of them. I mean, having them pop out of a glacier thirty years after an avalanche? Besides, I thought you were going to leave this to the pros."

"Mm. Well." She yawned and stuck out her empty cup.

Gideon filled it. "Okay, what are you thinking?" He was always interested in what she had to say, even when she wasn't a hundred percent awake. Julie had a way of coming at problems from shrewd, offbeat angles, raising questions and opening up perspectives that were surprising and often helpful.

Not this time. "I was thinking," she said, "that maybe the reason you didn't find any bones is that she wasn't killed."

"But you read what Tremaine said. He saw the crevasse close up over her."

"That's what he said. That doesn't make it true. Don't forget what Julian said: 'Who is there to argue with him?'"

"Well, all right, that's a point."

"Of course it is," Julie said, warming to the idea. "Maybe she got away alive and came back thirty years later to kill Tremaine to—um, to keep him quiet about what *really* happened on the glacier."

"Which was?"

"Who knows? Maybe that she was the killer, not James Pratt. Maybe Tremaine lied about the whole thing in his book, only of course Jocelyn wouldn't know that. Maybe . . ." She drained her second cup and thought for a few seconds. "Am I being a little fanciful, would you say?"

"Just a little. Aside from a logical inconsistency or two,

Tirku is forty miles from anything approaching civilization, and that's by water. By land it'd be three times that, if you could get there over the mountains at all. How could she possibly have made it off the glacier alive?"

"I don't know," Julie said.

"And where was she all these years?"

"Don't know."

"And how could she get here to the lodge, to his room, without anybody knowing about it? Nobody saw any strangers, remember? Sorry, it won't fly."

Julie's enthusiasm for the idea had visibly diminished. She put her cup on the nightstand, shaking her head. "I think maybe I *was* dreaming."

He reached for the pot. "Want some more?"

"Uh-uh. Hey, was somebody kissing my shoulder before, or was that a dream too?" She slipped her hand into the open front of his bathrobe and ran it down his chest. "Nice dream."

Gideon put the pot back on the nightstand and leaned toward her to take up where he'd left off, nuzzling the soft skin below her shoulder, gently working the sheet down. "Have I ever told you," he murmured, "what terrific infraclavicular fossae you have?"

"Mm," she said, "I love it when you talk dirty."

# 21

John turned out to be right about Fisk's diary. "Nothing in it," Minor told them, using his knife to scrape boysenberry jam from a foil packet and spread a thin layer on his wheat toast. "Just fragmentary rantings and ravings about a wide variety of subjects: alleged thefts of his ideas by Tremaine and others; unpleasant remarks about many people, of whom his fiancée was only one; self-inflating juvenile anecdotes. Hyperbolic rodomantade of the most puerile type. If you will."

"Come again?" John said.

"Hyperbolic rodomantade of the most puerile type."

"Don't forget to put that in your report," John said.

"There wasn't anything to connect to Tremaine's murder?" Julie asked.

"Not in my opinion," said Minor.

"Nothing in the journal, nothing in Tremaine's manuscript," Gideon muttered. "What are we missing?"

"Damn," John said abruptly, "we're not getting anywhere. Today's already Friday. You realize everybody leaves tomorrow?" He shoved aside the dish that had held his sausage and eggs and gloomily reached for a monstrous bear-claw cinnamon roll that overhung its plate at each end.

"That won't affect our investigation," Minor said. "We can get hold of them when we need to."

"It won't make it any easier, Julian."

Conversation halted as Shirley Yount came in and went through the buffet line a few feet from them. With her tray loaded, she gave them an awkward nod and went to a table across the room, as far away as she could get.

Julie, who had been watching her with an odd intensity, suddenly sat bolt-upright and clamped her hand on Gideon's forearm.

"She was here all along, that's how!" She turned toward John and Minor, keeping her voice down with an effort. "That's how she could get into his room without being noticed!"

"What's this we're talking about?" John asked, chewing pastry.

"Jocelyn! She could have been right here at the lodge all along."

"Oh-oh," Gideon said.

"Jocelyn," echoed Minor. "Jocelyn Yount?" Then, after a fractional pause: "I'm not sure I take your meaning."

"Julie has this thing about Jocelyn," Gideon explained. "She seems to think it was Jocelyn who killed Tremaine, that she wasn't killed on the glacier."

"Yesterday it was Pratt," Minor observed mildly.

"Killed Tremaine!" John said fiercely, then quickly lowered his voice. "Now how the hell—"

"There's no real proof that Jocelyn's dead," Julie said. "None of her bones have turned up."

"Is that right, Doc?"

"That's right, none that we know of," Gideon said abstractedly. He thought he knew where Julie was headed, and this time "offbeat" hardly did it justice.

"Which means," Julie said, "that she could still be alive."

"All right, sure, she could be," John said reluctantly.

"For the sake of argument," Minor interposed.

"But how could she kill Tremaine? How could she get here without anybody seeing her? We're really talking boonies here, Julie. There aren't exactly any crowds to melt into. And nobody saw anybody who wasn't supposed to be here."

"I know, but they saw *Shirley.*" Julie jerked her head impatiently, as John and Minor continued to look at her with tolerant incomprehension. "Maybe I'm not being very clear. Look, how do we know that woman over there is Shirley Yount? How do we know it isn't her sister Jocelyn?"

"No," John said, "it won't wash. Tremaine, Judd, Henckel—they all knew Jocelyn. They'd recognize her."

"Would they? It's been thirty years. They were twin sisters."

"Not identical twins," John said.

"Even so, everybody would expect them to look alike. And from what you told us, Shirley does look like Jocelyn."

"I take your point," Minor said.

"Yeah," John said thoughtfully. "I take your point."

"In fact," Julie said, heartened, "for all we know, maybe Jocelyn never *had* a twin sister. Maybe the whole thing was made up just for this."

Minor shook his head. "In point of fact, I'm afraid not. Shirley Yount quite definitely exists. She's been employed by Montgomery Ward for twenty-two years. She has a valid Social Security number, a driver's license—"

"Those can be faked," Julie said, like an old hand at false IDs. "Maybe after the avalanche she took on another identity, maybe—" She stopped with a laugh. "How do I get myself into these positions? All right, forget it. I hereby retire from the case. Again."

All the same, as if on signal, the four of them cast lidded, sidewise glances at Shirley, who was at that moment staring emptily across the misted cove and shoving a quarter of a buttermilk donut into her mouth with a large and spatulate thumb.

The Jocelyn-as-Shirley theory failed to survive the day. At 3:30 P.M. the *Spirit of Adventure* returned with Julie and the other trainees, back from their final field session; with Frannie and Russ, who had put in some more bone hunting; and with a small box of bone fragments. Pickings had been slimmer today. At Frannie's request, Gideon had given her a copy of Bass's *Human Osteology* field manual, and the ranger had been able to eliminate most of the nonhuman material herself. There were only three objects in the box. One was the sacrum of a large bird. One was the partial skeleton of a bear's foot, still held together by dried-out ligaments. And one was a complete human femur.

Jocelyn Yount's right thigh bone.

"It has to be," Gideon said half an hour afterward. "It's from an adult female, somewhere in her mid-twenties, obviously well muscled. Tall too, it looks like. Let's see . . ." He slid the adjustable segment of the osteometric board up against the end of the bone. "Maximum morphological length is 53 centimeters. Yeah, she's going to be big, all right." He flipped open the cover of his pocket calculator and punched in the Trotter and Gleser formula to calculate overall stature from the femur. "Yup, that's what I thought." More key-clicking to convert from centimeters to inches. "Estimated height between 71.37 and 74.30 inches."

He looked up from the calculator to Julie, who was

sipping tea and lounging deservedly in the contact station's only armchair after her day on the ice field. "Tall."

She was frowning over the rim of her cup at the long, gracefully bowed bone. "Can I ask a question, or will you go all defensive on me again?"

"I?" Gideon said. "Defensive?"

"Well, yesterday you said that, basically, the way you tell male bones from female bones is that the male ones are bigger and more rugged. Right?"

"Right."

"But here you have a big bone, a rugged bone, and what's your conclusion? That it's a big, rugged woman. I don't get it. Why isn't it a man?"

"If that's all I had to go on, you'd have a point. Fortunately, the femur has some good sex criteria of its own. Lateral pitch, for instance." He stood the bone upright on the board, resting it on the condyles, the smooth, rounded upper surface of the knee joint. "See how the bone tilts instead of standing straight up and down, when I just let it rest naturally? Well, that happens to be a seventy-six-degree angle. Anything lower than eighty is probably a female, and seventy-six is a near certainty."

She sighed. "I guess it's easy when you know how."

"And why. That inward tilt is there because women have wider hips than men, so they have to be built more knock-kneed to get their feet back under them."

"Watch it, Oliver," Julie warned.

"In a most attractive manner, of course," he added sincerely. "I wouldn't have it any other way."

Julie's openly skeptical reply was interrupted by Russ's arrival at the door. "Dr. Oliver? Ma'am? Mr. Lau sent me to look for you. The press conference started half an hour ago, and they have some questions for you. They're getting sort of impatient."

"Damn," Gideon said, laying the femur down, "I forgot all about it. Let's go."

They followed Russ up the path to the lodge at a trot. Julie, normally a faster jogger than Gideon, lagged a few steps behind.

Concerned, Gideon slowed. "Is anything wrong?"

"Oh, no," she said sweetly, "but running's not that easy when you're thick-hipped and knock-kneed."

Silence seemed the wisest response.

The sun had come out for the first time in almost a week, hanging twenty degrees above the hazy Fairweathers, flat and wan, but still able to burnish the air with a welcome, golden tinge of warmth. The meeting was being held outside, on the broad wooden deck at one end of the main building, and the attendees seemed less interested in the subject matter than in the sunlight. Folding fabric lawn chairs had been pulled into an arc facing the sun, and most of the people in them had their eyes closed and their faces tipped gratefully up.

It was an unusual press conference in that respondents outnumbered reporters. There were, in fact, only four journalists taking part: one reporter from the *Ketchikan Daily*, one from the *Juneau Empire*, and two wire-service stringers. The other two media people were a television crew from Anchorage who, having completed their filming for the day, were unashamedly sprawled on their backs on the bench that ran around the edges of the deck, soaking up sunshine. Tremaine's crew sat in attitudes ranging from detachment and indifference (Anna and Shirley, respectively), through boredom (Fisk) and glassy-eyed woolgathering (Pratt), to outright sleep (Judd).

John, his broad face up to the sun, was sitting next to Minor, his chair tipped back against the sun-drenched wall of the lodge, his interest level somewhere between Pratt's and Judd's.

One reason for all this lethargy was the unaccustomed effect of the sunlight. The other was Arthur Tibbett, who was holding forth and apparently had been at it for some time.

"Ah, here he is now," he said as Gideon and Julie arrived and took chairs at the end of the semicircle. "You can ask him yourselves."

The reporters turned their chairs to get a better look at Gideon. Notebook pages were flipped. A tape recorder was turned on.

"I've been telling them about your exploits," Arthur said, preening.

"Is it true that you've identified the murdered man from 1960 as Steven Fisk?" The speaker was one of the wire-service people, a thin-lipped, severe woman who spoke with a cigarette jouncing at the corner of her mouth and her eyes narrowed against the smoke.

"Yes, it is."

"There's no doubt in your mind?"

"No." The episode of the four-foot freaks had taught him to keep his remarks to the press short.

"Why do you think Professor Tremaine was murdered?"

Gideon spread his hands.

"Are there any suspects?"

Yes, and all of them were sitting within ten feet of her. Gideon glanced at them and saw John do the same thing from under half-closed lids. None of them did anything helpful, like making a run for it, or breaking into a sweat, or even stiffening guiltily.

"No idea," he said.

"But you think there's a connection between the murders?"

"Beats me."

The front legs of John's chair came lazily down on the deck. "Dr. Oliver's an anthropologist, not a cop," he said good-humoredly. "If you have questions about the murders, I'm the one to ask."

"All right, then," the woman answered curtly, "*is* there a connection?"

"Beats me," John said.

The reporter threw a poisonous look at him, a disgusted one at Gideon, and pointedly closed her notebook.

"I have a question," said a gangling kid of about twenty-two. He put a hand up to his mouth and coughed. "C. L. Crowdy of the *Empire*," he murmured, blushing. "Mr. Tibbett said that another human bone was found at the glacier today—"

"A right femur," Tibbett interrupted helpfully. "That's the thigh bone. F-e-m-u-r. Dr. Oliver's just come from the contact station, where he's been working on it. We've set up a lab for him there, and it's worked out very well. Hasn't it, Gideon?"

"Yes, it has, Arthur."

"Thank you, sir," C. L. Crowdy said. "Dr. Oliver, are you able to tell us anything about this latest find? Do you know whose leg bone it is?"

Gideon hesitated. He couldn't think of any reason to keep to himself the knowledge that they had found Jocelyn Yount's femur, but he couldn't think of any reason why the reporters needed to know, or the members of Tremaine's party, either, or Tibbett, for that matter. He was less sanguine than John about all of them sitting in on the meeting. From his point of view, it paid to keep a few steps ahead of one's suspects.

"No, I don't," he said.

"You can't even tell if it's a man or a woman?"

"No, I can't. Well, not yet. I've hardly begun my analysis. It takes time, you see, and I don't have all my tools with me, of course, and I . . ." He made himself trail off. He was an infrequent liar and a poor one. When he wasn't telling the truth he tended to babble. And, like young Crowdy, to blush, dammit. Casually, he put his hand over his warm forehead.

The *Ketchikan Daily* reporter, a beefy, bearded man with an eye patch, jumped in. "Sorry, but that's pretty hard to swallow, Professor. You're the Skeleton Detective. We've all read about what you can do."

"You can't believe everything you read in the papers," Gideon said with a smile, but the reporters didn't seem to find it funny. Maybe it was time to just shut up.

Tibbett came to his rescue. "Dr. Oliver's going to be delighted to learn that he has one more tool than he thought he had. I've managed to borrow an accurate double-beam balance scale from the university." He beamed at Gideon. "It'll be in the contact station tomorrow morning."

"A what?" one of the reporters asked without enthusiasm. A balance scale, Tibbett told them, with which Dr. Oliver would be able to apply certain regression equations (that was r-e-g-r-e-s-s-i-o-n) that would permit him to tell which bones went with which, so that he would know just who was represented in the Tirku remains.

Apparently Tibbett had forgotten that all but two of the bones were now in the FBI evidence room in Juneau, but there wasn't any reason to correct him. The reporters hadn't even bothered to write it down.

There was only one more question for Gideon, some twenty minutes later. C. L. Crowdy, the *Empire*'s loose-jointed, six-foot-three correspondent, wanted to know if—human beings being what they were—there would have to be nondiscrimination laws to protect tall people by A.D. 2050.

# 22

If you ask me . . . *nngh* . . . Arthur was looking pretty chipper . . . *gghh* . . . at that press conference," Julie said from the bathroom, the observation punctuated by the sounds of dental floss at work. "And later too, when he made his cute little farewell speech at dinner." She stuck her head briefly into the room, holding the strand between her thumbs. "I mean, for a man who's under suspicion of murder."

Gideon was sitting on the bed, his shoes off, leaning against the headboard with his fingers laced behind his head. They had dined with Bill Bianco and the search-and-rescue class, a long, convivial final dinner with coffee, cordials, and speeches afterwards—the cordials provided on the house by Mr. Granle. Whether this was out of gratitude for their patronage or relief that nothing even more ghastly had happened during their stay, no one knew.

"He doesn't know he's under suspicion of anything."

She was back in the bathroom. "John didn't . . . *ngh* . . . have that little heart-to-heart with him?"

I must really be in love, he thought. I even like the sound of her flossing her teeth. Something downright homey about it. When you tidy up your gingivae in each other's presence you must be in it for the long haul, all right.

"There's no hurry," he said. "Arthur lives here. He doesn't go home with the rest of us. Julian wanted to get his information in order before they talk to him."

She came out of the bathroom in a brief flannel shift, sturdy and curvy and scrubbed-looking.

"You," he said, "are as cute as a button."

This was deservedly ignored. "Could you really do what he said—figure out which bones go with which by weighing them?"

"Yes, with a little luck. But I don't see that it matters much anymore; not forensically, at least. Anyway, I dropped off most of the bones in Juneau. All I have left in the shack are the femur they found yesterday and the clavicle—damn." He swung his legs off the bed, slipped into his loafers, and pulled his jacket down from the clothes rack. "I'll be back in ten minutes."

"Where are you going?"

"I just realized—when we ran off to the press conference I never closed the window in the contact station. I better go shut it. Those bones are just sitting there on the counter." He rummaged in the dresser until he found their flashlight.

"What could happen to them?"

"Who knows? Raccoons, maybe even a dog . . . Those things belong in Owen's safe."

"I suppose, but what can you do about it now? It's after

ten o'clock. Owen's one of those early risers; he's probably in bed. You really want to wake him up?"

"I can bring them back here."

"Gideon, if you think I'm sleeping in the same room with somebody's clavicle—"

"Julie," he said, laughing, "I'm not planning to put them in bed with us. I'll stick them in the bottom drawer."

"On my sweaters? Forget it."

"Okay, I'll give them to the night clerk to go into the hotel safe. How's that?"

"Fine." She gave him a crooked little smile. "You might want to put them in a plain brown wrapper first."

The night air felt wonderful. Windless and moist. Crisp, and clean, and mossy-smelling, with a faint, nose-tickling tang of salt water. Gideon walked slowly along the wooded path, breathing in the primal, uncomplicated fragrances with pleasure, enjoying the thought that he was on some of the newest, freshest land on earth, out from under its icy mantle for only two centuries. He paused where the path came out of the woods onto the beach, and stood looking across the moonlit cove. A dense, still fog lay on the surface of the water, covering it like a skin of cotton. He shone the flashlight onto it, watching the beam bounce away into the trees on the other side.

When he'd put the bones safely away, maybe he could convince Julie to throw on some clothes and come back out with him. They could walk to the end of the pier and sit on the edge with their feet dangling; maybe drop in a few pebbles, watch them drill holes in the fog sheet, listen to the hollow plunk they made when they hit the water. They could lie back on the cool planks and look at the sky. A gauzy layer of clouds had moved in a few hours earlier, turning the stars to furry dots, like distant lamplights on a foggy night. He didn't think it was going to take much convincing.

The contact station was just a few steps farther along the shore. He flicked the beam of his flashlight at the shack, confirming that he had indeed left the side window open, and hopped up onto the wooden porch in front, searching for the key. The floor creaked beneath him. Inside there was a faint, answering creak. He found the key in the first pocket he looked in and turned it in the lock, then paused. An answering creak? *Had* an animal gotten in? Or maybe not an animal at all? The skin on the back of his neck prickled. He turned on the flashlight and shone it through the front window, playing the beam over the floor and the sparse furniture. Nothing. He went around to the side and aimed it through the open window. Everything was perfectly still. The beam lit up the clavicle and femur on the counter, just where he'd left them.

Well, of course. What had he been expecting? What would anyone want with them? There was nothing of forensic importance in them, no information that anyone had any conceivable reason to fear. The danger was animals, not people, and there weren't any animals in there. He let out his breath and went back to the front to open the door, feeling a little ridiculous. But also a little jumpy. He reached prudently inside to turn on the lights with his left hand, the right hand holding the flashlight.

He never got to the switch. The half-open door was driven against him with nerve-jarring force, the force of a human body flinging itself onto it. Fortunately he took the brunt of the blow on his shoulder, but still the edge of the door slammed his forearm against the jamb, sending a tooth-rattling jolt of pain from fingertips to jaw. He stumbled backwards onto the porch, the flashlight dropping to the floor inside the room and blinking out.

He doubled over, sucking in his breath, eyes streaming,

cradling his arm against his chest. His hand was numb, as heavy as concrete. *Not broken,* the rational gray matter of his cerebral cortex was smoothly assuring him. *Merely a sharp blow taken directly on the "funny bone," that exquisitely sensitive spot where the ulnar nerve lies directly on the bony medial epicondyle of the humerus just below the skin. Discomfort acute but short-lived. Not to worry.*

*Merely, hell!* the primitive, raging brain stem structures of his limbic system shrieked back. *That sonofabitch on the other side of the door just tried to break your fucking arm! Go get that mother!*

*I think we'd just better think this through, don't you?* his cortex sneered predictably. *That person on the other side of that door may well be armed. Wouldn't it make more sense to—*

For once Gideon went with his brain stem. Snarling half in pain and half in anger, pressing his arm to his side, he threw himself in a flying kick at the door, which was slightly open and still shuddering with the force of the impact against his arm.

Unfortunately, the sonofabitch on the other side of the door wasn't there. In the second or so that it had taken Gideon to react, he or she had stepped to the side. The door sprang unresistingly open to bang against the wall, and Gideon came flying through. His foot came down on the flashlight barrel, which spurted out from under his sole and sent him careening the length of the room until he was brought up short by the counter, the edge of which caught him painfully below the rib cage on the left side.

Meanwhile the door had rebounded to clatter shut again. The room was completely dark, utterly, startlingly silent after all the noisy door-banging and galumphing over the wooden floor. Whoever had slammed the door on him was still in the room; there had been no time for anyone to slip out. *Who's there?* almost sprang from Gideon's lips. *Where are you?* But he held back. Whoever it was couldn't see any better than he could. Why broadcast where he was? Quietly, he shifted his body away from the counter and turned back to face the area near the door, balancing his weight evenly over his feet, getting ready for whatever came next.

As usual, his cerebral cortex had been correct; the searing pain in his arm had been short-lived. Already it was becoming a buzzing, bearable tingle. He breathed quietly, shallowly, through his mouth, standing perfectly still, a little crouched, his hands away from his sides. Let the other person make the first move, the first sound.

The first sound was a soft click, followed by a burst of light; dazzling, pulsing, blinding concentric rings of white. Whoever it was had a flashlight of his own, a powerful one, and was beaming it into his face from a couple of yards away, fluttering it to keep him blinded. The floor creaked as the other person moved forward. Gideon narrowed his eyes to a squint and strained to see between his out-thrust fingers, but the brilliant, darting light seemed to fill his eyeballs, his skull. He could see only his own backlit hands and wrists, raised as if in supplication, exposed and vulnerable. There was another creak. The wobbling, blazing circles moved closer, full of menace. Was there a gun, a knife, a club in the other hand?

Gideon's cerebral cortex had no pertinent advice for him. He did the only thing he could think of, which was to launch himself at the light, or rather just below it, arms spread, hoping to get them around a body. But the person holding it was a step ahead of him. The flashlight was apparently being held well off to the side. Gideon's forearm brushed against what felt like a hip, but his arms closed around nothing, and he fell heavily to the floor, immediately going into a roll and scrambling toward the light again.

It went abruptly out, leaving him trying to blink away

the afterimages, then came on again a foot or two to the left. Was it farther away? Closer? He lashed out at it from his knees, feeling like an animal caught in a net of illumination, unable to get at its captors. The light went out as he thrust at it, and came on almost at once, a little more to the right. Out again. On again.

An abrupt rustling sound, a sudden movement.

Out again.

*Chug, chug, chug, chug.* Slowly, the train slipped peacefully away into the darkness, the steady beat of the wheels lulling him into a . . .

Train?

Gideon opened his eyes. He was lying on his back on the floor of the contact station, a few feet from the open door, with a throbbing head and an upset stomach. Rolling his eyes gingerly upward, he could see the narrow black tops of spruce and hemlock trees framed in the doorway against the not-quite-as-black sky. He realized at once that he had been unconscious only a few seconds; the chugging noise was running footsteps on the path back to the lodge. He could still hear them, or rather the sounds of someone mounting the wooden stairs leading to the main building and the boardwalks that led to the rooms.

He knew better than to try to give chase. It was going to be a few minutes before his legs would be able to take him anywhere; before the rest of him would *want* to go anywhere. He wiggled his fingers, moved his toes. His nervous system seemed to be working all right. When he became aware of a hot, wet stinging at the left corner of his chin, he touched it with a finger. It was nothing awful; a small, raw scrape coated with a thin ooze of serous fluid and maybe a little blood. That was where he'd been hit, then. Probably with the flashlight. Not over the head, but on the jaw, the way a boxer was knocked out.

That was fortunate; less likelihood of real damage this way. The mobile jaw automatically swiveled away from the force of a blow, diffusing it in a way that the more rigid cranium couldn't. All in all, he was sure he hadn't been seriously hurt. He felt no worse—no better either—than the couple of times he'd been knocked out several lifetimes ago when he was working his way through graduate school by boxing in local fight clubs. The disorientation and nausea were to be expected. And the fact that he couldn't remember the blow that had knocked him out was no cause for concern. That was normal. A transient axial distortion of the brain stem caused by a blow to the chin, which is what a knockout is, almost always resulted in retrograde amnesia that—

"Ah, shut up," he mumbled half aloud. Christ, what he didn't need now was another lecture from his cerebral cortex. Grunting, he pushed himself up on one elbow and waited, eyes closed, for the queasiness to subside a little. After a minute, he got cautiously to his feet. Everything ached, not just his jaw, but that was hardly a surprise. He switched on the ceiling lights and went to the counter. No surprise there either.

The bones were gone.

# 23

It's 9:00 A.M.," Julie said in his ear. "Do you really want to get up, or would you rather sleep some more?"

"Up," Gideon mumbled into the pillow. "If I sleep any more, I won't be able to move at all."

Softly she stroked the side of his head with the back of her fingers. "How's your jaw?"

Gideon gave the question some thought. "My jaw's okay," he said finally. "The rest of me feels like hell."

I know, I know, he told his cerebral cortex. Generalized malaise and stiffness went along with postconcussive trauma reactions. Big deal.

"Nothing to worry about," he said. "I'm just a little achy." He opened his eyes. Julie, already dressed, was sitting in an armchair she'd pulled to the side of the bed.

"Coffee's on," she said. "Want some?"

"Uh-huh. Maybe a couple of aspirin, too."

While she got them he worked up to a sitting position

against the headboard and checked himself over more thoroughly. His shoulder and arm were all right. The scrape on his jaw was not much worse than a razor burn. Only the area on his left side, at the base of his ribs—where he'd bounced off the counter—was truly sore, and that wasn't as bad as it would have been had Julie not made him press some towel-wrapped ice to it when he'd gotten back to the room. He probed it with his fingers, flinching when he pressed too hard. It didn't feel as if anything were broken, but maybe he'd cracked that twelfth rib. Best to have it x-rayed when he got back home. Not that there was anything to do about a cracked twelfth rib anyway, other than wrapping it with one of those awkward canvas belts for a month. He leaned against the headboard, tipping his head back, muttering to himself. God, he was getting just a little old for this.

He made himself get out of bed—otherwise he'd really stiffen up—got into his bathrobe, groaning under his breath, and shuffled carefully to the table and chairs near the window. It was a pearly, northern kind of day, gray but drenched with light. He grasped the arms of a chair and lowered himself slowly into it.

Julie poured the coffee, watching him settle creakily down. "Gideon, does it ever occur to you that for a scholarly type you lead a—well, a rather physical sort of life?"

"Yes, it does. I was just thinking about that myself. I don't know why it is. It's not as if I invite it."

"Mm," she said noncommittally, watching him down the aspirin and start on the coffee. "John stopped in about twenty minutes ago. He's been talking to all of them."

He looked up from the cup. "Has he gotten anywhere? Does he know—"

She shook her head. "No more than he did last night."

Which wasn't much. The three of them had sat around

the room for almost two hours trying to make sense of things. John had briefly considered a late-night search of the Tremaine party's rooms (on a voluntary basis; they had no warrants), but they had agreed there was no point. What would he be looking for? The chance that the person who had taken the bones had brought them back to his or her room was nil. They had probably been tossed into the thick woods, or buried under some brush or in a rotted log, or thrown into the cove itself.

So Gideon had lain back on the bed, holding the ice to his ribs, while John, with an attention to detail that was new to Gideon, had him describe three separate times what had happened in the shack. Then they had fruitlessly tossed around ideas on what anyone could have wanted with the bones. At midnight Julie finally threw John out, settled Gideon down, and turned out the lights.

Now she poured some coffee for herself and sat down next to him at the table, pursing her lips, frowning into her cup.

"Okay, let's hear it," he said brightly. Making it to the chair without hurting anything had cheered him up.

She looked at him. "Hear what?"

"Your new theory."

"What makes you—"

"Your expression. When you purse your lips like that it means something is being hatched."

She eyed him, her head cocked. "We've been married too long."

"Not hardly. Come on, let's hear it."

"Well . . ." She hesitated. "I keep coming back to Jocelyn and whether or not she's dead."

He smiled at her. "No one's ever going to accuse you of prematurely giving up on a hypothesis. How can she not be dead? We've finally gotten ourselves a female femur—or at least we *had* a female femur. Whose else could it be?"

"No, I was looking at it differently this time; the other way around. That femur is the only real evidence that Jocelyn *is* dead, right? Maybe somebody took it to get rid of that evidence."

"To get rid of the evidence that she was killed? What for?"

"I don't know, but why else would anyone take it? There wasn't anything special about it, was there? Just that it was female."

"Yes, but nobody knew that except you and me. Remember, at the press conference I told them I hadn't sexed it yet."

"All right, then, maybe they were trying to keep you from finding out. Maybe—"

"Julie, how would *they* know it was female?"

"Well, then . . ." She stretched and laughed. "You sure take all the fun out of it. Okay, what's *your* theory?"

"Oh, no, I'm not even trying to come up with a theory. I'll just stick to what I'm good at: pointing out the flaws in yours. You know what? I'm hungry."

"Good. John went to the dining room to get us all some breakfast. I could tell you'd be waking up in a few minutes, and I knew some food would do you good."

"How could you tell I'd be waking up in a few minutes?"

"Oh, you make these noises when you're starting to wake up."

"Like what?"

"Snork, unk, mrmp. Like that."

He made a face. "You're right; we've been married too long."

He had just finished getting into his loosest shirt and trousers when John got back.

"Hey, Doc, you look great; halfway human again. Breakfast is on the way. Ham and eggs okay?"

"Ham and eggs sounds wonderful." Gideon lowered

himself into the chair again, somewhat less stiffly than the first time. The aspirins were working, and moving around had loosened him up. "Julie says you haven't been getting much of anywhere."

"Not so's you'd notice. But I'm starting to get some ideas. That's what I wanted to talk to you about."

He had barely sat down when there was a double tap on the door. He got up to admit Cheri, the sunny, skinny waitress who'd been serving them at dinner.

"You guys must rate," she said. "We don't usually do room service." She edged in sideways to clear the big metal tray on her shoulder, then stooped in a fluid, practiced movement, to put it on the table as smoothly and noiselessly as a professional bowler lays down a ball.

"Ham and eggs, ham and eggs, ham and eggs," she said, pulling the covers off the plates and setting them out. "O.J. all around. Sourdough toast. Coffee. That do it?"

"Looks great," John said. "Thanks, Cheri." He rummaged in his wallet and came up with two dollar bills. "Wait a second. Doc, you got another couple of bucks? All I have is a twenty."

But Gideon was sitting as if suddenly turned to stone, staring hard at nothing, and it was Julie who had to supply the bills. "He's oblivious again," she said matter-of-factly to John. "Can't you tell from his eyes?"

And he was. When Cheri had come in lugging that heavy tray, something in his mind had popped open like a box. Theories, and hypotheses, and guesses all spilled out at the same time and fell into new niches. He'd had it all wrong. He'd been miles from the right questions, let alone the right answers. If not for Cheri he'd still be miles away.

He'd made a mistake, a bad one; he and Dr. Worriner both. They had failed to follow the advice they'd given hundreds of students. Don't jump to conclusions. Never assign sex, age, or anything else on the basis of a single indicator. Well, they'd jumped. Worriner had shown him two partial left humeri in Juneau, both identified as male, and Gideon had agreed with the identification. He had also agreed with the conclusion: The bones belonged to Steven Fisk and James Pratt, the only two males caught in the landslide.

Wrong. Wrong because one of those arm bones wasn't male at all. That piece with the prominent, rugged, oh-so-obviously masculine deltoid tuberosity . . . was *female*. He was ready to bet on that now, thanks to Cheri. Because—how had he allowed himself to forget?—there *was* one kind of habitual activity that could do that to a woman's humerus. Oh, there were plenty of things that would develop the bone overall, but just one, as far as he knew, that would exaggerate *only* the deltoid tuberosity without also developing the other muscle insertion points.

Waiting tables. Lifting trays, year after year, with the time-honored technique Cheri had been using all week. Male or female, anyone who hefted those thirty-pound trays five days a week was eventually going to come out of it with a hell of a deltoid tuberosity on the weight-bearing arm. If an anthropologist wasn't careful, if he relied on that criterion alone, he could easily misidentify the humerus of a hardworking waitress as that of a man.

Which is just what he'd done, and what Worriner had done before him. But at least Worriner had an excuse; anthropologists hadn't know about the "waitress tuberosity" in 1964. Gideon, however, had no excuse but carelessness; carelessness and wanting the old man to have done it right. The fact that the rest of Worriner's work had been competent, that the other identifiable bones had all been male, that the humeral fragment had simply given him nothing else to go on, all had led him into being sloppy and acquiescent.

My God, where had his brain been? What was it Cheri

had said a couple of days ago at dinner? *I got muscles on my muscles.* And how could he have forgotten what Shirley Yount had been shouting at Elliott Fisk the day Gideon had gone up to talk with them all about the bones? *She was killing herself taking classes full time and still working in a goddamn Chinese restaurant, humping dishes every night.* And hadn't Elliott countered with something about her having been a waitress since she'd been fifteen? How could Gideon have failed to remember that? How much more obvious could things be?

That was Jocelyn's humerus, he was positive.

Well, ninety-nine-percent positive.

"I made a mistake," he said aloud.

"A mistake?" John said lazily. He and Julie had begun their breakfasts.

"On the bones."

Julie put down her fork. "*You* made a mistake on the bones?"

"Is that so amazing?"

"It's just nice to be reassured that you're human once in a while."

"Come on, Julie, that's not fair. I never said I was infall—"

"Take my word for it," she interrupted in her gruff, funny imitation of his voice, "I've looked at ten zillion bones—"

"*One* zillion," he said, laughing along with them. "Not enough, I guess. Remember those two left humeri of Worriner's in Juneau?"

"Sure. Both male. That's how you knew there were parts of at least two bodies: Pratt's and Fisk's."

"Right. Only I was wrong. We were both wrong. One of them wasn't male."

He explained about deltoid tuberosities and waitressing. This took some time, and when he was done, John and

Julie were still looking at him with something less than total comprehension.

"Okay," John said a little suspiciously, "so it's Jocelyn's humerus; so what does that tell us?" He spread his big hands, knife in one, fork in the other. "What's the big deal? We already knew she was dead."

"Don't look at me," Julie said, chewing. "I seem to be missing something too."

"The big deal is this," Gideon said. "When we came up with that female femur yesterday—the one that got stolen last night—we concluded that we finally had parts of all three skeletons, right?"

John chewed slowly. "Umm . . ."

"Sure we did. We already had parts of two males, or so we thought, and now here was a female femur. That makes three."

"I guess so," John said.

"But if that's Jocelyn's humerus down in Juneau, then we *don't;* at least not for sure."

"We don't?" John said.

"We don't?" Julie said.

Gideon restrained his impatience. It had taken him long enough to put two and two together, and he was supposed to be an expert. "Look," he said, "we know we have some of Steve Fisk, all right; no question about it. That jaw was positively identified by the dental work, and then we matched the ramus and the punctured cranial fragment to it."

"Okay," they both said.

"Okay. And we have some of Jocelyn: the female femur they found yesterday and now that misidentified humerus I've been talking about."

Two cautious nods this time.

"But now—with that humerus reassigned from James Pratt to Jocelyn—it's possible that *all* the male fragments belong to Steve Fisk, since there aren't any other duplications. And *that* means, or it could mean, or it's at least conceivable—"

"Gideon, dear," Julie murmured, "I don't mean to press you, but you do have a way—"

He sat back in his chair and put his hands flat on the table. "I think I know who killed Tremaine, and why. And who clobbered me," he added with satisfaction. He drew a breath. "I think it's—"

"Gerald Pratt," John said.

Gideon looked at him. "John, you have to stop doing that. It's really irritating."

John laughed. "Is that who you're talking about? Pratt?"

"Yeah, that's who I'm talking about," Gideon said grudgingly.

John slapped the table and stood up. "I'm gonna pick up Julian and go have a talk with Pratt right now. Owen too," he added. "He's got proprietary jurisdiction. If there's an arrest, he oughta be the one to make it." He headed for the door.

"You're going to arrest him right now?" Gideon asked. "This minute?"

"I'm not sure." He paused, musing, with his hand on the doorknob. "Doc, how the hell did you figure out it was Pratt? Even with that stuff about the bones."

"How the hell did *you* figure it out?" Gideon responded.

But John was already gone. Julie stared after him at the closing door. "How the hell did anybody figure it out?" she muttered. She leaned toward Gideon, frowning.

"Figure *what* out?" she said.

Gerald Pratt was sitting by himself at one of the tables that looked out over the cove, a half-empty cup of coffee before him. He was wearing his orange coveralls; already looking like a prisoner, John thought.

"Mr. Pratt?" he said.

Pratt, caught predictably in the act of tamping his pipe, looked up from under his eyebrows to take in the three men. "Hm?"

"Could we speak with you, please?"

"Sure," Pratt said, and pointed with the pipe. "Have a seat." If he was made uneasy when none of them moved, he didn't show it. The pipe went into his mouth and was laboriously lit. "What about?" he said through the resulting fug.

"I think it'd be better if we talked in private." Around the room, a few other solitary members of Tremaine's group had looked up from their breakfasts to watch.

Pratt took the pipe from his mouth. He probed a cheek with his tongue. "They're warming up one of those jelly donuts for me. Kind of hate to pass that up. Why don't I look you up in ten minutes or so?"

"I'm sorry, that won't do," Minor said.

Pratt sat up straight. His long jaw tightened. A ropy tendon stood out on either side of his throat. "Well, sir, I'm afraid it'll have to do. I don't see that I have to sit here and be, well—" He looked directly into John's eyes. "Mister, are you standing there and telling me I'm under arrest?"

"I tell you what," John said, "why don't we just say—"

"Why don't we just say what you've got on your mind?"

John exhaled, then nodded, not at Pratt but at Owen. "All right, do it," he said quietly.

Owen took a laminated plastic card from his shirt pocket. "James Pratt," he said in a tight, unfamiliar voice, "you have the right to remain silent. Anything you say can be used against you in a court of law. You have the right at this—"

"Wrong," Pratt said.

Owen faltered.

"You people ought to get your facts straight," Pratt said,

looking from Owen, to Minor, to John. "James Pratt's been dead for thirty years. My name's Gerald Pratt. Gerald Harley Pratt."

John waited for what seemed like a long time before answering.

"No," he said, "I don't think so."

They had finally gotten out to sit on the end of the pier; to lie, rather, looking up at the thin, luminous cloud sheet, Julie directly on the planks, Gideon with his head propped on her belly.

"I understand," Julie said lazily, her fingers in his hair, "about deltoid tuberosities and waitresses. I understand that you and Worriner misidentified that humerus as male when it was actually Jocelyn's. What I don't understand is how you get from there to Pratt's being guilty."

Gideon covered a relaxed yawn with his hand. The effects of the aspirin were well along and, even with the cloud layer, enough sunlight was getting through to put a comfortable glow on his forehead. "Well, I just started wondering if it was simply a matter of chance that we never found any of James Pratt's bones—or if maybe he hadn't been killed after all."

"Hey—" Julie said.

"Which started me thinking about Gerald Pratt. Wasn't it conceivable—barely—that Gerald Pratt wasn't Gerald Pratt?"

"Hey—"

"That he was really *James* Pratt? After thirty years, with his hair thinning, and his nose broken, and a mustache, who was going to recognize him? He was claiming to be James's brother, after all, so it'd be perfectly natural for them to look a lot alike."

"Hey, wait a minute!" She sat up. His head, so tenderly

looked after a few minutes ago, bounced from her abdomen to her lap. "That's *my* theory."

"Your theory?" Squinting against the bright gray sky, he peered innocently up at her face. "What do you mean, your theory? You thought it was Shirley."

"I know, but you just took my theory and—and applied it to Gerald. I was the one who thought it was funny that we only had bones from two people. I was the one who—"

Laughing, he reached up to grab one of her gesticulating hands. "Of course it's your theory, Julie. I realized you were on to something the minute you brought it up. It just needed—"

"You did not. You told me it wouldn't fly, and then you changed the subject. To my infraclavicular fossae."

"Well, who could blame me for that? But on sober reflection I came around. You had it figured out long ago. You just had the wrong person." He smiled. "One of those little details."

"Well, I was sure doing better than anyone else," she said spiritedly. "In case you forget, I was also the one who pointed out—to universal derision—that Tremaine didn't actually *see* James Pratt killed, and for all we knew he was still alive. At which point I was sneeringly encouraged to leave it to the pros. Or am I remembering it wrong?"

"No," Gideon said ruefully, "you're remembering right. Had we but known."

There was a thin, fluttery buzzing in the southeast. They looked up to see a pontooned airplane dropping out of the cloud sheet over Icy Strait and making for Bartlett Cove. It looked like the same cheerful blue-and-white Cessna that had brought Dr. Wu and taken away Tremaine's body. This time it had come for Pratt, who was going to be turned over to the state for prosecution.

"Anyway," Gideon went on, as she settled back on her elbows, "I realized that if this guy really was James Pratt, it gave him a reason for getting rid of the femur. He didn't know I'd already sexed it, and he didn't want me to find out it was Jocelyn's."

"Why not? If—wait a minute, how could *he* possibly know it was female?" She cocked her head at him. "As I recall, you were raising the same objection when I was suggesting this, all of two hours ago."

"Yeah, but I forgot about one thing: I pretty much told him myself. When I met with Tremaine's group last Tuesday I told them the right femur they'd brought back from Tirku was male. Pratt knew it had to be Fisk's, because it damn sure couldn't have been *his*. Now we come up with another right femur. He'd know right away—and only he would know—that it was Jocelyn's, because who else was there?"

"Okay, I see that. Now go back for a minute. Why should he care whether you found out it was Jocelyn's? I mean, nobody aside from me ever doubted that she was dead in the first place. What was he worried about?"

"I guess he was worried about us putting it all together, which is just what we did. See, before this, only one person had been positively ID'd, and that was Steven Fisk. But now, with a female femur in hand, we'd have to know we had Jocelyn Yount too. That leaves only one person *not* positively dead: James Pratt. And that made him nervous. He didn't want people thinking too much about that."

"So he gets rid of the femur before it's sexed," Julie murmured, "or, rather, before he thinks it's been sexed." She lay slowly back down, her fingers laced behind her neck. Gideon resettled his head on her belly.

"Not only sexed," he said. "At the press conference Arthur very helpfully announced to the world that he was giving me a scale that would allow me to determine which bones belonged to whom, which Pratt couldn't have been too happy with, because none of them were going to belong to James."

"Obviously."

"Obviously to Pratt. He didn't want it to be so obvious to John."

"Now that I think about it," Julie said, "Arthur also told everyone where the bones were—at the contact station."

"The dark, isolated, *unguarded* contact station, yes. Pratt really wasn't taking much of a risk going there, you know. It was just luck that I came back when he was there."

"Yes, you've always been lucky that way," she said drily. The little airplane was already on its way back out. They both sat, arms around their knees, and watched it skim over the water, pick up speed, and finally lift off, beelike, to quickly disappear against the flat sky. Nearer, only a few yards away, a line of small, stubby-winged birds shot over the surface of the water like so many black bullets in pursuit of it.

"Pigeon guillemots," Julie said absently. "Gideon, why did Pratt have to kill Tremaine? Why did he steal the manuscript? What difference did it make if—"

Gideon held up his hands. "Hey, lady, all I know is bones. Ask John about the rest."

"And—now wait a minute, how did he get off the glacier?" She turned to him, eyes narrowed. "When it was *my* theory we were talking about, you said it was impossible. And where has he been all these years? And—"

"Bones," Gideon said. "That's all I know."

# 24

John prodded the gelatinous cube tentatively with his fork. "What is it?"

"Tofu lasagna," his wife said patiently.

"Why is it green?"

"It has spinach in it."

He continued his unenthusiastic probing. "Do I like it?"

"You love it. Trust me."

"I don't know, Marti . . ."

"Mellow out, babe," said Marti, who was sometimes given to this kind of locution. "Give it a try."

John looked skeptically at her, used his fork to cut an almost invisible wedge, and put it cautiously in his mouth. "Not bad," he admitted.

"Of course not," she said, pleased. Marti Lau was a loose-limbed Chicagoan (née Marsha Goldenberg), good-looking in a long, big-jointed way; candid, flip, and perpetually happy. "You know," she said to Gideon and Julie, "he only *thinks* he's a junk-food freak. Actually, he likes anything once he tries it. The guy's a human garbage disposal."

"I wouldn't argue with that," Gideon said.

They were in the Laus' Queen Anne Hill apartment, the first time they had gotten together since Glacier Bay, ten days earlier.

"What was the question again?" John said as they all made their way dutifully through Marti's cheeseless, meatless version of lasagna.

"How he got off the glacier," Julie said.

"Oh, yeah. Easy, he thumbed a ride."

Gideon glanced up from his plate. "Come on."

"Really. Look, Glacier Bay had tour boats in the summer in those days too; out of Gustavus, out of Juneau. And if you were going backpacking or kayaking, they'd let you off along the way. They still do. They'd also stop to pick you up if you got out where they could see you and you waved 'em down." No longer doubtful about the lasagna, he helped himself to seconds. "Which is what Pratt did. Simple."

Through the rest of the dinner he explained the reasoning that had led him to Pratt, an entirely different path than Gideon had taken. There had been several questions nagging at him. Why, for instance, had Pratt agreed to come? Tremaine's manuscript didn't seem to mean a damn to him, and his attendance was costing him a week's fishing. And why, really, was he there instead of his sister, who had been the one approached by Javelin Press? And why, when it came to that, had Javelin approached his sister and not him in the first place?

The last question was taken care of first: Javelin hadn't known about his existence until his sister had turned down their invitation and suggested her brother Gerald attend in her place. A telephone call by John to Pratt's sister Eunice in Boise had produced vague, edgy, evasive answers. These in turn prompted some more of Minor's meticulous research, from which it was learned that Gerald Hanley Pratt had been born in Sitka on March 19, 1936, that he had brown hair and brown eyes, and that he weighed seven pounds at birth.

And that he had died of congenital cyanotic heart disease in Spokane on November 26, 1936, at the age of eight months.

From there it had been simple for them to piece together what must have happened in 1960. Like Tremaine, James Pratt had survived the avalanche. Unlike Tremaine, the life he had to go back to held little appeal: Sea Resources, his cholesterol-reduction scheme, was in deep and inextricable trouble with creditors, investors, and the law. Even worse, he feared, as soon as Tremaine told what had happened on Tirku, a warrant would go out for his arrest on a charge of murder, or manslaughter at the least.

Once out of Glacier Bay he had holed up in Juneau to nurse his injuries. There he had read that he had been killed in the avalanche, along with Steven and Jocelyn, and had decided, understandably enough, that he was better off staying that way.

Fortunately for him, there was another identity waiting to be slipped into. The following week a man identifying himself as Gerald Hanley Pratt filed a request for a copy of his birth certificate at the Sitka City Hall. The required information was neatly and accurately filled out, and the request was routinely granted. With the birth certificate in hand, a driver's license and Social Security card were not hard to get, and early in 1961 "Gerald Hanley Pratt" took up residence in Ketchikan, purchased a boat, and joined the fishing fleet. Taciturn, solitary, unsociable, he fit right in.

There he had stayed until he received a worried telephone call from his sister Eunice, his one confidante. Tremaine, silent all these years, was writing a book about the Tirku survey, and God knew what he was going to say.

Pratt had to know too, of course. Was the ancient murder finally going to come to light? It had been thirty years, and Tremaine had been badly hurt, in a coma. Would he even remember it? Equally to the point, what did he remember, what had he seen—what would he write—of what had happened to Pratt after the avalanche struck? Would the official version be that he had been killed in the cataclysm, that the matter was closed? Or would it leave the reader with the idea that he might still be alive, still be within the law's reach? There was, after all, no statute of limitations on murder in Alaska.

"So we started thinking," John said. "What if Pratt's story about hearing Tremaine's voice through the wall was a smokescreen? Maybe he'd been listening until he heard Tremaine's shower go *on*, not off, and maybe that was when he used that key to get into the room and hunt around for the manuscript."

"Is that the way it happened?" Gideon asked.

"Looks like it. According to him, he got spooked when he heard you found out about Fisk's murder. He stole the key from the laundry cart, waited till he heard the shower go on, and snuck in."

"How do you know all this?" Julie asked. "Has he confessed?"

"No, but there's probably some plea bargaining in the works, and they filled me in on where he's coming from." He shrugged. "I think he's telling the truth."

"Plea bargaining!" Marti exploded. "For a double murder? What kind of rat piddle is that supposed to be?"

"Well, if you believe what he says, there wasn't any premeditation either time. As far as Fisk's murder goes, the manuscript backs him up on that. They might even go for self-defense there. And murder-two on Tremaine."

"Second-degree murder?" Julie said.

"Right. According to Pratt, he was poking around, see, looking for the manuscript, when Tremaine surprised him. Then there's this big confrontation, with Pratt trying to talk his way out of it. But after a couple of minutes this weird expression comes on Tremaine's face, and he points his finger and says, 'Why, I know you. You're James Pratt.'"

John swallowed the last of his lasagna, shoved his plate away, and sipped from his glass of white wine. "Well, Pratt panicked. He started to threaten Tremaine, and then to shove him a little. To scare him, he says. But Tremaine kept getting more excited. And then—"

"Let me guess," Marti said. "He blacks out. He can't remember what happened next."

"That's it," John said genially. "He blacked out, came to with Tremaine dead, *really* panicked, and set up the fake suicide."

"Sounds like first-degree murder to me," Marti grumbled.

"Marti, things'll get sorted out. Don't you have any faith in the American system of jurisprudence?"

"Ho," Marti said. "Does anybody want some more lasagna?"

"What happened to the manuscript?" Julie asked.

"He threw it in the lake, he says. I guess he was hoping it really was the only copy, the way Tremaine said. And the bones got tossed in the woods. What's for dessert, babe?"

"Tofutti," announced Marti, who took a thematic approach to dinners. "You love it."

John looked pained. "How about walking down to the Pacific Dessert Company for something?"

"Chocolate Decadence?" Julie murmured plaintively.

"Fine with me," Marti said, unoffended, "but it's gonna be guilt burgers in the morning."

"I'll risk it," John said.

"I wonder what will happen to Tremaine's book now," Julie said as they got into their jackets.

John had the answer to that too. "It'll get published. Javelin's asked Anna Henckel to finish it up. Do a foreword in her own name, expand the scientific stuff, edit the whole thing."

"Anna Henckel?" Julie said. "But I thought she hated him. She'll destroy him."

"No," John said slowly, "I think she'll do just fine."

They were sitting over their coffee and dessert in the big, bright pastry restaurant at the base of the hill when Gideon raised something else.

"John, how could you make all those assumptions about Pratt not being dead, when I kept telling you we had bones from both men?"

"Yeah, well . . ." John said with a grin. "No offense, Doc, but I don't always believe everything you tell me."

Gideon smiled. "A good thing, too," he said.